Never Trust a Gemini

Never Trust a Gemini

FREJA NICOLE WOOLF

WALKER BOOKS

First US edition 2023

Library of Congress Catalog Card Number 2022915278
ISBN 978-1-5362-3054-3

LBM 28 27 26 25 24 23
10 9 8 7 6 5 4 3 2 1

Printed in Melrose Park, IL, USA

This book was typeset in ITC Usherwood Medium.

Walker Books US
a division of
Candlewick Press
99 Dover Street
Somerville, Massachusetts 02144

www.walkerbooksus.com

SUSTAINABLE FORESTRY INITIATIVE
Certified Sourcing
www.forests.org
SFI-00854

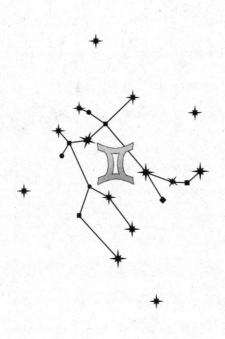

Libra
SEASON

1

Conversations with Taylor Swift

I cannot stop dreaming about Alison Bridgewater. This could be because it's Libra Season . . . Love and relationships are on everybody's minds during Libra Season, according to my *Bible to the Stars*—or my *Book for Blithering Idiots*, as Dad calls it. But it could also indicate that I'm reaching dangerous and dizzying new heights of my Alison Bridgewater Obsession, which is not good news, as I'm dizzied almost to death already!

They're very innocent dreams: Alison and me walking hand in hand across Tower Bridge in London . . . Alison and me playing tag on a white-sand beach . . . Alison and me lying side by side on a queen-size bed and then, just possibly, shuffling close enough that our lips can touch, and we brush fingertips, and I say under my breath, "I love you," and in my dreams, Alison's perfect face will glow, her smile like pure sunlight and rainbows . . .

She opens her mouth to say, "Love you, too . . . !"

But I always seem to wake up before that happens.

It's Tuesday morning in Lambley Common, Kent, and I have school soon, where I'll have to see Alison face-to-face and not be awkward: not easy when you're a born clown like myself! I stay in bed for ages feeling troubled. Specifically, about the fact I just dreamed about kissing Alison again! Then I hear Mum's singsong morning call.

"Cat, come down for breakfast! I've made porridge!"

In that case, I might as well stay in bed forever! Mum is far from competent in the kitchen. Her porridge is like cat food! But when I've raised this with her, she just says, "It's a good thing we named you Cat, then!" Then she laughs a lot with Dad.

But woe alas, I do have to get ready (a time-trousering process indeed if your gang has the überest of standards like mine does), so I stumble to my mirror and examine my blond curls. They're basically a bird's nest, so I quickly comb my fingers through them, then add mascara. To my eyelashes obviously, not my hair, though a bit does get caught in the wand.

Then I sigh a tragic sigh—because I do this every day . . .

My morning routine is simple: Get up, get dressed, pray to Almighty Aphrodite (she is the Goddess of Love, and nothing is more important than that), then make myself as beautiful as possible for my friend and romantic obsession, Alison Bridgewater.

But today, before I've even applied my lucky lavender deodorant, my phone buzzes and my eyes almost explode. Which would be really messy and traumatic, to be honest. But I have a text from Alison herself!

Alison, 8:09 a.m.:
Hey bb! Can we talk after school, just us? xox

"Gooseberries!" I exclaim (my favorite curse word). Alison Bridgewater wants to talk to me ALONE? After school? ON A TUESDAY? About what?! Then my bedroom door flies open, and I Frisbee-fling my phone and shriek, "I'M NOT ON MY PHONE, MUM, HONESTLY, I'M JUST COMING DOWN!"

My phone smashes through my nail polishes on the dresser and right into the pinky-purple lava lamp, which teeters dangerously. I have to jump to catch it and end up face-planting in the pile of dirty underwear on the floor: a true moment of knickerbocker glory.

Then I look around and see it's not Mum but my tree-hugging terror of a sister, Luna, who is interrupting my celestial flows. She really is the WORST person—this text from Alison could be the most important conversation of my life! And that includes my conversation with Taylor Swift (Luna says it's "not a conversation" when she's never once replied, but I disagree).

Oblivious to my woes, Luna waves her phone around and says, "Cat, have you seen your horoscope? Apparently, Aquarius Lives are being blessed today. Maybe that fungal infection on your leg will clear up!"

"It's just a bruise, Luna!" I snap, swiping her phone. "I've told you already!"

Usually, I'd be deeply unamused that Luna is rabbiting on about astrology now. I'm the one with the *Bible to the Stars*, and she's already claimed pacifism, anti-consumerism,

3

intersectional feminism, and radical veganism! Can't she leave anything for me?

But reading her phone, I realize I may have to Elsa-style Let It Go. Because my sister, who is so bizarre that she grows mushrooms in a shoebox for fun, might actually be right. According to my horoscope, my life is about to change forever, which sounds pretty outrageous for a Tuesday morning.

Deep in my knickers pile, my phone buzzes again. I dig it back up and gasp.

Alison, 8:10 a.m.:
I really need u!!! xxx

Head spinning with a thousand Taylor Swift lyrics, I feel the stars align . . . Well, that might be my stomach rumbling. But could today really be the day Alison Bridgewater falls in love with me?! It's a lot to take in. Especially given that, as I might have mentioned already, it's a Tuesday.

I'm in an Alison-induced coma all through Mum's horrendous breakfast and all the way to school as well, which is a wonderful distraction from Luna raving on about Mum's "anti-animal" shopping agenda. Last night's dreams are all over my skin like pollen . . . You can't see it, but you can feel it clinging to you.

Gosh, that was a very poetic thought! Maybe I should be writing Alison one of my amazing poems . . . She's bound to fall in love with me then! I try to think poetically, but Luna won't shut up! It's no wonder I never get anything done.

". . . just because it said 'farm fresh' on the label—farm

fresh?! Everybody knows that's code for factory farm!" Luna gasps in annoyance. It isn't unusual for my sister to be angry at our parents—or "symbols of a capitalist dystopia," as she calls them. I'm only fourteen, but she makes ME feel like a boomer. I guess I'm nearly fifteen, so I'm not far off. "Mum seemed to think the picture on the front justified it as well," Luna rants. "As if that chicken ever really saw a field! Then she's bought those sausages for dinner—again!"

My sister (a Scorpio, Aphrodite save me) is very passionate. Last Christmas, aged twelve, she announced she wanted to change her name from Lauren Anna Phillips to "Luna Anaïs Celeste Phillips." She'd printed the official forms and everything! Apparently, she wanted this or nothing as her Christmas gift.

"At least she's keeping the surname," Dad grunted, not even lowering his paper.

Mum told her to "try it out" before making it legal. Then when Luna left the room, she turned to my utterly shocked face and said, "Don't worry, love. It's normal to play with identity at this age. Just let her work through it, and she'll be Lauren again before you know it."

Nine months on, Luna is more Luna than ever! No one calls her Lauren anymore, so I suppose I'll have to start taking her seriously . . . But seeing as she's currently wearing an embarrassingly enormous pin saying VEGAN FROM MY HEAD TOMATOES on her blazer, perhaps I won't call her Lauren *or* Luna. I'll just call her ridiculous instead.

But you know who isn't ridiculous?

Alison Bridgewater. She really is so perfect. She's half-Ghanaian and her hair is gorgeously dark and curly, and her golden-brown skin glows even in the depths of winter . . . Gosh. I actually slightly hate how poetic and stunning she is.

"Perfect . . ." I sigh out loud, then my eyes widen. Oops.

Luna stops talking about the crimes of the farming industry. "Excuse me? Did you just say 'perfect' when I was talking about animal genocide?!"

"No?!" I pause walking. "I'm tired. I was thinking about something else!"

Luna rolls her eyes. "You know, if you listened to me, you might learn something! Why are you tired? Were you writing *Frozen* fan fiction until four in the morning again?"

"Yes," I say. "I mean, NO! I've never done that!"

Gooseberries . . . how does Luna know about that?

"Whatever." Luna adopts her peak zen face. "Libra Season is sending everyone into a frenzy. Just because they're scared of being alone another year. Maisy McGregor literally fainted over it yesterday . . ."

That catches my attention. I pause trying to mentally compose a sonnet.

"Wait, for another YEAR? Luna, what do you mean?"

Luna gives me a smug smile. Which is also a very annoying smile, but that's just her face. "Haven't you been reading your *Bible to the Stars*? Some people believe if two don't become one in Libra Season, you'll have to wait until next year to find someone. And that's a long, long time. Eight million metric tons more plastic will have gone into the ocean by then, which is a lot of tons, Cat . . ."

She rambles on. But I am ozone-layering out all over again.

A whole year?! I'll basically be almost sixteen and I won't

even have had my first kiss! Suddenly, my conversation with Alison Bridgewater is even more important. Really, I deserve some sort of award just for holding it together! I'm like Florence Nightingale, if she was a blond fourteen-year-old with a crush on her best friend. Which she isn't, so I suppose I'm not actually like Florence Nightingale at all, but I'm still very virtuous and saintly. Today could be bigger than Disney's silence on Elsa's true romantic persuasion!

Because no way, Swift-Tay, am I going to wait another year to find true love.

2
For the Love of Alison

The first thing I see when I walk into homeroom is Alison Bridge-water, pressing flowers into her scrapbook like some kind of creative demigod. She really is the Prettiest Pisces Princess who ever walked this cruel, cruel earth . . . Big, poetic sigh.

Back in seventh grade, me and Alison sat together in science, and because science is properly Yawnsville Express, I doodled a flower in my planner.

Alison spotted me. "Aww, that's so pretty! Do you draw a lot?"

"Um . . . sometimes," I replied, thinking about my entire portfolio of kissing-princess drawings. Probably best Alison didn't see those. "Do you?"

"I make scrapbooks!" Alison reached into her bag to show me. The scrapbook was a mix of newspaper clippings, photos from magazines, postcards, scraps of fabric, all thrown together in a way that somehow looked beautiful, like all the chaos in the world sorted out.

"That's . . . so cool!" I murmured, and Alison beamed, and her teeth looked so perfect, and her hair looked oh-so curly and gorgeous, and my stomach clenched like a sour grape, because how did I never notice this before? She's actually mesmerizingly beautiful!

But sour grape became full-on LEMON when, one sleepover, Siobhan (THE Queen Bee of Queen's School Kent) instructed me to bring my *Star Bible* and much-admired grand and impressive zodiac wisdom so we could study our star charts and find our perfect match. She's been bleating for a Capricorn ever since. But then we tried Alison's details and the website just reloaded MY chart. I thought it was a mistake at first, like falling in love with a Gemini, but no . . . Everything aligned. Every single planet. WE were the perfect match!

"Well, that's a massive coincidence," Siobhan said, blinking in surprise.

I could barely breathe. But Alison just wiggled her (perfect) eyebrows. "I don't know, Cat . . . What if it's written in the stars? I've always loved your adorable button nose . . ."

Everyone shrieked with laughter, and I went *AHAHAHA* as convincingly as possible, but inside, Aphrodite was throttling my heart with a glittering garland of roses, and ever since, I've been stupidly and pathetically and intergalactically in love with Alison Bridgewater.

Nobody knows except for my so-called best friend, Zanna, who is currently observing me, one eyebrow raised in complete and utter judgment. I snap back to the present. It's rather like being thrown into a swimming pool . . . and I should know; it's how Dad wakes me up on our summer holidays in France. I'm late, Zanna knows I'm staring at Alison, and I still have no idea what Alison wants to talk about later.

To put it simply, I am stressed in a vest. And the rest of my clothes as well.

I take a deep breath, then beeline toward my seat in the most unnoticeable way possible. But at once I hear, "Cathleen Phillips, well, well, well."

Gooseberries! I judder to a halt, internally groaning. Then I turn around with the fruitiest, fakest smile I can muster. "Good morning, Mrs. Warren!"

"Good morning, Cathleen." Everyone says Irish accents are dancing-dingo divine, but I'm not sure I'll ever trust one in all my life thanks to Mrs. Warren. She taps her pen on the surface of her desk. "Why don't you come over here," she says, sing-song-stomach-churningly, "and explain to me why you're five minutes late to homeroom?"

I slide to the front desk. "Sorry I'm late, Miss," I recite. "My sister got up late."

Not strictly true, but I'm hardly going to tell her it was my fault! Me and Mrs. Warren have had a mutually hateful under-standing since FOREVER. Well, since she caught me drawing Shrek ears on her photo in the hallway anyway.

After I have agreed with Wicked Warren that no, I am not my sister, and therefore yes, it's a fair-and-square "late" mark, I slump down next to Zanna and do everything in my power not to gaze longingly at Alison Bridgewater. Sadly, everything in my power is like a Capricorn's capacity to love (meaning: not much), and I gaze longingly at Alison after all.

She sunbeams back with all the usual summertime and

rainbows, and I almost fall off my chair. For the love of Libra Season, this is hard! What does she want to talk about? Aphrodite above, please give me a sign . . .

Zanna clears her throat. "Good morning, my useless blond friend."

Pausing midprayer, I scowl. "What are you judging me for now?"

"Possibly the way you stared at Alison for five painful seconds before you came in?" Zanna tuts, tapping her owlish glasses like she often does when she's disapproving. Which is basically all the time. "There's such a thing as subtlety, Cat."

Zanna Szczechowska is an utterly horrendous friend who mocks me on a daily basis for absolutely everything. But I've known her since primary school, and she knows far too many of my shameful secrets to ever risk falling out with her. Also, unlike me, she knows my class schedule by heart, so I really can't afford to lose her. I can still glower at her though.

"A real friend tells you the truth," Zanna says, shrugging. "You've got to get over that girl!"

"That's a valid opinion," I agree as Mrs. Warren trawler-drags through the announcements. "But here's a better idea. What if Alison falls in love with me back?"

Zanna frowns. "Falls in love with your back? What about the fungal infection?"

"IT'S A BRUISE, ZANNA!" I shriek. I really shouldn't have posted about that on Instagram. Then I remember we're in the middle of class. Oops. Everyone and Alison Bridgewater goggles at me in shock. After Mrs. Warren has logged my second caution of the day, I whisper on with Zanna . . . "It's on my leg anyway!

And I didn't even say that . . . Although she'll hopefully fall in love with my back as well. But first, she has to fall in love with my front, my sides, and the rest of me! And that's where the poetry will help."

Zanna's eyes widen in horror. "Sorry. The poetry?"

"I've decided it's now or never," I explain. "I'm reliably informed by my horoscope that today is the day I should tell Alison how I feel, so I'm going to write a poem and give it to her after school. It's a new chapter—sorry, *stanza*—of my life, and Alison is definitely going to fall in love with me, because poetry is the language of the soul."

"That's the worst idea I've ever heard," Zanna replies. "*Please* don't do that. You will ruin our friendship group and make everything awkward forever."

"It's too late, Zanna," I say. "It's not even an idea. It's a concept."

"Good grief," Zanna murmurs. "That does sound worse."

She might be more annoying than my fungal infection. Gooseberries galore.

By lunchtime, I still don't have so much as a haiku to give to Alison Bridgewater. And the moment I find a quiet corner to write something spectacular in my notebook, Jamie Owusu appears with his Ninja Turtles lunch box, sounding off about how desperately hard his life is.

I really have no choice but to be friends with Jamie. Our mums are besties and host this sad-fest "sewing group" in my house together every weekend. Jamie always comes along because he's scared of being home alone, and mostly we lounge in my bedroom and he complains. I usually don't mind because

I'm used to not listening, but today it's too much. How am I supposed to write wondrous poetry if tragic, non-poetic types keep bothering me?

Today Jamie's problem is that no girl in Lambley Common will date him. "Why do nice guys always finish last?" he moans, halfway through a mouthful of Keebler cookies. I'm only half listening, because I'm sketching the most cute-alicious sketch of Elsa from *Frozen* marrying Merida from *Brave*. And writing my poetry . . . of course.

"Girls only want white guys, don't they?" Jamie mourns on. "Like Chris Hemsworth or Tom Holland."

"But the bathrooms are covered in graffiti about Chidi Unigwe," I muse, drawing Merida's curly hair and sighing wistfully because it's so much like Alison's. "Everyone fancies him."

"Chidi's TikTok famous!" Jamie protests. "Literal Stormzy called him a legend!"

"Well, maybe you should start making music," I suggest. "Then you can be as cool as Chidi! You're bound to find a girlfriend then."

Jamie jogs my elbow, almost ruining Elsa's bouquet of flowers! I scowl as he points across the playground to where Siobhan is talking to her latest boy obsession, Kieran Wakely-Brown. She's letting out an annoying gibbonish laugh every five seconds and bobbing up and down like a rubber duck as Kieran boasts away about his collection of signed tennis balls.

"That's the kind of guy all you girls want," Jamie says decisively.

I'm not sure what he means, saying "all you girls" like that, but somehow it really prickles my pumpkins, so I slam my notebook shut and say, "Well, maybe if you stopped moaning all the time, Jamie, some girl would notice how secretly good-looking you are, or whatever, and go out with you!"

Jamie gapes at me. Oops. Was that too harsh?

Then he says, "So, you think I'm good-looking?"

I widen my eyes. Really?! That's the part he chose to hear?! I flap my lips about like a salmon, trying to articulate that I didn't mean it *like that*, because I don't want Jamie thinking I fancy him when I certainly in a million-billion years do not!

Unfortunately, I end up saying, "I don't mean—I mean . . . good-looking, but—I mean!" I decide not to mention that he's sadly no match for Alison Bridgewater. But I suppose he's okay, if that's what sinks your submarine, so I say, "You're all right!"

But he keeps grinning like I made his day, week, or entire zodiac year. "That's special," he goons on. "A proper compliment from a girl like you."

I'm worried he's reading far too much into this. Gulping down the merry-go-round of panic that's spinning in my chest, I watch Jamie slowly bite into another cookie, maintaining eye contact the entire time. What now?! Then someone smacks their hands onto my shoulders, and I jump out of my knickers.

"O-M-ACTUAL-G! Did you SEE that, Cat?!" And Siobhan Collingdale leaps onto the tabletop, obliviously barging Jamie's lunch box to the ground. "Über-special moment with Kieran— were you watching?!" She tosses her hair back and whips Jamie right in the eye.

Siobhan's hair is famous: she uses five different conditioners mixed together, and although I'm secretly sure it's just brown, Siobhan insists her natural color is "burnt umber." She's probably just blinded Jamie, but she's exploding with Kieran news and doesn't even look at him. Although I notice she swipes a cookie while he's busy groaning in pain.

This is the last strawberry. I'm never going to come up with a poetic masterpiece! Anyway, Siobhan's been talking about Kieran Wakely-Brown all day, and I'm beyond over it. We all have crushes, but for the love of Alison, she takes hers way too seriously!

"He's not like other boys," Siobhan raves on. "He's a CAPRICORN, and he knows what mascara is, because his mum is a professional MUA, and he's even met Cara Delevingne! Which is great because everyone says I have her eyebrows. I'm so over Chidi!" Jamie chokes on his cookie. "Having a new boyfriend is the best natural cleanse, Cat. I never even think about Chidi anymore! That's why my skin is so clear these days . . ."

Jamie keeps googly-eyeing me all through Siobhan's Kieran Catch-Up Special, but I pretend not to notice. I've got quite enough on my platypus: Libra Season is clearly taking effect! Siobhan is on the verge of a sparkling new relationship, and meanwhile I still have nothing to give to Alison Bridgewater. Sappho strike me down!

WHAT RHYMES WITH ALISON???

1:45 p.m.—

- Madison? Atkinson?
- Smalison . . . ? How about . . . ALISON! Oh.
- Badminton? Although . . . In sixth grade, I *might* have broken Sporty Habiba's perfect front tooth when a badminton racket slipped from my hand midswing . . . Maybe best not to remind Alison of that.
- Hag-ridden? I'm not sure "Hags" really experience true love though. I'd have to ask Mrs. Warren to be absolutely certain . . .
- Sally's son? Frustratingly, the only Sally's son I know is Nigel the Nibbler from nursery school. He chewed my second-favorite gel pen so much, it practically turned into a twiglet . . . Not very romantic.

1:55 p.m.—

- "Salishan"! Thanks, internet!
- Meaning: "a family of Native American languages from the northwestern USA and Canada . . ." Time to get inspired!!!

2:35 p.m.—

- I can now introduce myself in Halq'eméylem, but I do not have a poem.

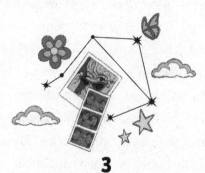

3

Sappho Strikes Me Down

Unfortunately, Sappho (who the most poetic among us, like myself, will know is an extremely famous and ancient lesbian poet with HER OWN ISLAND) does not strike me down, and by the end of the day, I have what can only be described as a "nice try" in my hand. I read it over while I'm waiting outside the school gates in the drizzle. Which probably means Sappho is crying.

How can I give Alison this?! I should have illustrated it, then she'd have been too distracted by my drawing skills to notice the actual words. But it's too late now. I slide the poem into my blazer pocket, my heart already boom-shaka-lakering the house down.

"Are you good?" I hear, and I look up to see this edgy-looking girl with green glasses smirky-eyeing me. "You look stressed," she adds, in a rather nifty accent I wish I had.

"Um . . ." I flounder. "Well, I'm definitely not . . ."

She nods slowly. "I've started counting to one hundred in Korean. By the time I get there, I've nearly always forgotten what I'm nervous about. If that helps."

Then she does this really chillaxed smile and walks off. I stare after her blankly. Korean? How is *that* going to help me? I'm not the Duolingo owl. Some people have such easy-von-Teese-y lives; they wouldn't know stress if it hit them like a school bus!

To distract myself from the tsunami of anxiety, I take out my phone and scroll through Instagram. Siobhan's posted a selfie that has already gotten over two hundred likes from her terrified brethren of followers. (Siobhan says she has "almost three thousand" followers, although I'd say 2,400 is "just over two thousand" personally.) I double-tap . . . then I hear a familiar laugh.

I look up and gasp. Alison is chatting to a boy across the road! She must have been waiting for me—how did I miss her?! Between the buses and parents driving like bumper cars, she hasn't seen me, so I leave the railing and raise a hand to wave. I don't recognize the boy, but to be honest, all boys look the same to me. His blazer is pretentiously purple though, which stands out among the deeply uninspiring blue of the Queen's uniform. Purple means he's from the private school, Lambley Common Academy. We call them the "Beetroot Brigadiers."

But now is not the time to get sidetracked by pretentious blazers! I take a deep and grounding breath. This is it: the most important conversation of my life! (Sorry, Taylor Swift.) Gulping down my nervy-nervousness, I step off the curb, opening my mouth to call her name . . . then Private School Dude leans forward and kisses Alison Bridgewater. MY Alison Bridgewater. Right on her perfect brown cheek.

WHAT?! I stop right where I am in the middle of the road.

My mind is reeling. He kissed Alison on the cheek! I mean, it's not a full-blown lippy-lullaby make-out session. But a kiss is a kiss! Should I feel happy because Alison is my friend? Am I thrilled? Okay, I'm definitely not. I want to punch his lights out! Or maybe I just want to cry?! Really, I don't know what to think, but it suddenly feels like I've been blown sideways.

Then I notice I actually have been blown sideways—something has smacked me from the side, and I'm sailing through the air in real-life slow motion, and that's when I realize that, GOOSEBERRIES GALORE, I'VE BEEN HIT BY A BUS!

I hit the pavement and roll. Next thing I know, I'm flat on my back and looking at the great poetic sky—which is rapidly turning a spirited sepia—and would feel very Shakespearean if this weren't real life. Or is this real death?! The shadow of the netball team's minibus looms over me; gasps and cries fill the air as onlookers gather round.

Then I see Alison's horrified, beautiful face leaning over me like Aphrodite welcoming me to the sunny, glorious afterlife. "Cat?!" she gasps. "Oh my goodness! Are you okay?!"

Even in this moment of great tragedy, she looks gorgeous. And I only hope I'm not going to wet myself if I die in front of her, because Siobhan said her cat peed when it died, and I'd literally never live that down if it happened to me. But then it's too late because everything goes dark. Perhaps I'm getting my romantic poetic ending after all.

"Right," I can hear someone saying. "Everybody, stand back!"

Is that Aphrodite? Luna says it's utterly nonsensical believing in astrology AND Greek goddesses, but what does she know?! I like having all bases covered. Still, I don't think that is Aphrodite. I'm vaguely aware of the cold air, a crowd around me, lots of murmuring and gasping. I'm still lying in the road, which is damp and icy beneath my palms.

I suppose the fact I'm aware of all this means I'm not dead. Though there's still time! What if I'm bleeding out, slipping in and out of consciousness? Alison's face still in my mind, I part my lips and try to tell her before it's too late . . .

"If I die . . . I want you to know that you're truly beautiful . . ."

Then I open my eyes. I'm staring right at Mr. Derry, my history teacher. He looks surprised behind his Tetrisy glasses . . . And I suddenly realize what I just said. TO HIM.

"Oh . . ." I murmur, and everyone is chattering and giggling, and I wonder how loudly I just told Mr. Derry that he was truly beautiful and what I'm going to do now. "Um . . ."

"Don't worry, Cat," Mr. Derry says, though his cheeks do seem a little pink. "You're probably feeling a bit confused. There's a doctor on the way—you've had an accident."

An accident?! I really hope he just means the whole getting-hit-by-a-bus fandango. If I've soiled myself as well, I may ask the bus to full-on run me over . . .

Then Alison does appear, and I could headbutt her for the pain and torture she puts me through every single day without even knowing! Well, I possibly wouldn't actually headbutt her. But I'd give her a very stern look, which is also pretty brutal broomsticks.

"Cat!" she gasps. "You're alive!"

"Stay back, Alison," Mr. Derry says annoyingly. "I've got this."

But I reach out a hand and Alison kneels beside me in the road, squeezing my hand in hers. Her skin is cool from the October air, but she rubs a thumb across my palm and suddenly I

20

don't feel so dizzy anymore. Or maybe I feel dizzier? Either way: SCORE!

Alison shines down upon me with the smile where all her teeth show, and it's like the clouds have parted and the sun has just broken through. Thank you, Aphrodite . . . !

"You daft thing," she says, shaking her head.

Not the best compliment in the world, but I'll take it.

"Sorry," I croak back. "Was I knocked out?"

Alison grimaces. "Not for long—"

"We're not sure," Mr. Derry cuts in. I wish he'd leave me to faint in Alison's arms in peace. It's not like this kind of thing happens every day. This might be my only opportunity!

But then a man with a first-aid bag snatches that opportunity from my grasp when he barges his bald head in and Alison has to back away. I suppose this is the paramedic, but since he interrupted my moment with Alison, I'm already not a fan, whether he saves my life or not.

There's a long wait at the emergency room, especially once they see I'm not actually dying, or even hurt at all really. They do a weird brain-scan thing though.

"Anything in there?" Dad asks the nurse, and Mum chuckles away.

My parents like to think they're professional comedians, but they're literally bankers. They're boring for pay! Try telling that to Dad's baguette-themed tie collection though. Just so he can loaf around saying he's "the bread maker" of the family . . . Truly crusty scenes.

Frowning at Dad's croissant-crazy tie, the nurse explains to my clown parents that I'm mildly concussed and (as if I haven't been punished enough) will need to stay home for a few days, but it's nothing to worry about. Easy enough for her to say! Mum will be vroom-vrooming on about road safety for the rest of my life now, so I'm VERY worried actually.

"Your father's had to leave work early for this!" Mum gabbles on the car ride home.

I'd have thought that was a relief, given Dad's job—he should be thanking me! But before I can make this extremely valid point, Mum changes the subject to Luna. Apparently, Luna invited Niamh (her best friend and Siobhan's little sister), who shares Luna's cuckoo-clock cacophony of bizarre beliefs. It seems that despite my getting hit by a bus, Niamh came over anyway, and Luna's still expecting her to stay for dinner. Unbelievable!

"I can see she's really concerned," I grumble.

"Oh, don't be so dramatic, Kit-Kat," Dad chuckles. "You're fine."

"I nearly died!" I protest. "I was hit by a bus!"

"Might do you some good," says Dad.

Mum laughs out loud at this, and Dad pats her knee across the gearshift. Then Mum switches on the radio, and they're playing "Walking on Sunshine." She turns up the volume and begins singing along with Dad, joyously clapping her hands.

I sigh hopelessly. If getting hit by a bus can't earn me some sympathy, Aphrodite knows what can! Maybe I should get hit by a plane next time? Then I remember Alison. And the poem, still lurking in my pocket, which, reading it now, sounds a bit less Shelley and a bit more shell-shockingly awful. Gooseberries. What was I thinking?!

I suppose it had to happen eventually. Libra Season would

come, Alison would find a boyfriend, and I'd have to watch it happen. It hurts deeply, being in love with your friend. I suppose it doesn't happen to most people. I should be crushing on some boy I don't know properly, like Kieran Wakely-Brown. But I just . . . can't.

Gooseberries, now my eyes are stinging! And not just because I got disinfectant gel in them at the hospital. I'm crying real tears. Zanna's right to call me a "messy clown." And she was right about something else as well:

I really, really, REALLY need to get over Alison Bridgewater.

It could all be so perfect though. I know Alison! So much better than Private School Dude does. I know she likes pineapple juice, she's left-handed, she likes rom-coms . . . She's wanted a Dalmatian since she was seven. And I never turn on overhead lights when I'm with her, because Alison once told me lamplight is softer. We have the same favorite color: orange. And according to the STARS IN THE ACTUAL SKY, we're soul mates!

But none of that matters because she just doesn't see me that way.

Perhaps I'm being a selfish sardine. I should just be grateful I have an amazing friend like Alison Bridgewater, even if I am officially going to be alone for another zodiac year. But when you've been hit by a bus on the same day you've seen the girl you love so very painfully and poetically getting kissed by some random, stupid boy in a pretentious blazer, I think it's fair enough to feel a little sad and tragic.

I wonder if it's too late to go back to the hospital and offer my heart to organ donation services. I won't be needing it myself after all.

☆ THE PISCES PRINCESS POEM ♥
—BY CAT PHILLIPS

Alison is so sunny! And buzzy like a bee!
I wonder if she notices the buzz she's giving me?
The sun is made from fire, and Alison is not.
But they have this in common: they're both really hot,
Emotionally speaking. Objectifying is wrong.
But Alison is as pretty as a really pretty song!
She's like a real sunbeam: really, really bright,
In creative subjects. Not in science, right?
So now this poem's over, I finally have to say
I secretly really like you, as more than friends . . .

   Yay . . . ?!

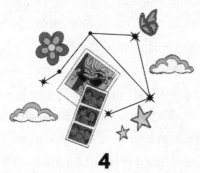

4
Concussed and Traumatized

As soon as word spreads that I've been hit by a bus, Siobhan springs into full Queen Bee action: bludgeoning everyone into signing me a giant "Get Well Soon" card, writing a "Serious Letter of Complaint" to the bus company, even opening a fundraiser in my name.

The school quickly puts a stop to the fundraiser—especially when I have to admit that (a) I'm not that badly hurt, and (b) the accident was mostly my fault anyway, because I was "dancing about in the middle of the road like a bloody idiot" (Dad's words).

So instead, Siobhan insists on arranging a Recovery Party at my house on Friday. I suspect Siobhan just wanted to organize an event, but it's still a nice gesture, especially since my parents are not taking my traumatic experience seriously at all.

All the gang comes over: Siobhan, Alison, Kenna, Habiba, and Zanna, and even Lip Gloss Lizzie makes a special guest appearance. Lizzie Leeson-Westbrooke is sometimes in the gang and sometimes not, because she's staggeringly lip-glossy and popular and has several groups of friends. On her phone, she numbers her group chats, or so I've heard.

"Wow!" says Kenna, who's never been round before. "Your house is amazing!"

"Christ on a bike, Kenna!" snaps Siobhan. "You're so easily impressed. It's not like she has a butler or anything! Anyway, pay attention: Cat's had a TERRIBLE accident! She doesn't need you sweeping in here and making a fuss . . ."

Siobhan proceeds to order Kenna and Habiba about, making them lay down a picnic rug in the middle of the floor, where they spread out hundreds of cakes, cookies, dips, and snacks. Lip Gloss Lizzie posts a picture of me on Instagram to "show everyone Cat didn't die after all," and I'm given pride of place in Dad's leathery armchair.

Siobhan instructs me not to lift a finger to help.

"I'll take care of absolutely everything, Cat," she assures me. "Don't worry at all. KENNA! DON'T MIX UP THE HUMMUSES! ARE YOU *ACTUALLY* STUPID?!"

I subtly throw Kenna a life-jacket smile as she carefully places a teaspoon in each dip. She's too busy gazing in awe at the "digital fireplace" to notice though.

My house is so modern, I'm practically living in the future. Me and Luna ceremoniously named it the "iPhone Box" when we moved in last year, because it's all wall-height windows and a completely open plan, a privacy nightmare. Dad said we couldn't put "The iPhone Box" on a sign though, so it's just called 11 Beech View Lane.

Personally, I'd prefer somewhere whimsical and Tudor, with beams and uneven walls. Any walls at all would be nice actually. My dream house is the cottage we always used to visit in Cornwall, which *actually* had a beach view. I even suggested we buy the cottage one summer, but Dad just laughed and said, "Wouldn't that be nice!"

Which it would, obviously. Why else did he think I suggested it?

The theme of our kitchen in the iPhone Box is "Things That Slide Shut Automatically So You Can Never Leave Anything Open" and "Is That a Wall Panel or a Cupboard, They Both Look the Same." It takes Habiba about twenty minutes to find any glasses. Eventually, everything is set up, and we sit around and they all listen in detail to my story . . .

"I got hit by a bus," I tell them.

"You're so strong," says Lip Gloss Lizzie, gripping Kenna's hand.

"You're unbelievable," says Zanna.

"We're just all so glad you're okay!" says Alison, hand on her heart, and I melt like a chocolate bar. Alison looks especially glowy and beautiful today, wearing soft pink nail polish and a sunny yellow sweater. Her eyes are creased in dewy concern, mascara licking her long eyelashes, and I gaze at her and . . . suddenly remember I'm not saying anything, and everyone is looking at me, waiting. Gooseberries! "You *are* okay, aren't you?" Alison asks, and I feel my face redden.

Zanna smirks, knowing exactly what I am.

"Oh, she's fine," she drawls, and I glare at her to shut up at once, or else I might get Siobhan to kick her out.

"She's obviously still concussed," Siobhan announces all-knowingly, and she snaps her fingers. "Kenna, pour Cat an apple juice! Actually, get me one, too."

Kenna and Siobhan have been friends since kindergarten. Kenna is basically her Number Two and Personal Assistant. Sort of like the minion who drives the White Witch's carriage for her in Narnia. Not that Kenna is a minion, though she is only five feet tall. We all think Kenna is a little hard of hearing due to the low success rate of shouting "HEY! KENNA!" across the school grounds (which Siobhan does often). Her grandparents, older sister, and basically all her friends apart from us are Deaf, so Kenna knows British Sign Language. And because Siobhan hates not knowing something, she learned some, too. Sort of. She did an exchange with someone at Marta's Deaf school and was praised by the teachers for her "expressive and highly unique" style of signing . . . so she must be doing something right!

Kenna runs around getting apple juice, then out of nowhere, Siobhan says, "Habiba, is there anything you'd like to share, since we're all gathered here?"

Kenna freezes while pouring juice, and even Zanna looks up from her phone.

Habiba's fairly fearless: she's captain of both the netball AND trampolining teams, as well as head cheerleader and tennis county champion—true Fitstagram royalty. She's actually brought one of her tournament trophies today just to drink her juice from. (I think she wants to make sure none of us forget her power.) She looks quite Sweaty Betty nervous now though.

"Something . . . to share?" Habiba repeats.

"Don't act thicker than you already are!" Siobhan snaps,

nostrils flaring. "I spotted your tragic and vapid attempts at flirting with Nico Benneston after netball on Wednesday! Did you really think we wouldn't find out? Spill. Now."

"RIP," Zanna whispers, shuffling closer to me.

Habiba wavers through some shaky account of how her and Nico have been "practicing ball techniques" (Zanna spits her drink at that), and I find myself gazing at Alison again. I suddenly notice her shoulder, which is showing because her gorgeous yellow sweater has slipped.

Aphro-DAYUM, I think I might have an Alison Addiction! I've seen shoulders before, but *Alison's* shoulder is like a whole new creation! She looks so smooth . . . Her face lights up in a perfect, glorious smile, and my heart swells like a water balloon. Alison adjusts her sweater, touching her shoulder, and I sigh. If I were the hand upon that shoulder . . .

"Cat, who do *you* fancy?" Lip Gloss Lizzie asks, ripping me right out of my music-video moment. Habiba's stopped talking, and everyone's looking at me again.

"Wh-who do I wh-what?!" I stutter.

"Don't be so insensitive, Lizzie!" Siobhan gasps, barging Zanna aside and clutching my hand in her manicured talons. "Cat's far too busy going through life-changing trauma to think about boys!" Then her grip on my hand loosens. "Some boys are ravishing though. Like Kieran . . ."

I roll my eyes at Zanna, who's scrolling through her secret Tumblr and carefully not getting involved. The last thing I want at *my* Recovery Party is for Siobhan to sound off about Kieran Wakely-Brown again! But the gang seems to have other ideas.

"Kieran is dreamy, to be fair," Habiba agrees as Kenna signs "beautiful" over her shoulder. "He's so tall and blond, and have you seen his forearms?! Kieran is everybody's type. You're so hashtag-blessed, Siobhan."

"Well, no offense," I snap, without thinking. "But Kieran is not *my* type at all, actually."

There's a shocked silence. Zanna mouths, "Uh-oh." Then Siobhan explodes.

"NOT YOUR TYPE?! Did that bus liquefy your brain?!" Siobhan stomps around the picnic rug, waving her arms about like she's on fire. "Kieran is an exquisite fusion of human DNA! How is WALKING ART 'not your type'?! If Kieran Wakely-Brown isn't good enough for you, Cat, then actually you'll almost definitely DIE ALONE!"

"It's because Cat likes someone else," Zanna says, still glued to her phone. Then she freezes, eyes widening. I gawp at her like a catfish. WHAT THE ACTUAL FRUIT JUICE SMOOTHIE?! Zanna's eyes dart between me and Siobhan. "I mean, probably," Zanna says, in a teeny-tiny voice. "It's *probably* because Cat likes someone else."

I could strangle my Sagittari-USELESS friend! Now everyone is looking. Siobhan ogles me like a seagull. Kenna grips her juice in trembling suspense. Lip Gloss Lizzie has even stopped applying her lip gloss. Habiba just looks relieved the attention is off her and heckles me with "Who? Who is it, Cat?!"

And then it's like I'm being swarmed by owls, everyone going "who, who, who," and I stare at Alison, who is looking right into my soul, only I pray to Aphrodite she isn't really, else I will be ruined. And I open my mouth, grasping for a name, a face, anything apart from Alison Bridgewater, who is still staring right at me and—

"JAMIE!" I blurt, then clap a hand to my mouth.

Too late. There's an uproar of screaming and shrieking. Mum appears at the top of the stairs, looking alarmed and mum-like in her cardigan. "Is everything all right, girls?"

"No, it's absolutely not!" Siobhan gesticulates, but I think Mum is scared of Siobhan because she goes, "That's all right, then!" and disappears back into her study.

"You fancy Jamie Owusu?!" Siobhan rages. "I can't believe you didn't tell me!"

"I'm surprised," Alison says.

"Why?!" I squeak, already defensive.

Alison shrugs her gorgeous shoulders. "He's really quiet and you're kind of . . . loud, you know?" She smiles, then reaches over and squeezes my hand. Gooseberries, I'm about to incinerate! "In a *good* way, obviously," she adds.

LOUD?! I swallow, not sure how to take this. Alison sees me as LOUD?

"I sit next to Jamie in science!" Kenna squeals, and I feel my soul leave my body through cringe-fest embarrassment. "He asked if you were okay three times today."

"That's not so many!" I protest, but Siobhan is having none of it.

"That confirms everything!" she exclaims. "He's obviously totally infatuated with you. Don't worry about a thing, Cat! We'll make this happen."

I'm not sure I've ever heard anything so ominous. I look

to Zanna in despair, but she's being about as helpful as, well, Zanna—who is the most unhelpful person of all. I think my panic is showing, too, because Alison squeezes my hand and says, "Well, nobody's asked me who I like." And Siobhan goes into cardiac arrest for the third time in five minutes.

Alison, probably thinking she's totally saved my knicker-bockers, tells everybody about Private School Dude, and I think I'd rather be on a West End stage performing a naked salsa with Mrs. Warren than where I am right now, listening to this.

"That's why I wanted to talk to you, Cat, so you could check his sign in your *Star Bible* . . . But then you got hit by the bus! Anyway, his name is Oscar, and he's a Gemini." Alison grins as I retch up my voice box. ALISON FANCIES A GEMINI?! This is too much. My cousin Lilac, aka the Queen of Everlasting Evil, is a Gemini, and she's literally cut my hair while I'm sleeping before. You can NEVER trust a Gemini!

But before I can warn Alison off, she says, "We're going to the park together this weekend! So that's my secret out." Alison winks at me, and I am positively beaming to hide the tornado of horror brewing in my stomach.

Alison Bridgewater is going on a date. Just like that, my heart is officially broken, and I am destined to never-ending solitude.

An Aquarius Alone will probably be the title of my biography.

Chat Thread: Zanna Szczechowska

Zanna, 10:11 p.m.:
Hey, umm, didn't mean to say that out loud
Sorry lolz. Are you all right?

Cat, 10:13 p.m.:
I'M FINE!!! PERFECTLY SPLENDID HAHAHAHAAA!!!

Zanna, 10:13 p.m.:
Are you laughing hysterically via text message?
You know there really are other fish in the sea, right?

Cat, 10:14 p.m.:
That's an unfortunately Piscean metaphor you've chosen :(
And Zanna, what if I'm a terrible fisherman!!!

Zanna, 10:17 p.m.:
You probably are, you're terrible at everything tbh

Cat, 10:17 p.m.:
???

Aren't you supposed to be comforting me???

Zanna, 10:17 p.m.:
Oh yeah lol
There are other fish in the sea!

Cat, 10:18 p.m.:
YOU SAID THAT ALREADY!!!

5

Lid to Your Saucepan

It rains over the weekend, so Alison and Oscar are going to the shopping mall instead. The shopping mall. Apparently, that was his idea, which is the most loathsome Gemini idea ever! But I still reply to Alison's message and say I'm glad it's not canceled.

I'm not glad though. I'm heartbroken and upset. I lie in bed all morning eating cereal directly out of the box and wallowing (the best word for such activities). Libra Season ends in two days, and I'm still no closer to finding true love.

Unfortunately, it's Saturday, the day Mum and Jamie's mum, Fran, have their "sewing group," so there won't be much time to search for romance today. It's not much of a group: it only includes Fran and Mum and seems to consist of a lot more cookies and cups of tea than it does sewing. "It's escapism!" Mum always claims, which is valid. If I were a banker, I'd want to escape, too. "My job can be hectic. And that's only the job I'm *paid* for."

Then she'll laugh annoyingly, like I'm too young and stupid to understand she's talking about being a mother as well.

After some more wallowing, I get up and go to my mirror, which is covered in Disney princess stickers but has a small opening so I can actually see my face. Perhaps I need more stickers though, because this morning I look horrendous. Like that painting *The Scream*.

Ironically though, screaming isn't going to help. Alison is going on a date with Oscar, and I'm spending the morning with Jamie, whether I like it or not.

HINT: I do not.

When the doorbell rings, I'm already downstairs trying to stealthily return the cereal before anyone notices I had it in my bedroom, so I answer it myself. "Coming!" I even call, to cement my false-sunny mood as I swing open the front door.

Mum appears behind me, chuckling cheerfully (too cheerfully) at Fran as Jamie hops out of his mum's little red car like a rabbit out of a hat. "You're very keen to play butler this morning! That's a pleasant change. You should see her on Sundays, Fran—never up before two in the afternoon! Not sure why she's so excited today . . ."

They witter on. Jamie is grinning ear to ear, and I wonder right away what *he* has to be so happy about. Something awful I expect. Mum and Fran head to the living area, and I hear Fran say, not too quietly, "She'd be good for him, Heather!" Excuse me?! Good for him?! You'd think I'm being married off like a princess in Tudor England!

"Hey there, Cat," Jamie says, weirdly sauntering over with a weird sauntering sort of smile. "Should we go upstairs or something?"

I'm not sure where "or something" would be, as it's literally just upstairs or down, so I turn on my heel and head to my room—which, quite luxuriously for the iPhone Box, has four entire walls. Usually, I lie on my bed and Jamie sits on the floor to complain. Jamie (not unusually for a Cancer) has many sorrows, such as his friend Lucas never letting him win at computer games, or his mum forgetting to wash his bed socks, so his feet get cold at night.

Today though, Jamie seems to want to talk about my friends. Luckily, not my bed socks. "Siobhan—she's your friend, right? Isn't she dating Kieran Wakely-Brown?"

"She just likes him," I mutter, eye roll incoming. "Apparently, everyone does."

"Do you?" Jamie asks, and I splutter offendedly.

"No! I wouldn't date Kieran if you threatened me with crocodiles!"

"Oh, cool," says Jamie, grinning strangely. "So, about Alison . . ."

I freeze. "What about her?"

"Her mum goes to our church! She knows *my* mum." He says this like it's an achievement, cracking his knuckles. He winces, then rubs them mournfully. "They're both from Kumasi, the Garden City of Ghana," he adds proudly. "So they're friends."

Ghana sounds gorgeous when Alison talks about it. Apparently, her middle name means "Tuesday," the day of the week she was born, which is a Ghanese tradition. Or is it Ghanaian? I consider this, then realize I'm just thinking about Alison's smile . . . Big, poetic sigh.

"Alison said you mentioned me at your recovery party," Jamie says.

Ghana vanishes. I sit up sharply. "She said WHAT?!"

Jamie has a twinkle in his eye that gives me the heebie-jeebies. "At church. She said you told your friends you'd date me."

I might be about to throw up my skeleton. Freaking Alison! "I mean, I talked about you!" I babble. "You're, like, my friend, right?! I didn't think you'd mind, and everyone expected me to say someone, so . . . !"

"I didn't mind at all," Jamie says, then he jumps from the floor to the bed with remarkable speed. "I thought it was . . . Well, you know." He smirks. "Cute."

I gulp. "Well, good! I'm SO relieved, Jamie, thank you for understanding! And I hope you know that, well, if you ever need to tell anyone you've kissed a girl, for example, I'd be HAPPY to put my name forward in return—not that we HAVE TO kiss, just . . . !"

I'm feeling faint. How can I explain my way out of this? Maybe I should tell Jamie I'm in an arranged marriage with a German prince? But then Jamie might ask his name, and I don't know any German names. My mind races. Strubert Humbervink. Rudolph Strudolph. Just as I'm beginning to wonder if an Italian prince would be more believable, Jamie says, "I'd love to take you up on that offer, angel," and he leans forward and KISSES me.

WHAT IN THE NAME OF RUDOLPH STRUDOLPH?!

It's my first-ever kiss. I don't know what to do! What if I dribble in his mouth? I don't even remember to close my eyes! My balance, propped up on the bed on my elbows, is not ideal, and his weight against me means my neck is straining to hold up my head.

"Mmfmmphmhrmph!" I go, and Jamie pulls back. "Um, I'm falling!"

Jamie winks. Oh, gooseberries. "Head over heels in love, I hope."

I cough. "Um, wow, how swoony is that? Listen, I actually—"

"I took your advice and started writing songs like Chidi Unigwe," Jamie says, flicking his eyebrows up. "Wrote one about you the other day."

I naturally assume he's kidding, so I laugh right in his face, but he doesn't laugh back, so I stop laughing. "Wait, really? You're serious? That's . . . um . . . so sweet!"

Taylor Swift me down, I didn't tell Jamie to write songs . . . did I? Oh, perhaps I did. But I didn't mean it! And perhaps I'm a terrible actress, as well as a terrible kisser and advice-giverer, because Jamie goes all sheepish. "You think it's cringe, don't you?"

He looks like he might cry. I look to the door, wishing for once that Luna would barge in ranting about veganism, but no such luck. Jamie sniffs. Gooseberries! What am I supposed to do? Quickly, my lips squeezed all the way shut, I kiss him super-fast on the cheek.

"It's not cringe!" I squeak. "Don't be upset!"

Jamie looks round, eyes brimming with hope. "I can play it for you, if you like," he says, eager as a puppy. "I know the lyrics by heart."

I gawp at him. "Play it for me? Like, here? Like, now?"

Before I know what's happening, Jamie is fixing me with an intense stare. First, he starts clapping. Then he's singing! I quickly clock the tune. It's "Jolene" by Dolly Parton.

"Her smile is like Marilyn Monroe's,

Her skin is white and soft as snow,

And she has got the nicest nose, Cathleen . . ."

It's awful. It doesn't even scan! If Dolly Parton could hear this, I am certain she would drop dead from shame. But what can I do? He's in my bedroom! I keep my smile plastered on like my life depends on it, and Jamie continues his ballad.

"Cathleen, Cathleen, Cathleen, Cathleen . . .

I'm begging you, please let me be your man . . .

Cathleen, Cathleen, Cathleen, Cathleen!

Please let me be the lid to your saucepan . . ."

There seem to be a lot more verses than I remember being in "Jolene," but eventually he stops slapping his knees and pauses dramatically, eyes squeezed shut with emotional intensity. Then he breaks into a grin. "What did you think?"

Slowly, I clap. "It was . . . *very* good, Jamie! Thank you *so* much."

He leans forward to kiss me again. I let him, because at least he can't sing if his lips are occupied. Then my phone lights up. I make out Alison's name on the screen, so I break away from Jamie to read the message.

Alison, 12:29 p.m.:
CAT! Date is going GRATE. He's so cute!!! Details to come!!!
xxxxx

She's right about that: her constant updates are definitely GRATING on me. I open the keyboard to reply like a decent friend and bombard her with support, but woe alas, I can't find

39

the words. Alison Bridgewater is on a date with a boy, and the boy is cute. I sit in silence and stare at the screen. Jamie waits awkwardly.

Finally, he clears his throat. "Who's texting?"

I hastily lock the screen. "No one!"

"Not a guy, is it?"

I don't meet his eye because I might cry. I force a smile, but I actually might have to rip my face off to cope. (Which would still be less painful than this.) "Why? Jealous?"

He shrugs, aloof as a loofah, but his mouth droops and he's clearly the most jealous jelly bean ever. He looks almost as miserable as I feel! Did the stars plan this? What with the bus and now Jamie kissing me, slap-bang in the middle of Libra Season, maybe the universe is trying to tell me something? Perhaps I can't save Alison from a Gemini, but I can save myself from needing to write *An Aquarius Alone*! Siobhan swims dangerously to mind . . . "A boyfriend is the best natural cleanse, Cat . . . I never even think about Chidi anymore!"

I nudge Jamie with my foot. "It was just a friend. Don't worry."

My phone vibrates again, but this time I ignore it. Licking my lips determinedly, I grab Jamie's collar and yank him in so we can kiss some more. I'm not sure what to make of the kisses: they're more *hard* work than fireworks. But maybe I've been watching too much Disney? I kiss Jamie and try very hard not to think about Alison Bridgewater. Then I realize that there's a problem.

I'm actually always thinking about Alison Bridgewater.

WHAT I LIKE ABOUT JAMIE OWUSU

- He's . . . there. Yes. Good start!
- He always has cookies on him.
- I mean on his person, not on his clothes . . . although that, too.
- He has really, REALLY good . . . intentions?
- He's bad at texting, so we don't have to talk lots.
- He's a Cancer, the easiest sign to order about.
- He already visits every Saturday, so we don't need to arrange dates.
- He's not Alison Bridgewater!
- I slightly wish he was though.

6
Nine Rules of Necking

Alison gives her date rave reviews on Monday, but I remain unconvinced. I mean, a shopping mall? I still can't believe Private School Oscar took Alison Bridgewater to a shopping mall. Boys can get away with anything! I scowl across the playground.

It's coming up to snake-ridden Scorpio Season, but because Siobhan says "the library is for nerds and losers," we're outside huddled in our blazers like penguins. We always occupy the same picnic table by the art studios, which Siobhan claimed as our group's space in sixth grade. Her initials are literally carved into the tabletop, so no one else dares sit here now. Not even the teachers.

". . . then he loaned me five quid!" Alison reminisces. "For an ice cream at the café."

"Sorry," Zanna butts in. "*Loaned* you five quid?"

Alison's smile doesn't even flicker. "His dad works in finance," she explains. "So Oscar's very careful with money. I'm going to pay him back next week."

Then Siobhan demands, "Did you guys make out?"

Alison's smile tightens. "Not on the first date, Siobhan!"

Siobhan goggles at her. "This isn't medieval England, Alison! Are you dense? How is it even a date if you don't make out with each other? Boys aren't good for much else . . ."

"Well, she could always talk to him," I suggest.

Siobhan does not look impressed at that. "If a boy took me on a date and didn't try to kiss me, I'd assume he was a frigid weirdo. What are you supposed to talk to boys about anyway? I don't think that's natural, to be honest."

On that, we possibly can agree. Alison smiles at me in ally-ship though, so obviously that makes everything worth it, even if I am now in the foolish position of defending Private School Oscar. "Thank you, Cat," she whispers as Siobhan rants on. "Love you the most."

Blushing like a clown, I hastily look away from Alison and accidentally make laser-precise eye contact with another girl on the other side of the grass. Wait—I recognize her! It's the girl with the green glasses who counts in Korean. She's slouched against a tree with Marcus and Maja, these two goony goths with bleach-blond hair from the drama crowd.

She has dark hair with blond highlights and bold black eyeliner, which is shockingly outrageous all by itself, since fashion-loathing old fossils like Mrs. Warren usually sniff out makeup like bloodhounds. Perhaps she's too Avril Lavigne rebellious to care though. Her shirt is untucked and her socks are pulled up to her knees.

Basically, she's über-cool as can be. She's the überest.

The girl looks at me and I look at her, then I frown, because it's almost like she was looking at me already. She tilts her head curiously, then turns back to Marcus and Maja, like our moment of intergalactically intense eye contact never even happened.

I nudge Zanna. "Zanna. Zanna. Zanna. Who's that girl?"

Zanna looks round from Siobhan, who's occupying the tabletop, cross-legged like some sort of deity, and reciting her Nine Rules of Necking to Kenna and Alison. Habiba's had a lucky escape today—she's teaching tae kwon do to sixth graders with anger-management issues.

"What girl?" asks Zanna.

"That girl, over there!" I try to point without pointing. "Under the tree."

"Why are you twitching like that?" Zanna frowns. "Have you been Tasered?"

For the love of Coraline Jones, she truly is useless. "There is a girl, Zanna, standing under that tree. She was looking at me! She has blond highlights and huge socks and—"

"Oh, *that* girl," Zanna says finally. She might need new glasses. "That's Morgan."

Then she stops. I blink at her. "And?! Who's Morgan?"

"*That's* Morgan," Zanna says, nodding to the tree.

Rattlesnakes galore. I'm just about ready to throttle her!

"Yes, I understand that *that's Morgan*," I reply. "But who is she? Do I know her?"

"Well, obviously not, if you're asking me," Zanna replies. I have to close my eyes at that point. I am a true beacon of patience. Then Zanna says, "She's new this year. Julia from Slavic Society is in her homeroom and said she was in a band, which is cool." Then Zanna smirks. "So really, Cat, it makes no sense that she'd be looking at someone as uncool as you."

Before I have time to box Zanna's ears, Siobhan overhears our conversation and spins round on the tabletop. "Morgan Delaney? URGH! You're wrong, Zanna. Morgan isn't *in* a band, she's just banned. Banned from Starbucks, I think is what Habiba said."

"Banned from which Starbucks?!" Kenna glances at Morgan fearfully.

"*Every* Starbucks," Siobhan says with conviction. "So she must have done something truly evil. My useless cousin— Scrounging Samantha—once worked in Starbucks and told me you can get away with anything! I heard she's Irish or something twisted like that."

I widen my eyes. "Siobhan! You can't say that! Anyway, aren't *you* Irish?"

Siobhan stares at me like I'm thicker than brown bread. "Why would you think I'm Irish?! My parents are both from Sevenoaks! Anyway, she didn't group with me and Lizzie in psychology, even though I asked her because she's new and has an all-right nose. She said she'd already promised Marcus! And he's an utter freak show on wheels—he literally plays chess for fun like some dying old man—so we won't be friends with her."

"I guess she does have a streaky hair dye," says Kenna, wrinkling her nose.

Siobhan smirks. "It looks like she dip-dyed it in mustard."

Siobhan and Kenna exchange glances, then fall about cackling like bats. I'm just wondering what Morgan Delaney could possibly have done to get banned from every Starbucks in the country, when Alison puts her hand right on top of mine. I freeze and Alison smiles like everything is normal. Which it is, obviously. I am completely in control of the situation.

"Cat," says Alison, eyes crinkling in that crinkly and sympathetic way that absolutely ruins my life. "Can we partner up in PE? I'm awful at tennis, and last time Siobhan was raging with me for losing—she's too used to practicing with Habiba! But you're used to losing, right? Would you mind?"

"Sure!" I squeak. "We can team up!"

"Great!" Alison gives me a gorgeous-as-a-Greek-island smile. Over her shoulder, Zanna rolls her eyes. "Cover me while I check my phone?"

I turn so that I'm hiding Alison from passing teachers, trying to ignore my cheeks heating up like I'm on that Greek island myself. What is wrong with me? It's just tennis! Why does every tiny moment feel like the biggest deal since Jupiter when it's her?

"Oh my goodness, Cat!" Alison gasps, and I whirl round. What now?!

Alison turns the screen, showing everyone at the table before she shows me. Siobhan gasps, then Kenna, then Zanna goes, "Oh, yikes," and finally, the screen reaches me. My lungs practically explode out of my nostrils! Jamie has posted a picture of me from Saturday on his Instagram (@owusuperman) and the caption says "Saturday is Caturday! Isn't MY GIRL-FRIEND a piece of heaven?" Tagged: @cathezodiaclown

We're in the PE locker room, being awkward and silent. You'd think we'd all turned into Zanna. Unusually, none of us know what to say (or sign, in Kenna's case). I didn't tell any of them about kissing Jamie on Saturday and, given their reactions, I'm guessing they feel rather betrayed. And me? I'm positively flabbergastrocopied! Or is it flobberghosted?

Whichever it is, I am that, because I never told Jamie we were a thing! What does he think he's playing at?! For Alison to find the post as well . . . Coming to school in a clown costume would be less embarrassing.

"I can't believe you didn't say anything!" Siobhan hisses.

"I didn't . . ." I begin, but I trail off. Because I can hardly tell everyone he was wrong. I don't want to make Jamie the laughingstock of the school. Anyway, I still have to see him every Saturday, so this is quite the hullabaloo of a situation.

"Didn't what? Didn't think I was important enough to know?!" Siobhan unbuttons her shirt. She always takes off all her clothes before changing, just to make everyone feel bad about her toned and perfect figure. She goes jogging with Habiba twice a week, like some sort of masochist. She always has matching underwear: today it's snakeskin green.

"Sorry," I mumble.

Alison nudges me. "It's okay, babe. I'm sure you'd have told us at lunch. I spent the whole break talking about *my* date—you couldn't get a word in edgewise!"

But Siobhan doesn't look convinced. "Whatever!" she chimes, sliding on her PE top and yanking up her shorts. "Zanna? I'm partnering with you today."

"Um, cool?" Zanna is still tying her shoelaces.

As usual, the slowest to change is Millie Butcher. She's pale and wispy, and shorter than any other girl in ninth grade, which is why Siobhan calls her "Millie the Micronaut." She hasn't taken off her uniform yet, and Siobhan eyes her up like a boa constrictor.

"What's taking you so long, Mills?" she calls across the locker room.

Millie flushes red. "Nothing, thanks."

Siobhan mimes not hearing, one hand on her ear. "What was that?"

"Nothing," Millie repeats louder. "I'm fine."

"Okay, there's no need to shout!" Siobhan staggers backward, fake-gasping, and the other girls laugh, leering at Millie in hope of a snappy comeback. But Millie is like a depressed ninja: she never fights back. She just takes off her top and Siobhan snorts. "Still in a bralette! Adorable. Anyway, I'm changed! Zanna?"

She snaps her fingers and strides out of the locker room. Zanna groans, then slopes after her. I'm watching Millie though, feeling oddly uncomfortable. I should say something positive! Tell her Siobhan's only joking, even if it's, um . . . not always a TOTAL giggle-fest? Then Alison brushes my arm. My skin tingles dangerously.

"Are you okay?" Alison asks. "Don't worry about Siobhan."

"Oh, I'm not." I definitely am. "Thanks though."

Alison smiles. "Anytime! Now come lose at tennis with me."

Perhaps, if I'm really lucky, I'll get knocked out and re-concussed by a speeding tennis ball, and I won't have to deal with any of this later.

Group Chat: The Gang

Habiba, 4:35 p.m.:
Cat, my Auntie says she's so happy for u getting a
#BOYFRIEND!!! xox

Cat, 4:37 p.m.:
Doesn't your Auntie live in Morocco? How did she find out???

Siobhan, 4:39 p.m.:
OFC she found out, you DUNDERHEAD! You're in a
RELATIONSHIP, ppl have to know, or what's the point??? So I
told Jasmine McGregor, problem SOLVED

Cat, 4:40 p.m.:
YOU TOLD **LOUDMOUTH JASMINE MCGREGOR**???
SIOBHAN!!!

Zanna, 4:41 p.m.:
Maybe Cat should just change her @ to @cat.owusu now . . . You
wouldn't want Jamie to feel like a shady secret . . . Share ur pride
with the world! :)

Cat, 4:42 p.m.:
GO AWAY ZANNA!!! Me and Jamie had a very mature
discussion ACTUALLY and he's agreed to keep our relationship
QUIET online so it can blossom without interference from the
outside world . . . It's very romantic and I'm very VERY happy
about this!!!

Alison, 4:42 p.m.:
Awww . . . That's so cute! I'm so happy you're happy babe!! xo

Zanna, 4:42 p.m.:
Same, bestie :) SOOO happy!

Scorpio
SEASON

7
Snogging Snow Whites

Well, at least I'm not diving into Scorpio Season alone. Having a boyfriend changes everything! No sooner have I "bagged" Jamie (Siobhan's words), Siobhan announces that she and Kieran have "decided to go exclusive," too. I'm not quite sure what she means by "go exclusive." It's not like she's been seeing anyone else. Maybe it just sounds more adult that way? Siobhan takes her relationships rather seriously . . .

But, as Siobhan explains in detail on the phone that weekend, having a boyfriend means you have to allocate your time. Basically, if I spend break with my friends, I have to spend lunchtimes with Jamie, or vice versa. It's all very complicated and unnecessary.

Back in school on Monday, I realize I could suggest Jamie just come and sit with us, but I also want to keep Jamie as far from Alison as I can. I don't want her to *see* me with him! He keeps putting his arm round me and kissing me on the cheek at random intervals . . . It's a waking nightmare!

"I don't know why you're surprised," Zanna tells me in the cafeteria. "He's your boyfriend. That's what boys do. They kiss you all the time and get really annoying."

I sigh in frustration. "But is it normal for them to kiss your ear?"

Zanna looks me up and down, then smirks. "My poor blond friend," she sighs. "You've got a big storm coming. Speaking of which . . ."

Then Jamie appears, bounding into the seat next to me with his Ninja Turtles lunch box. He grins at me, then at Zanna, too. "Zan-Zan!" he says, holding up his hand, and I almost choke on my hot chocolate. "Put one right there!"

I gawp at him. Is he joking?! Zanna Szczechowska does *not* high five.

Zanna narrows her eyes. "I'm good. I'm actually going to the library. See you in French, Cat." I beg her with my eyes to *please, please stay*, but Zanna, useless as always, abandons me. I slowly turn to Jamie, *my boyfriend*, with the best smile I can muster.

"What's her deal?" Jamie asks.

"Zan-Zan?" I repeat. Like, duh!

"I'm just being friendly!" He spreads his arms. "Your amigos are my amigos, right?"

Absolutely not, I want to tell him. Also, I think it's "amigas," but all I can do is smile awkwardly and appreciate that he's doing his best. Even if his best is absolute garbage.

Siobhan was right about boyfriends distracting you: fending off Jamie's advances takes up an enormous amount of time. But Scorpio Season is all about passion, and I am very passionate about not dying alone. So, Jamie and I are going to have to work at emotionally connecting this November, or else we'll be sad slippers together for the entire zodiac year!

One sunny afternoon, we go to the riverbank together, which runs across the end of the sports fields. I take out my notebook while Jamie sits there like a nuisance, holding my hand. Drawing one-handed isn't easy though, and eventually I have to shake him off. My drawing today is Elsa from *Frozen* experiencing her first kiss with Moana. I'm just wondering whether to draw them in the tropics or the snow when Jamie harrumphs.

I look up from sketching Moana's hair. "What's wrong?"

Jamie sniffs. "Nothing."

I drop the pencil and scowl because he's really dampening my blossom by now. If he doesn't switch it up soon, I may have to murder him before our three-week anniversary! "Well, it's obviously something," I retort. "So maybe you should just tell me."

"Why are you always drawing girls kissing?" Jamie asks.

I gasp, then hug my notebook to my chest. "I'm not *always* drawing girls kissing, actually. Sometimes I draw girls . . . getting married!"

"But why?" Jamie picks at the grass. "Don't you ever draw anything else?"

"Well, obviously I do!" At once, I'm flipping back through my notebook. "Look, there's . . . There's definitely one here." I flip back. And back . . . And back . . . "Somewhere."

I gulp. Okay, Jamie's not entirely wrong. There are lots of

kissing princesses in my notebook. But it's not my fault princesses are so aesthetically pleasing! They're just so pretty and flowery and . . . pretty.

"I can draw what I want," I mumble, avoiding Jamie's eye.

Jamie reaches for my notebook, but I snatch it away, suddenly self-conscious.

"What's the problem?!️ Let me look!" he says, but I shake my head.

"No," I tell him. "It's private!"

"Lovers don't keep secrets from each other, Cat," says Jamie, and I go so limp with horrified shock that Jamie has just called us "lovers" that the notebook slides right out of my hand! He begins leafing through the pages, and I yodel in panic.

"Jamie!" I rush at him. "Give it back!"

I leap through the air, and Jamie, eyes widening in shock as I launch myself toward him, throws the notebook away like a Frisbee. It spins across the sky and falls:

Right. Into. The. River.

We goggle at the water. My notepad is floating away.

"Oh," Jamie mumbles. "Sorry."

"You did that on purpose!" I cry, tears in my Aquarius eyes. All my drawings! My hours and hours of princesses, my stanzas of tragic romantic poetry, all gone just like that, bobbing down the river to be some duck's living room curtains.

Then there's a splash.

I look round in alarm and, with my utterly-disbelieving-and-almost-crying eyes, see Morgan Delaney. She steps right into the river without even taking her shoes off. The water reaches her knees! Everybody on the riverbank is watching. Morgan must be as reckless as they say: everyone knows that entering the river will get you a detention!

Morgan slips on the slimy stones. I gasp. What if she's swept away? What if she drowns for the sake of a few snogging Snow Whites? But Morgan is fearless, flinging back her hair and splashing through the water toward my nautical notebook. She whisks it out of danger and holds it up like King Arthur's sword for all the gathered crowd to see.

"SHE'S GOT IT!" Loudmouth Jasmine McGregor bellows, and everybody cheers. You'd think Morgan Delaney had just walked on water! Then again, if she could walk on water, jumping into a river probably wouldn't be quite so heroic. I watch in awe as Morgan climbs back onto the riverbank. She's soaked up to her waist, and there's green slime on her shoes.

"You saved my notebook!" I exclaim, tumbling over to her.

Morgan is still catching her breath. She gives me the funniest look, like she can't quite believe I'm talking to her. "Yeah, looks like it," she says, shaking her head like she's waking herself up, and she lifts the notebook, which is tragically soggy and crumpled. "Although it might be too late. Maybe you can dry it out in an airing cupboard or something?"

Siobhan was right: Morgan is Irish. Irish enough to have the accent anyway. But her voice is soft and slightly throaty, and she definitely doesn't sound evil, like Mrs. Warren, so perhaps Irish accents aren't so bad after all. She also has the palest blue eyes, a sharp contrast to her dark hair and brows. Water droplets pepper her green-framed glasses.

Then I realize I'm just staring at her, speechless as an apricot.

I look away from her aquatically amazing blue eyes and down at her slimy green shoes instead. "You're soaked!" I breathe. "Are you okay?!"

"Oh, I'm fine," says Morgan. "Just a bit of water, right? Totally worth it to save . . ." And then, before I can stop her, she opens the notebook, right onto Elsa and Moana. Morgan blinks, looking more than a little surprised. "Your drawing of two kissing princesses."

I think I am a little lost for words. It isn't every day a heroic Irish girl jumps into a river and saves your book of secret lesbian princesses. I'm just conjuring up a very clever and believable excuse for why I have such a notebook when Morgan's friend Maja comes over.

"That was insane," she says. "Are you cool?"

UM, YES?! Morgan is possibly the coolest, in fact. But then Jamie clears his throat annoyingly, reminding me he's actually still alive.

"I was totally about to jump in myself," he says. "But, er, you were pretty fast, so I just, er . . . waited here."

I glare at him, ready to tell him exactly where he can jump next, but then Morgan cuts in. "Jamie, right? We met on the field trip—I gave him a bandage when he cut his pinkie on a thistle," she explains to me with a grin. I look at Jamie, and Jamie looks at me.

"No," he says. "That . . . No, that wasn't me."

"I'm Morgan, by the way," says Morgan Delaney, handing me my notebook. "I'm new this year, but I've seen you round. You're Cat, right?"

I'm taken by surprise. She knows me?!

"Yes, I'm Cat! Meow!" My cheeks heat up like thermometers. Meow?! What?! "I mean, *ni hao*," I cough hastily. "Which is Japanese for hello. Or maybe it's Chinese? I'm not sure, I'm not actually from China. Or from Japan. Um . . ."

I trail off. I might have to execute myself.

"Cool," says Morgan eventually, justifiably looking a touch confused. Her cheeks are actually pink! But maybe I'm wrong . . . Morgan quite possibly has hypothermia.

I want to say something cultured and clever, something that will mean Morgan doesn't walk away thinking I'm the epitome of absolute clownery, but my head is emptier than a Scorpio's soul. Then Maja goes, "Uh-oh . . ." and a shadow looms over us, obsidian and ominous, blotting out the sun. I whirl round in fright, right into Mrs. Warren.

"Well, well, well," Mrs. Warren says, her hag-ridden eyes gleaming across Morgan Delaney. "Tell me, young lady, in your previous school, did they teach you to read?" Mrs. Warren raises a finger and points. We all turn silently to the sign on the riverbank. Unfortunately for Morgan, the message is pretty hard to misinterpret: DO NOT ENTER THE WATER.

Quivering like queasy violins, we all watch Morgan Delaney. But Morgan folds her arms right back at Mrs. Warren and replies, "Sorry, Miss. I must have mislaid my glasses wherever you mislaid your manners. I can read just fine, thank you very much."

I find this very funny. Mrs. Warren evidently doesn't though. She gives Morgan two detentions: one for rudeness and one for jumping into the river to save my notebook.

"I'll have to write her a poem to say thank you," I tell Zanna, in class afterward.

"She'll wish she'd drowned," Zanna says, which is very rude indeed. I tell her I wish *she'd* drown, but Mrs. Warren overhears and gives me a caution for making death threats!

I explain that death threats are to be expected when under the influence of Scorpio Season's scorching passion, but she doesn't think that's very funny, either.

It is though.

Chat Thread: Siobhan Collingdale

Siobhan, 5:30 p.m.:
CAT, you useless haggis-muncher. Give me a horoscope for
Scorpio!!!
What should I avoid? Bonus points if it gets me out of LAME-
FEST h/w

Cat, 5:43 p.m.:
Ummm yes Siobhan ofc!!! Hmm ...
Scorpio Season is about PASSION and CERTAINTY. So avoid
writing or reading anything in quiet, doubtful italics. Only losers
use italics anyway. BOLD CAPITALS are the safest! Send
messages at times you'd find in the five times table (5:00, 5:15,
5:45, you know?) and don't wear indecisive patterns ... BOLD,
PRIMARY COLORS only!
Oh, and DON'T hang out with any Geminis ... THEY'RE ALL
TWO-FACED!

Siobhan, 5:55 p.m.:
THANKS IDIOT NOW I HAVE TO BURN MY FAVE SCARF
URGH

8
Incredibly Good Pushover

Over the weekend, I cannot stop thinking about Morgan Delaney. Every time I close my eyes, there she is, like a mythological vision: dashing out into the water, often in slow motion, throwing back her dark hair . . . Although I'm possibly making it slightly more dramatic than it actually was. That's what Zanna tells me over the phone anyway.

"You should have been there, Zanna," I gush, sprawled on my bedroom floor.

Zanna sighs impatiently. "I feel like I *was* there. You've told me what happened about five hundred times. Haven't you got anything better to do?"

"As a matter of fact," I reply haughtily, "I have two entire essays to write."

"Two?" Zanna says. "Cat, you can barely write one essay. What are you talking about?"

"Well, I have to write my own essay . . ." I hesitate. "And I also may have slightly agreed to write Alison's." There's a long silence. "Zanna? Are you still there?"

"Unfortunately, I am." Zanna sighs. "Are you being serious? You're doing Alison's homework for her now? And to think we say Siobhan is the stupid one."

I frown. "Do we?"

"Well, I do." Zanna pauses. "Cat, I think you might be the biggest pushover I've ever met in my fourteen years of living. Can't Alison write one basic essay by herself?"

"Of course she can!" I say at once. "She's just . . . not very academic!"

"Oh, and you are? Just because you know who Mary Oliver is?"

"Well, I mean . . ." I bluster a bit. "Look. It's not her fault she hasn't read the book!"

"Cat, my pathetic blond friend, don't take this the wrong way," Zanna says. "But if Alison Bridgewater spelled her own name wrong, you'd blame the pen before you blamed her."

"Well, Alison wouldn't spell her own name wrong," I retort.

"She always spells my name wrong," Zanna grumbles. "She spelled it 'Shakiraska' once. Like, what? That's literally just 'Shakira' with a Polish-sounding ending."

"Zanna," I say, calm as a clam at a clam convention. "Nobody can spell your name. I'm surprised even Polish people can spell it, to be honest. Maybe you should change it to Shakiraska."

"Am I going to have to get Luna to talk to you about casual xenophobia?" Zanna asks.

We hang up and I send her a text that just says "ZANNA

SZCZECHOWSKA" to prove that I'm not really a terrible friend and can absolutely spell her name. Zanna sends back an eye-roll emoji.

Then I get going on Alison Bridgewater's English essay, trying very hard not to get distracted by thinking about Morgan Delaney.

Splish, splash, splosh.

You'd think, given that I wrote her entire essay for her, Alison Bridgewater would be delighted as a daffodil to see me. But at break, she's drooping about at the back of the library like a rain-swept blade of grass.

She's found a table safely out of sight of the librarian, Miss Bull (yes, genuinely), who hates me because in sixth grade I spilled water over the library's new copy of Mary Oliver's *New and Selected Poems*. I told Miss Bull I loved the poems so much, I'd nearly cried myself to death and here's the evidence, but she didn't find that very funny.

As I walk over, Alison doesn't even look up. "Ta-da!" I announce, dropping the carefully printed essay on the desk. But Alison glances over mournfully. In fact, her eyes are misty and Piscean, like she's about to cry.

"Hey, Cat. Oh, is that my essay?" She gives me a watery smile, then looks away.

"Are you okay?" I ask. "Look, if this is about Zanna implying you're stupid . . ."

Alison sighs. "No, it's actually about Oscar. It was all so perfect, but now everything's gone wrong, and . . ." Then she trails off and frowns. "Wait, Zanna did what?"

"Let's talk about you." I hastily take a seat. Alison sighs, looking so terribly sad, I could weep myself. I do what Alison would do and place my hand over hers. Of course, as soon as I've done it, I wonder if I should have wiped my palm on my skirt first, but it's too late for second thoughts. I just sit there with my sweaty hand on hers. "What happened?"

Maybe it's my lucky day and Private School Oscar has been hit by a speeding truck!

"Oscar turned out to be a jerk. That's all." Then Alison looks at me and forces her sunniest Alison-like smile. "Sorry. You don't want to hear about this! I should be thanking you! You wrote my whole essay for me and didn't even ask me to pay for printing . . ."

"Of course I want to hear about it!" I assure her, mentally scrapping my plan to ask Alison to pay for printing. "What did Oscar do? Do you want me to murder him?"

Alison does a snotty laugh. Which could be gross, but Alison's snot probably tastes like honey . . . sigh. "He didn't really do anything. It was something he said." She hesitates, glances over the bookcase toward Miss Bull's desk, then pulls out her phone! "Look, why don't I just show you? Maybe I'm being too sensitive . . ."

I try to keep my expression to one of true care and concern. After all, Alison is my friend. Oscar being mean to her would be very, very sad. Then again . . .

NO! I mentally slap my own wrist. I am absolutely not going to be happy about this. I lean over to peer at Alison's phone. She's currently scrolling through a worryingly large number of texts, and I gulp away the pain.

"Here," she says, and she reads out loud: "*You're really hot and actually a black girl has been on the menu for some time.* I asked him what he meant and he just said *yummy*." Her voice trails off and a tear—an actual, real-life tear—trickles down Alison's perfect cheek.

I grab the phone and read the text myself. Shockingly, I didn't mishear! Oscar really said that to Alison Bridgewater. My mind flounders about like a flustered pelican as I try to process this most ghastly of ghastlinesses. "But, Alison, that's . . . Well, that's really racist!"

"Thank you!" Alison says, and she puts a hand right on my knee. Oh, Aphrodite . . .

Then Alison keeps talking, hiccuping occasionally, as I try to ignore her hand on my shivering knee, because I'm supposed to be Alison's supportive best friend: not easy when your heart won't stop clowning around like a circus marching band!

"I know it's not the biggest deal. Some people even think it's a compliment to say my hair is cotton candy or my skin is cara-mel. But it's always food, like I'm there to be eaten, you know?" She flutters her dewy lashes as I wonder whether dreamy-dreaming about her snot being honey-flavored is equally problematic. "Sorry. Am I even making any sense?"

"Absolutely," I assure her. "True love and raging cannibal-ism don't normally go hand in hand . . ." I pause and think. "But, Alison, I'm really sorry people say things like that."

Geminis really are intrinsically evil beings. I really want to give her my highly wiseful zodiac assessment of the situation, but unfortunately I'm now just thinking about Alison's snot, and it's breaking me out in a nervous sweat! I tug nauseously at my shirt collar and pray to Aphrodite that my face hasn't gone completely Scarlett Johansson.

Alison frowns. "Are you okay? You've gone red!"

Gooseberries! "I'm fine! Just, er, a little warm in here, isn't it? Um . . ." Distract her, quickly! "YOU SHOULD JUST BE GAY!" Me and Alison blink at each other. Did I just say that OUT LOUD?! I babble on, "I mean, if boys are so awful, maybe dating girls would be better, you know? I mean, *you* wouldn't know, and I wouldn't, either, but . . . !"

"Urgh, I wish!" Alison says, and my chest practically explodes. "I mean, never say never, right? If only attraction worked that way. Liking girls must be so much easier . . ."

I widen my eyes. "Well . . ."

Then, like a sign from Aphrodite that I really need to shut my mouth instantly, the air blossoms with heavenly music. I'm just wondering if the stress of this conversation has genuinely killed me and sent me into the great beyond when the music breaks into rap, and Nicki Minaj starts swearing loudly, which rather shatters the atmosphere.

"My phone!" Alison hisses, and I see her phone vibrating noisily along the tabletop.

We both dive for it at the same time. Unfortunately, I jog Alison's hand and the phone is knocked onto the floor, where Alison's ringtone carries on rapping. I dive under the table, grab the phone, and finally switch the music off. Then I leap to my feet in victory.

Only, there's a table right above me, so I actually end up smashing my head, upturning the desk, and saying, "Fizzlesticks!" which is (bizarrely) the first word that comes to mind.

Pain blares through my skull. When the world swings back into focus, I see Miss Bull, the worryingly-beige-clad-for-a-thirty-five-year-old librarian, glaring at me, along with half the students in the library.

"Um . . ." I clear my throat. "Sorry . . . ?"

"Whose phone is that?" Miss Bull demands, and I stare at it, right there in my hand.

Alison's eyes are as wide as wheels of cheese and, speaking of cheese, why the fresh cheddar isn't she saying anything?! I gawp between the phone and Alison and Miss Bull, then I say, "Um, it's mine! But you see, Miss, I was actually just . . . !"

Miss Bull holds up a rickety finger. "Just breaking the rules, I think you'll find. Cathleen, do you know the punishment for using your cell phone in school?"

"Um, is it a forgive-and-forget type of deal?" I suggest hopefully.

"It's a detention, Cathleen. Your phone will be confiscated until the end of the day."

I hand the phone over, still rubbing my throbbing skull. Maybe Zanna was right after all . . . I'm the worst pushover of them all! Then again, I pushed over that table very successfully indeed, so perhaps I'm actually an incredibly good pushover.

I decide I probably *shouldn't* ask Zanna about this later.

Chat Thread: Zanna Szczechowska

Cat, 3:31 p.m.:
I need to pick up Alison's confiscated phone!! Come with??

Zanna, 3:32 p.m.:
Why do u need to go if it's her phone

Cat, 3:32 p.m.:
Well u see Zanna, they actually think it's my phone???

Zanna, 3:33 p.m.:
Why do they think that?

Cat, 3:33 p.m.:
Probably because I told them it was

Also . . . I got a detention today!!!

Zanna, 3:35 p.m.:
Are those two things related?

Cat, 3:35 p.m.:
Ummmmmmmmmmmmmmm

Zanna, 3:35 p.m.:
Omg

Clown college called

They want their nose back

Cat, 3:36 p.m.:
Very funny Zanna, hahaha

Zanna, 3:36 p.m.:
:o)

Kate Bush in My Kitchen

Mum is far from happy to hear I've got a detention. In fact, when I tell her, she flails all over the kitchen-living-dining area of the iPhone Box like she's Kate Bush—which, as anyone who has seen the music video for "Wuthering Heights" will know, is a lot.

"There's no need to make such a fuss," I assure Mum as she clatters about like a poltergeist. "It's not a massive deal! I've had, like, twenty detentions already this year."

That stops Mum's clattering. For a moment, I think she's possibly calmed down. Then she slowly turns to face me, and her eyes are bulging, meaning that perhaps she has not.

"You've had twenty detentions this YEAR?! Cat Phillips! You haven't even reached the Christmas holidays!"

Then Mum yells a lot about how if I don't change my ways, I'm going to slip down a very slippery slope indeed, and I yell back that I can't help slipping if my slimy teachers keep making so many slippy slopes to slip on. Then I stomp upstairs with the intention of slamming my door as loudly as I can.

Unfortunately, Dad's just waxed the floors, and I slip on the landing and bruise my elbow.

9

The Lace-Trimmed Menace

Wasting an afternoon in detention is school-dining-depressing already. But when I find that Mrs. Warren is the teacher on duty, I honestly could inhale Buddha's bed socks with despair! Mrs. Warren must have prayed for my ultimate suffering in her vampire cathedral. Her face glows with satisfaction when she spots me shuffling into the cafeteria.

There are a few weepy-looking chairs spread about the floor and ten or so students sitting there, glum as plums. I recognize Brooke "the Crook" Mackenzie, Queen's most notorious redhead, running a coin through her fingers. Normally, I wouldn't look twice at anyone else because I'm pretty and popular and they are not, but I suddenly clock Morgan Delaney, slouching at the back in a really slouchy, über-awesome way.

She looks up just as I notice her and, despite the dingy tragedy of our situation, she smiles. Hesitantly, I smile back, subtly waving my hand. It's the first time I've seen her since she heroically dived into the river, and all at once, I get the flappiest butterflies.

Honestly! If I weren't quite so in love with Alison Bridgewater, I'd say I fancied her or something. Morgan *is* really pretty and striking, with her pale blue eyes and effortlessly cool sense of coolness . . . And her green glasses. And that scattering of freckles across her nose. She'd be amazingly easy to fall in love with. But compared to Alison Bridgewater, the prettiest, loveliest Pisces Princess in all of Lambley Common . . . ?

"Well, well, well, Cathleen Phillips," says Mrs. Warren, her voice positively dripping in lace-trimmed menace, and I am rudely awakened. "How nice of you to join us. Of course, as you're two-and-a-half minutes late, I haven't started the clock yet, so you'll all be here a full hour from now. You can blame Cathleen's lateness if you were hoping to leave sooner."

Everybody groans, and I blush at my shoes. She really does loathe me! Even Morgan is going to resent me now. I squirm into a seat and fold one leg over the other. They don't even give you a table in detention: you just sit around and slowly die. I jiggle my leg, and Mrs. Warren takes her seat at the front. Of course, *she* gets a table. She creaks open a folder.

"Stop bouncing your leg, Cathleen," Mrs. Warren says without looking up. I go still and sigh, gazing around the room. There's a cleaning lady mopping the floor with wet squelches, and the clock behind Mrs. Warren ticks loudly.

Five minutes later, my will to live is ebbing away. One boy seems to have dozed off, but perhaps he's just died? If Mrs. Warren notices, she doesn't wake him, which is unfair. If it were me, she'd probably clash cymbals above my head! Scowling, I fold my arms and—ouch! Something jabs me. I reach inside my blazer pocket. I have a pen.

In these dust-bowl desperate times, a pen is the most exciting discovery in the world! Slowly, I tug off the cap, then carefully roll back my sleeve. The patch of white over my wrist is particularly tempting, so I write my name in elegant calligraphy . . .

Cathleen

I smile at how sophisticated it looks. Like an author wrote it! Then, just to experiment aesthetically and quite fictitiously, of course, I add a last name in the same swirly hand . . .

Cathleen Bridgewater

Just for if I ever married Alison, you know? Then again . . . I bite my bottom lip. With two girls, how do you decide which name you're going to use? I've never thought about that before. I add on my last name as well. Just for the sake of imagining.

Cathleen Bridgewater-Phillips

Or does Phillips-Bridgewater sound better? I consider, tapping my pen on my knee.

A shadow falls across me. I gasp in alarm and look up, right into the spectacled glower of Mrs. Warren, who has glided silently across the cafeteria toward me like a hammerhead shark. She adjusts her tweedy-looking jacket, possibly the most tragic and Victorian piece of clothing I've ever seen. "Cathleen, what have we here?"

I gulp. "Um, just a pen, Miss!"

"Oh, *just* a pen!" Mrs. Warren chortles revoltingly. "Because I suppose a pencil would be worse?"

"Well, I'm not really one to judge, but . . . !"

"Silence in detention, Miss Phillips." Mrs. Warren holds out her hand, and I place the pen sheepishly in her palm. "Unless you want me to restart the timer of course."

This gets some concerned shuffling from neighboring chairs. She can't mean it, can she?! Not even Wicked Warren would do that! It's not like she wouldn't have to stay here longer as well. Then again, maybe she'd enjoy that. Maybe the suffering nourishes her. Maybe she's High Priestess in a vampiric cult, where they store human misery in glass jars—

"Show me your arms, Miss Phillips," Mrs. Warren demands, and my high-concept fantasy of Mrs. Warren's secret religion evaporates. I'm dropped back into my plastic chair.

I can feel my face going beetroot-rouge. "My arms, Miss?!"

Mrs. Warren blinks slowly. "You were writing on them, were you not?"

"W-well, I w-was," I stutter. "But, Miss . . . !"

"Then your arms, Miss Phillips."

Mrs. Warren waits like she has all the time in the world, and given that she's a teacher, she probably does. I glance over to where Morgan Delaney is sitting, watching my unfolding humiliation with an expression of mild interest. But not even Morgan can help me now.

Wordlessly, slowly as I can, I roll up my right-hand sleeve and show her my blank wrist. But Mrs. Warren just nods to my left arm instead. I feel the room swaying. She's going to know. She's been Alison's homeroom teacher since seventh grade! I'm shaking more than Dad's tragic hero, Shakin' Stevens. I can't even look. I roll up the sleeve of my left arm and hold it out to

Mrs. Warren. I sense her eyes scanning left to right like a Dalek's antenna thing.

"Interesting," I hear.

Then she walks away.

WHAT?! I sit rigid as a flowerpot man, flushed and dizzy, like I'm seasick, travel-sick, and lovesick all at once. Mrs. Warren returns to her desk and reopens her folder without another word. "Interesting." What the flipperless sea lion does "interesting" mean?!

Several times for the rest of detention, I glance warily at Mrs. Warren, and I get the feeling she's just been watching me, too. It's rather unsettling, but I'm probably being paranoid.

Doubtless, she's just plotting how to ruin my life even more.

When Mrs. Warren releases us, I'm practically cartwheeling toward the exit. I even forget to ask for my pen back! So now I can add "theft" to the extensive list of ways in which Wicked Warren has wronged me. Her seeing my romantic fantasy arm doodles is quite possibly the most traumatic experience of my life so far. And remember: I've been hit by a BUS!

I'm reaching the school gates when I hear, "Hey! Cat, wait up!"

Morgan is jogging to catch up with me, which is most flattering indeed. I don't think I could be persuaded to jog even if it were Queen Cate Blanchett herself I was chasing.

"I didn't realize we'd be buddied up in detention." She elbows me, smiling, and my stomach does its very own somersault, independent of my torso. Gooseberries, I'm really going to have to pull myself together. It's not like she's Alison

Bridgewater. I should be able to get through a basic conversation without wanting to transcend my body.

"No . . ." I say very normally. "I didn't realize, either."

"What were you in for?"

I hesitate. Perhaps I should fabricate a bold and dashing story to impress Morgan! I rugby-tackled a walrus on the art department's recent trip to Brighton, or I was caught selling stolen stationery on the Lambley Common black market . . .

I'm not sure Morgan would believe me though, so I just say, "Phone."

"Oh, bad luck." Morgan and I are now walking together, down the road outside Queen's toward Lambley Common Green. "But hey, at least you don't have to do it all over again tomorrow. Thanks to that notebook of yours, I'm in double trouble."

"Ah. Yes. Sorry about that." I pause walking. "It was very dashing of you though, Morgan. You were my heroine! Like, heroic, I mean—I'm . . . I don't do drugs."

Morgan frowns. "Wow, really? But you look like such a badass."

"HAA!" I laugh stupidly. "Well, thank you, it's my mascara; it's the darkest shade . . ." Then I trail off. "Um, you were probably joking, weren't you . . ."

"I was," Morgan confirms, and I go all blushful.

Awkward avocados galore! I stare at my shoes. Mine are boring black with buckles, but Morgan's have tiny stars subtly grooved into the leather, almost as if she carved them herself with a penknife. Stars! Because I'm a massive clown and can't think even the smallest thought without blabbing it out loud, I say, "I love your shoes!"

Morgan tilts her head. "Thanks. I love your hair. It reminds me of Madonna in *Desperately Seeking Susan*. Get a leather jacket and you'd look exactly like her." At my blank expression, she laughs. "Sorry—it's a movie from the 1980s. I'm kind of a film nerd."

I swallow, trying to think of something equally intelligent to say. "Oh, really? That's so cool. I'm a fan, too. I mean, not really of movies, but of, er, something. You know?"

Sappho-*no* . . . This is going disastrously!

But Morgan only nods earnestly, then bursts out laughing. Her laugh is carefree as a dandelion—almost a cackle actually. Like she's not ashamed or embarrassed. I can't even imagine not being ashamed of my laugh. I sound like a goblin with a blocked nose!

"You're funny," Morgan says. "A fan of something, huh? I like that. It's really, you know . . . really inspiring." She narrows her eyes and smiles, and she might be making fun of me, but before I can be sure, she's stopped walking again. "Anyway, this is me."

"And this is me!" I reply, and Morgan frowns.

"Um . . ." She points over her shoulder, down the cul-de-sac we've reached. "I meant this road? I turn off here. Marylebone Close is where I live. That house with the blue door."

I'm possibly the stupidest human who has ever lived!

But before I can redeem myself, Morgan opens her arms and I realize we are about to hug. Even I can hug without embarrassing myself, although I do get a face-full of Morgan's hair. She smells dark, smoky, deep . . . not like Alison's bubbly fruitiness at all. I really want to ask what her star sign is! But that might be weird and nosy. And I'm not a Libra.

"See you round, Cat," says Morgan, and she walks up Marylebone Close. Then she glances over her shoulder, and I have to walk away in a hurry, or else she'll think I was just standing around staring after her like a clown with googly eyes.

Which I was, but I'd never want her to think so!

Chat Thread: Alison Bridgewater

Alison, 3:35 p.m.:

Hey babe . . . I'd love a horoscope! xxx

Just paper-shredded my homework by mistake, worried I'm cursed :(

Cat, 3:35 p.m.:

HEY ALISON! OMG how unfortunate, stupid shredders!!! Why don't they have an undo button?? If you need help redoing the homework I'm always here!!! xxx

For Pisces like you, Scorpio Season is about broadening horizons, developing awareness, and becoming more well-rounded. So make sure to eat LOTS of donuts. Blueberry muffins should also do the trick! Then open your bedroom windows as wide as you can and walk up lots of hills—mountains are even better if there are any lying around! :)

Hope that helps!!! xxx

Alison, 3:45 p.m.:

Omg you're the best! Love you!!! xxx

10

Divine Feminine Energy

Saturday, and Jamie is back at my house. I'm still waiting for our Scorpio-steamy soul-bond to happen, but after Jamie's torturous rendition of "Dove Laboratory" ("Love Story" by Taylor Swift), I'm becoming seriously concerned. How are we supposed to bond over that? Not even my terrible poetry is terrible enough to spiritually connect with him.

After, Jamie wallows around my floor, moaning about how his mum won't buy him a gym membership, so he'll never have a six-pack, and it's all her fault. Then he tells a long and tragic tale about how he outgrew his favorite flip-flops, and I'm just about ready to cease.

"That's why I have my music," he's saying. "An outlet for my trauma."

I nod along pretending to listen, but actually I'm catching up with the gang's group chat on my phone. Siobhan's sent a screenshot of Millie Butcher's Instagram:

Siobhan, 1:33 p.m.:
[sent an image]
She sure knows how to BUTCHER my timeline!!!

Which is rather mean actually. But Habiba says she's SCROL-ling, which is scream-LOL-ing—a new term Siobhan and Lip Gloss Lizzie invented last month. Now every second comment on Instagram says SCROL, and anyone who doesn't live in Lambley Common gets confused. It's very funny. SCROL-level amusing, in fact.

"You never know when inspiration will strike if you're a singer-songwriter like me," Jamie prattles on. "In fact, now that I mention it, I'm feeling the vibe right now . . ."

I drop my phone and blurt, "Let's watch a movie!" Anything to stop Jamie from composing another song! I grab my laptop before he can disagree. Jamie doesn't watch anything other than *Gilmore Girls*, so the pressure to find something entertaining is on me. Then I remember what Morgan said after detention about Madonna and my blond hair, so I look up *Desperately Seeking Susan*.

"What's this?" Jamie asks as I find it online and hit play. He's all sulky-salads about not being able to write his songs, so I shuffle right up to him to cheer him up. Unfortunately, this means he puts his arm around me, but I decide I'll take one for the team. The team being me, Aphrodite, and the entire celestial sphere of the zodiac.

"It's just a film Morgan recommended!"

Jamie glowers. "I didn't know you talked to *Morgan* . . ."

I frown. "Why do you say *Morgan* like that? Just because she saved my notebook?"

Jamie shrugs, still pouting. "I feel like, I don't know, she'd be into heavy metal or something. She's a bit try-hard. She isn't musically refined like me."

I resist the urge to SCROL. "So what if she's into heavy metal?"

"Well, it's not your thing," Jamie sniffs. "That's all."

Jamie is right. Heavy metal is not my thing. But I'm not sure I like him telling me that, so I say, "Well, maybe you don't know me as well as you think. Maybe you're too busy being Mozart himself to notice that I'm very much into heavy metal and all sorts of craziness!"

That puts Jamie into a properly mopey mood. We watch the film in silence. Then Madonna appears with a Polaroid camera and her leather jacket, just like Morgan said, and she looks so stunningly amazing and perfect, I actually gasp.

"Who's that?" Jamie mumbles.

"Shush!" I hiss back. Because that's Madonna, obviously. That's *me*.

On Sunday, I'm rather looking forward to some me time, so I can de-traumatize myself from my horrifying week in peace. I think about messaging Morgan (seeing how she's granted me access to her über-VIP private Insta) to tell her I watched *Desperately Seeking Susan*, but then I remember that she's banned from every Starbucks in the country, and Siobhan doesn't like her, so maybe I shouldn't be her friend.

If only I knew her star sign . . . then I'd know whether she's trustworthy or not!

Suddenly, Mum strides into my room like she owns the place. She sort of does, I suppose, but it's still very annoying. "We're going to Maidstone to do some shopping!" she chimes. "Put your shoes on, love."

I'm lying flat on my back in the middle of my floor. "Why do I have to go?!"

"You need new tights. You've got holes in nearly every pair."

"I don't need to come with you for tights!"

Mum sighs, then lowers her voice to that level she uses when she's pretending to treat me like a grown-up. "Luna needs a new coat, but she'll never trust my opinions. Just last week she was rooting through my wardrobe to determine how heavily I've 'financially contributed to sweatshops.' I need you, Cat. Your sister's a nightmare to shop with."

I groan. That's peak Mum, guilt-tripping me into going for her sake. But I lever myself off the floor anyway and grab my coat in a very organized and adult way. I really am a saint.

In the car, Luna babbles on about the lack of TV representation for East Asian women. "I mean, name one East Asian actress with a leading role. Even one!"

"How about Sandra Oh from *Killing Eve*?" Mum suggests.

Luna scowls. "Another one, then."

"You didn't say two, Luna, you said one!"

"One example isn't going to tear down systemic racism, Mum!"

"Systematic what?"

Luna and Mum rave away all the way to Maidstone. I think

I deserve an Award of Endurance for coming on this shopping trip at all. The daily doses of clown-shoed chaos I have to put up with would push even the steadiest person over the edge.

"Why don't we forget the communist manifesto, Luna," Mum says as we walk from the parking garage to the department store, "and talk about what sort of coat you want instead? How about a nice, warm furry one?" Then her eyes widen in panic. "Faux fur, of course . . ."

But she's too late. Luna is already at her wit's end (which isn't saying much, given that my sister is already barking-sparking-multistory-parking-lot bizarre).

"Faux fur is just as bad as real fur, Mum!" she raccoons on. "It promotes the idea that humans can use animals' bodies for the sake of fashion. It's basically appropriation!"

"Do you mean it's inappropriate?" Mum asks, and Luna starts hyperventilating.

Maidstone is bleak today, like a town in midwinter. Probably because it *is* a town in midwinter. The soulless department store lurks next to a canal, and the air smells of moldy seaweed. The first shop Mum drags us through is an instant no-no. Everything is either faux fur or looks like a robe. By shop four, Luna has rejected more coats than I have vegan cheese alternatives, finding some minor problem with each one. Then she finds these "biodegradable boots."

"But we're not here for shoes, Luna!" Mum grumbles, and I sneak to another aisle, because I think if I have to listen to another clown fight, my head might implode.

That's when I spot a rack of leather jackets. Morgan and *Desperately Seeking Susan* come to mind, so I abandon my raging relatives to check them out. There are burgundy jackets and brown ones, too, but because I'm not forty-five, I reach right for the black. There's only one left, and it's probably too big. I still slide it on—if anything, I can send a funny picture to the group chat . . . But as soon as my arms are through the sleeves, I feel . . . different.

Luna is strutting around in the boots while Mum stands, hands on hips, giving the most useless opinions, such as "Can you really walk in those?" so I cool-glide to the mirror. The jacket has a rose stitched into the shoulder: a little flare of detail in red and green. I breathe in sharply, because ooh-la-la, Morgan was not wrong! I could be Madonna.

I toss back my blond curls. I am powerful. I decide right away that this jacket truly gives me divine feminine energy, so I dash over to where Mum and Luna are hullabaloo-ing.

"Mum, I need this jacket!" I announce. "It gives me divine feminine energy."

"Oh, not you as well," Mum groans in her usual supportive way. "A jacket? Do you need a jacket? You have that short coat, don't you?"

"But it's cheetah patterned." I smirk. "I wouldn't want to offend Luna."

Luna whirls round. "Shut up, Cat! And is that jacket leather?! You're literally a MURDERER—"

"All right, all right!" Mum holds up her hands. "Yes, you can get the jacket, and, Luna, you can get the boots. But now can we please look for what we actually came here to get?!"

"What about this one?" I suggest, pulling a lovely emerald coat from a hanger. Luna frowns, maybe wondering where the joke is. But there isn't one—I genuinely think it's nice. Goose-berries, why is everyone so suspicious? I trick Dad into wearing a sports bra ONE TIME and no one ever trusts me with fashion advice again!

Ten minutes later, we're at the register with the coat, the boots, and my divine-feminine-energy jacket, which Mum hands me with a grateful nod. I've definitely earned it. As we head back to the car, I put my coat in the shopping bag and wear the jacket instead.

"You're walking different," Luna says by the canal.

I roll my shoulders, very iconic indeed. "Am I?"

Luna nods, looking me up and down. "I hope you're not going to invent a whole new personality just because of a jacket," she says. "That's such a trope and implies that women can only show individuality through material possessions, which is actually very patriarchal."

But Luna's rambling cannot bother me when I'm looking as queenly as this. I regard her down my nose. "It's probably just my divine feminine energy from Madonna."

"Why would Madonna waste her divine feminine energy on you?" Luna asks, and I realize her rambling can still bother me after all. I chase her all the way back to the parking garage, cha-otic as a nun on a tractor.

Group Chat: The Gang

Cat, 5:09 p.m.:
Guys, is the Morgan getting banned from Starbucks thing . . . true??

Siobhan, 5:10 p.m.:
ARE YOU INSINUATING I WAS WRONG? MY INTEL COMES FROM TOP-NOTCH SOURCES, INCLUDING RICH ELIZABETH GREENWOOD HERSELF!!

Zanna, 5:15 p.m.:
Didn't Elizabeth make up an Azerbaijani pen pal to lie about being bilingual?

Siobhan, 5:16 p.m.:
AZERBAIJAN SHOULD BE HONORED ELIZABETH EVEN THOUGHT OF THEM FOR HER SLIGHTLY EXAGGERATED STORY. MORGAN DELANEY WAS ABSOLUTELY BANNED FROM STARBUCKS. I WILL NOT DEBATE THIS!!!

Zanna, 5:17 p.m.:
I texted Maja from Slavic Society and she says it's not true

Kenna, 5:17 p.m.:
Omg, doesn't Maja have a nose ring on the weekends?

Siobhan, 5:18 p.m.:
EXACTLY. TOTALLY UNRELIABLE!!!

11
Death by Dungaree

Jackets as amazing as mine deserve a debut event. Luckily, the most elevated event of Scorpio Season is around the corner: Siobhan Collingdale's birthday party. I was actually looking forward to it, but then I realize I'm going to have to go with Jamie.

Having a boyfriend is really beginning to grate my gherkins. We're halfway to Sagittarius Season, and still no soul-bonding in sight. Perhaps the party will help?

Anyway, I can't stay festering and irritated for too long because Siobhan shows up at school on Monday wearing a crown (a plastic one, but it's still rather fabulous) and parades around like Empress Catherine the Great of Russia while Kenna issues invitations on her behalf.

"Who's coming?" asks Lip Gloss Lizzie when we're gathered round the picnic table.

"Everybody's coming," Siobhan informs her. "And the theme is ROYALTY, for obvious reasons. I expect you all to dress ravishingly, which means NO CORDUROY! I don't appreciate having to waste my time burning your tragic choices, Habiba . . . !"

Siobhan rants on as Kenna pats Habiba comfortingly. Alison is scrapbooking, and I'm just admiring her for being so talented and gorgeous, pressing flowers into paper like that, when I notice that the Triple M's (Morgan, Maja, and Marcus) are by their tree again.

Slowly, Morgan raises her hand. I hesitate, but I wave back in the end. I can't just sit there and not wave. I'd look like some sort of clownish goose! Of course, as soon as I do, Siobhan's eyes are snapping between us like rubber bands.

"Why are you WAVING at Morgan Delaney?!" she demands.

"I'm not!" I squeal, quickly lowering my hand. "She was waving at me. I just, er, waved back!"

"What a salmon-slapping FREAK!" Siobhan explodes. "Who does she think she is, waving at you like that?! If she shows her ugly face at my party, I will throw her into the river."

Before I'm able to say that's a little (well, a LOT) on the harsh side, especially since Morgan's face isn't actually ugly, Habiba lowers her tennis racket (which she's spinning on her finger for no apparent reason) and says, "Maybe she has some weird lesbian crush on you!"

I almost choke on my tongue. "She does not!"

But Siobhan's already gesticulating wildly and even Alison gasps. Everybody giggles away like a lesbian crush is cringe-fest pantaloons galore, and a positively pumpkin-size bubble of panic swells in my chest. I just pray to Aphrodite that none of my friends are secretly telepathic. Thank Sappho that Zanna isn't here.

It's only when we're on the front path of the iPhone Box that Luna pauses her babbling and goes, "Why are you asking though? Are *you* gay?"

"No!" I retort, my pumpkin-size panic returning. "I have a boyfriend, remember?"

"Oh, yes," Luna says. "Him." There's a pause. "No offense, Cat, but I don't think Jamie is all that great. He's actually a bit of a desperate donut."

Tragically, I cannot disagree with Luna on that one.

One o'clock in the morning, and I cannot sleep at all. I want to blame my parents. They have been very irritating all evening. At dinner, Dad accused me of being quiet, and Mum said that would make a pleasant change. Parents think they're so funny, don't they?

I think the real reason I cannot sleep is because I do not love, or even slightly fancy, my boyfriend. I can't imagine that changing any time soon, either, especially if Jamie performs "Your Song" later this week like he's promised. The "VIP Preview" I received made me wish time travel were real. That way, I could travel back to 1969 and bash Elton John on the nose before he wrote "Your Song," so that it would never have existed for Jamie to discover.

I lie awake with my lava lamp, which is pinky-purple and makes my room look like a jellyfish's insides. Then I try reading a book with my flashlight, but my flashlight goes out. The lava lamp isn't bright enough to read by, so I'm forced to sneak about downstairs like a cat burglar (ho-ho) in search of batteries.

Sadly, I'm not a very good cat burglar, because I can't find any.

When I go back upstairs, I notice a light flickering above Mum and Dad's door. The fire alarm! The front isn't even screwed on, so I pop the batteries out, then return to my room. If we all die in a fire, Aphrodite can just apologize to my family on my behalf.

I return to my book. I'm reading *To All the Boys I've Loved Before*, and it's supposed to be a distraction. Sadly, I can't stop thinking about how I haven't loved ANY boys before, so I drop the book and sigh mournfully at my blobby pink ceiling. When I read in my *Bible to the Stars* that Scorpio Season was about "going deeper," I never expected it would mean plunging even deeper into despair and desolation!

I got a boyfriend during Libra Season. That was supposed to make me happy! But following my astral path hasn't made me happier at all. I'm still totally in love with Alison Bridgewater, and having a boyfriend hasn't cleansed me in the slightest. So that confirms it: I am truly doomed and destined to be unhappy forever. I should probably buy some cats.

Then I remember I'm allergic to cats, so even being a Crazy Cat Lady isn't going to work. I'd just be a Crazy Lady, and that doesn't have quite the same ring to it . . . I'd basically just be Mum! Then again, even Mum has Dad.

Über, über sigh indeed.

Chat Thread: Kenna Brown

Kenna, 8:35 p.m.:
Heya ... Can I have a Leo horoscope?
I'm nervous for Siobhan's party
Like, I'll have to talk to people, right? :/

Cat, 8:45 p.m.:
That is usually how parties go Kenna
But OFC I have advice!!! When have the stars EVER let me
down???
(Don't answer that)
Okay, so ... Scorpio Season is a PASSIONATE and FIZZLING
time for Leos to make CONNECTIONS ... Try making daisy
chains or necklaces from pasta! And have a deep talk with
someone you wouldn't EXPECT to like ... (Mum is always my
go-to for this). Get back to your excitable Leo roots (painting your
toenails yellow might work) and mostly, DON'T remain silent!!!
USE THOSE LIGHTNING HANDS AND MAKE THUNDER!!!

Kenna:
Read—9:07 p.m.

12
The Lucky Laundry Basket

Mum makes the most hysterical hullaballoo of me going to Siobhan's party *with Jamie*. He shows up wearing a waistcoat, which is as horrifying as it sounds, and Mum coos away, even insisting she take pictures on her phone! Of course, because she has the amazing adult talent of breaking a piece of technology just by looking at it, getting one photo takes about four thousand decades. But eventually, we're able to escape.

Jamie spends most of the walk complaining that his new shoes are giving him blisters. And although I am a beacon of patience, even I have my limits. By the time we arrive, I have a stress headache. You'd think I'd hopped the whole journey there upside down.

Siobhan's house is like the iPhone Box, all modern and glassy and pretentious with no walls downstairs. There's a wavy fountain thing in the driveway (*a custom décor de jardin*, in Siobhan's words), and Jamie goes Bruno Mars ballistic over her dad's red sports car.

"One day, I'm going to have a car just like this," he announces, and I resist the urge to tell him I hope he's right so he can drive it fast and furiously away from me!

Inside, I roll my shoulders, feeling *sehr iconique* in my jacket. Headache or not, I still have my divine feminine energy. I'm sure Morgan would see it but, alas, Morgan isn't here.

Everyone else is though, all dressed up to the seven seas. Loudmouth Jasmine McGregor is hooting about with her daffiest disciple, Cadence Cooke, and even Zariyah Al-Asiri from tenth grade is here, in a sparkling silver hijab. Zariyah is cool as cream cheese: she's Head Girl of Queen's and once hugged Lady Gaga! That didn't help her pass her pledge to make "Poker Face" the school anthem though. Habiba is playing Ping-Pong against three boys simultaneously and is single-handedly slaughtering them.

Siobhan herself is draped in a ridiculously glittery gold dress and receives her guests one by one from the bottom of the stairs like she's Cleopatra. I have to squint to look at her! She's posing next to Rich Elizabeth Greenwood, the richest girl at Queen's. According to Siobhan, Rich Elizabeth is so rich, she never washes her knickers; she just buys a new pair every day. That might not be entirely true, but I wouldn't know. I've never seen Rich Elizabeth's knickers.

"Hey, Siobhan!" I shrug Jamie off to hug her. "You look amazing!"

"Obviously, I look amazing!" Siobhan retorts, shoving me away like I'm infectious. "I'd never host a party looking like, I don't know, Kenna."

Kenna is wearing aubergine purple, but she doesn't look

that bad. I suppose Siobhan would know best though: she is the one who did an internship at Balenciaga. I wait for Siobhan to pass judgment on my fabulous jacket. If I were her, I'd be most flattered indeed that I'm using her birthday party as my jacket's debut event!

But Siobhan just says, "Oh, if you see my tragic cousin, Scrounging Samantha, will you talk to her? I'm supposed to be keeping her company, but she's so boring and I hate her. If she asks for money, tell her you're saving for laser hair removal— she'll believe that. Cool, laters!" Then she's gone, flicking Jamie in the face with her hair again. Not a word about my jacket!

"My eye!" Jamie moans on. He really is impossible, no matter the zodiac season . . . I search around for someone else to care about my jacket and divine feminine energy.

All the gang are here (except Zanna, who is selfishly in Poland for the weekend, attending her great-aunt Marcelina's funeral). Alison looks abracadabra amazing in a flowy gold top, and I achingly ogle her chatting to Posh Josh O'Conner on Siobhan's gigantic corner sofa (which Siobhan calls her *corner settee de la mode*). Her eyelids shimmer with gold flecks. Every time she laughs, I feel another sun being birthed inside me . . .

It's going to be hard as rocks not to be distracted by Alison Bridgewater tonight.

Meanwhile, Kieran Wakely-Brown is telling some story to his Lad Friends that ends with "and that's how you reel them in," so I suppose he's talking about fishing? Lip Gloss Lizzie and her glossiest girl brigade are touching up their many lips in the mirror, and Jamie's cookie-nibbling side bros, Losery Lucas and

Unoriginal Ryan, are googly-gazing at all the dancing girls in awe. I cannot BELIEVE Siobhan invited them! Although . . .

"Look, Jamie, your amigos are here!" I nod at them encouragingly. "You should go chillax with them—I truly don't mind!"

Jamie's bobbing about, dancing tragically in his tragic waistcoat. It's SCROL-ling levels of awkward. "I'd rather stay with you," he says, and I give a strangled laugh, manic as a matchstick already. Then I notice he's just taken a cookie out of his pocket.

"Did you have that cookie loose in your pocket?" I ask, horrified.

He frowns, taking a bite. "Yeah, why? You want one?"

"No!" I say firmly, then I snatch a drink from the side counter, where Siobhan has Kenna serving people like a member of staff. I'm not sure what the drink actually is. Kenna says a mysterious concoction "from Chichester." I think it might be Ribena.

I finish my first drink and move on to a second, mainly because if I'm drinking, Jamie can't kiss me. He keeps trying though, as the evening drags on, so I have to keep drinking. Alison is dancing with one of Kieran's Lad Friends and, suddenly, I notice the room swaying. Perhaps it's the dizzying weight of my disappointment. Although now that I think about it . . .

"Are we on a boat?" I mumble, then I clutch my stomach. I'm suddenly nauseous as a gnome! I lean on the snack table for support. Then I hear Rich Elizabeth drawling on to Siobhan, "What's in the juice, chicka?"

"Oh, the red one?" Siobhan lowers her voice, which is still very loud. Her gold dress glitters painfully, pummeling my headache with tiny sequined fists. "It's cranberry juice, but I added vodka. This is a REAL party. Not like that sad event of Jasmine's in September—"

"Hey!" hoots Jasmine McGregor, who is unfortunately right there, and then it all kicks off. Jasmine and Siobhan flap at each other like furious pelicans, and I feel my lungs swap places with my digestive system. Because did Siobhan just say VODKA?!

"What's gotten into Siobhan?" Alison appears by my side, and my stomach swirls like a panicking pancake. Alison frowns. "Cat? Are you okay?"

I gurgle at her gluggily, trying to remember how many cups of red juice I've had. I count to four . . . Then I forget what I'm counting. I cling to Jamie's arm as my knees go wobbly, which I think he's rather happy about, because he grins goonishly.

"Feeling all right, my angel?" he asks.

"She looks a little sick, Jamie," Alison simpers, which is the last thing I ever want to hear Alison Bridgewater say. "Maybe you should take her to the bathroom?"

"Uuuuurgh," I groan, and Jamie nods.

"I get it," he says. "Sometimes I'm also lost for words when we're together." Then he's leading me to the staircase. Gooseberries, I feel rough. I want Alison to come with us, but she's too distracted by Siobhan challenging Jasmine to a duel, using serving forks for swords.

Jamie drags my potato-sack form upstairs. I gaze at the childhood pictures of Siobhan and Niamh on the walls, bouncing around like I'm inside a surrealist painting. "Are we supposed to go up here?" I try asking, but I actually say, "Awee s'pose-go ah-hee-hee-hee?"

Aphrodite above. I might in fact be drunk as a doorknob.

·★·⋆⃰·★⋆·

We find the bathroom, and I groan about like Lana Del Rey over the sink. I splash some water on my face, but it only makes me sneeze . . . and my snot does *not* taste like honey. Jamie gives an impressed whistle. Then he begins humming. "Wow! The acoustics in here . . ."

THE WHAT?! For the love of Marina's diamonds! Hurriedly, I force myself to stand and grab Jamie's hand. Because if anything is likely to tip me into vom-volcano, it's Jamie singing. Instead, I drag him to Siobhan's bedroom. Siobhan's bed is so huge, I'm amazed she can find her way out of it each morning. At least her many "Ural Mountain Goose Down" pillows will make good earmuffs if Jamie gets too "inspired."

"This is better . . ." I collapse into the all-consuming duvet, squeezing shut my eyes, and clutch my stomach, moaning like Dad does when he's hungry. But I'm not hungry at all. In fact, if I eat a single chip, I might hurl. "Urghhh . . ." I groan. "My head is spinning!"

"Mine, too," Jamie says, which makes no sense: he didn't touch the red juice! "It's this energy, Cat! This tension in the air between us . . . I've felt it brewing for a while, and finally you've led us to this room, this moment . . . which tells me you feel it, too!"

I haven't the foggiest fog what Jamie is talking about, and I open my eyes to tell him. That's when I see, to my absolute alarm, that Jamie is no longer in his tragic waistcoat or his tragic shirt, either. In fact, he's topless, all skinny and chesty, his twiglet arms spread wide. I'm having flashbacks to our paddling-pool days, aged seven. Which is definitely not sexy.

"Jamie!" I gurgle. "I think you've . . . !"

I try to sit up and explain that he's definitely, DEFINITELY misunderstood, but my hand slips and I end up rolling right off the duvet, onto Siobhan's fluffy white carpet with a thud. I'm just blinking at the ceiling, dizzied to Delhi and back again, when Jamie looms over me, grinning down like a clown on the moon.

"I love your passion, Cat," he breathes. "How you throw yourself into everything like . . ." He pauses, biting his lip. "Like a . . . Frisbee! Cat, can you make me the happiest man alive and throw yourself into me? What should we do now? Tell me your desires!"

I almost point out that if I threw myself into him, he'd probably crumple like a dead leaf, but he's nodding so passionately, earnestly stroking my hand, and waiting for my answer. What in the name of Barack Obama's much-memed mic drop am I supposed to say?!

"Um, I've always wanted to travel!" I splutter. "I want to see Uzbekistan!"

Jamie frowns. "You do?" he asks, and I nod profusely, racking my brains for every Uzbekistan fact I know. Luckily enough, I did a school project on Uzbekistan in sixth grade. Mainly because it's called Uzbekistan, and I found that oozingly funny indeed.

"Did you know," I babble, "Uzbekistan is one of only two doubly landlocked countries?! That means it's landlocked only by other landlocked countries, which is cool, unless you like the sea of course, in which case, it's probably not that cool . . ."

Uzbeki-STAMP on my lungs, I've run out of Uzbekistan facts already! What in the name of Tashkent am I going to do now?! Do I know anything about Tajikistan next door?! Then, like Aphrodite is finally reading my prayers, the door crashes open and Siobhan comes cascading in, clutching one hand to her face and howling profanities. "Jasmine McGregor is dead!" she's screaming, and my eyes widen in alarm.

DEAD?! Jasmine McGregor is DEAD?

Then Siobhan carries on, "She's so freaking dead when I get my hands on her!" and I blow air in relief. A serving-fork murder is the last thing I need! Then Siobhan notices Jamie and me, staring at her like startled chickens. She removes the hand from her eye. "What are you two doing here?! Upstairs is OFF-LIMITS!"

Jamie begins floundering about like a flabbergasted fool, so I open my mouth to explain. But before I can speak, my stomach goes topsy-turvy again and my throat begins bubbling like an anxious volcano. Oh, giddy-goodness: THE VODKA!

I grab the bin by the desk and throw up right into it, shoulders heaving. Jamie leaps back in shock. My throat is on fire, but at least I found the bin. I made it just in time!

"WHAT THE ACTUAL GUCCI HANDBAG?!" Siobhan shrieks. "THAT'S MY LAUNDRY BASKET, YOU INCANDESCENT IDIOT!"

Group Chat: The Gang

[Siobhan sent a post from @jazzy.mcgreggs to the chat]

Siobhan, 4:55 p.m.:
WHAT THE BLAZES IS THIS???????
JASMINE MCGREGOR HAS POSTED A SELFIE WITH A SERVING FORK
MY SERVING FORK
HABIBA WHY HAVE YOU LIKED IT

Habiba, 4:57 p.m.:
Omg I'm sorry babe, what a #snake . . . I unliked!! xox

Siobhan, 4:57 p.m.:
WHAT USE IS THAT!!!! IT HAS 495 LIKES ALREADY!!!!!!!
YOU ARE SO *DEAD* ON MONDAY ISTG

Zanna, 5:01 p.m.:
Lmaoooooooooo

Cat, 5:02 p.m.:
Don't blame Habiba, Siobhan, everyone makes mistakes . . . !!!
Speaking of which . . . I'm still VERY sorry about the laundry basket . . .)

[Siobhan has removed Cat from the chat]

13
Egg-Breakingly Evil Undertakings

Zanna becomes completely hysterical when I recount the laundry basket incident to her over the phone on the weekend. She literally can't stop laughing. "That's amazing," she chuckles, without even a hint of sympathy. "That's made my entire week, Cat, thank you. It's very depressing here, what with the funeral and all."

I wish I were at a funeral. Preferably, mine.

Zanna keeps on wheezing. "You threw up," she repeats, as if there's a chance I might have forgotten, "in her laundry basket. That's brilliant!"

I hum glumly. Safe to say, I didn't hang around after the laundry-basket incident. Siobhan didn't just scream blue murder: she screamed the full-color spectrum. Especially since the basket turned out to be WICKER and my vomit leaked onto her fluffy white carpet.

Jamie hurried back into his shirt (Aphrodite be praised) and walked me home in silence. Big sigh. I don't think a million Scorpio Seasons could make me fall passionately in love with Jamie Owusu. He doesn't inspire so much as a couplet from me.

"Zanna," I interrupt, before she gets carried away reciting Polish hymns. "I think I might have to break up with Jamie. I don't actually fancy him at all."

"Well, I could've told you that," Zanna says, and I scowl.

"How did this even happen?!" I explode, because it just seems so unfair.

All I wanted was to stop being in love with Alison Bridgewater and not be tragically alone for another whole zodiac year. Can it really be so hard? I know the ocean levels are rising and there's a hole in the ozone layer and we're losing the rain forest at an alarming rate, but really I think me being in love with Alison Bridgewater is possibly the most frustratingly unsolvable and problematic problem in all the world, because—

"Cat?" Zanna cuts in.

"What?"

"You're an idiot," Zanna says. "That's how this has happened."

I hang up on her after that. She really has the sootiest of souls.

Fourteen letter attempts, three farewell poems, and two very intense readings of the "Cancer" chapter in my *Star Bible* later, and I'm still clueless detectives about how to break up with Jamie on Monday. In the end, I decide there's only one thing for it: I'm going to have to *talk* to him. I march all the way to Queen's with conviction. So much conviction, in fact, that I walk right into an old woman on Lambley Common Green and have to waste two precious minutes searching for her dentures in the grass. I walk with a little less conviction after that.

"So you're really going to dump him today?" Luna asks, jogging along behind me. She's the only person other than Zanna who I've told about my grand-but-still-rather-nonexistent master plan.

"Yes," I reply, striding through the school gates. "And I'm not chickening out."

"Cool," says Luna. "Can I watch?"

"Luna!" I exclaim. "No, you cannot. I'm going to have a very mature conversation. Probably, it will be too mature for you, in fact. You are only twelve."

"I'm thirteen!" Luna protests, and I stop walking.

"But your birthday isn't until the twentieth of November!"

"Which was yesterday!" Luna splutters. "Why did you think all my friends came over? We literally threw a party right in front of you! You're so self-absorbed!"

I goggle at her. "You were making protest banners for Extinction Rebellion! How is that throwing a party?! There wasn't even music!"

"I had my *Tones of the Orca* album playing the whole afternoon," says Luna, folding her arms. "I can't believe you forgot my birthday! If I weren't so passionately against consumerism, I'd say you owed me a present."

"Well, it's a good thing you're a massive freak, then!" I retort, and things are about to get heated, but that's when I see Jamie walking through the gates with Lucas. My eyes widen and Luna frowns, glancing over her shoulder to see what I'm gawping about.

She turns back with a smirk. "Well? Are you going to talk to him?"

"Yes," I say, trying to ignore the cardiac prosecution attempting to take place in my chest. "That's exactly what I'm going to do. I'm going to talk to him."

"Right now?"

"Yes, right now and right here."

"Well, go on, then," Luna says. "What are you waiting for?"

I'm about to tell her that obviously I'm waiting for Jamie to see me, but then he's standing right in front of me and we're blinking at each other like cock-a-doodle-doos. I open my mouth to speak. I'm just going to tell him. It's going to be fine. I'm just going to say it.

"Cat," says Jamie. "About the party—"

"We'll talk about it later!" I blurt, because in the name of Humpty-Dumpty's yolk, I cannot break Jamie's eggshell heart this early in the morning. I turn on my heel and whiz toward my homeroom before Jamie or Luna can say another word.

Breaking up with Jamie is actually of time-sensitive importance. Scorpio Season ends tomorrow, and then it's Sagittarius Season. According to my *Bible to the Stars*, this is when people feel more experimental—it's the most adventurous time of year! Who knows what fresh horrors could come to fruition if Jamie becomes adventurous?! He even suggested folk dancing as a couple yesterday. I've never been so jingly with fright!

And then there's this to consider. Alison Bridgewater is single again! Might *she* feel a little "adventurous" as well? What if I was too hasty, giving up? Sign me up for chemistry because I am ready to experiment!

Well, don't, obviously. I'd probably blow up the school. But still . . .

Even so, as Miss Jamison drones on about MacBother-Me-Much, by Snoozy Shakespeare, in English, the prospect of breaking up with Jamie at break looms over me like a great blue whale swimming by the classroom window. Despite the brilliant wordplay, it doesn't sound fun at all, so when class finishes, I rush to the school gates to hide. It's the sad corner of the playground where sixth graders hang out, and they all watch me strangely as I sit there like a stuffed animal.

But if I'm really going to avoid Jamie all day, I have to constantly keep on the move: a true outlaw's existence. At lunch, I spend a confusing twenty minutes asking Mr. Derry strange questions, just so I can avoid the picnic tables. I'm sure Mr. Derry still feels uncomfortable from when I called him "truly beautiful" after the bus incident because he says "um" and "ah" a lot and stares at me like I'm asking to change my name to Loopy Tuesdays.

Maybe I should, because I end up explaining SCROL to him, just to keep us talking.

Then, before I've even blinked, it's Tuesday, and I've accidentally put off breaking up with Jamie for twenty-four nightmarish hours. I'm just loitering in the staff parking lot to avoid the picnic tables *again*, when I spot Morgan and Maja climbing over the fence, using the roof of the headmistress's sportscar as a stepping-stone. Gooseberries galore!

At least they're climbing back *into* school. Morgan jumps off the hood onto the concrete, then she spots me. Her face lights up into a smirk. "Don't judge me," she says as Maja hops down after her. "We only snuck out for milkshakes."

"Oh!" I say, blinking in surprise. "Um, no judgment here! I escape from school whenever I can, um . . . I'm very rebellious like that."

Maja snorts a laugh, and Morgan narrows her eyes. "Mmm-hmm. I can totally tell. Only the most rebellious people spend their lunchtimes in the staff parking lot."

"Ah . . ." I look over my shoulder like I've only just noticed I'm here. "Yes, well, um . . . I'm an Aquarius, which is actually the most rebellious of all the signs! Uranus, our planet, even spins counterclockwise, you know?! So, you should, um . . . watch out."

Morgan nods slowly, then bursts out cackling. "I will definitely look out," she says, sincerely as a Scorpio giving a compliment (meaning: NOT). "Thanks for the warning."

"Are you always this sarcastic?" I ask, trying to sound indignant, and Morgan smiles.

"Probably," she says, shaking back her hair and instantly transporting me to the river. Gooseberries, that really was dashing . . . "I'm a Gemini. Sarcasm is sort of our thing."

I stare at her for about four million years. Which wouldn't actually be so bad: she does have the loveliest blue eyes. But what good are blue eyes if you're evil to the stone-cold core?!

"Um, I h-have to go!" I stutter. "To, um, another parking lot!"

Then I skedaddle like a scarecrow on stilts. Because I may not know why the sky is blue or the grass is green, or why men have nipples. In fact, I don't even know basic math. But I do know that you should never, EVER, in any weather, consider trusting a Gemini.

WHY YOU SHOULD NEVER TRUST A GEMINI

- They have two entire sides, which is thoroughly greedy. People should only have one side MAX. We are humans, not Rubik's Cubes!
- Even though they're THE WORST, they're usually very beautiful. It's all just a distraction from their satanic Gemini souls.
- They are between Taurus and Cancer in the zodiac year, the most boring sign and the most wimpy, aka right where you least expect them . . . then BOOM! They've got you. They're very unexpectedly evil like that.
- Compare GEMINI with DEMON as a word. Coincidence? I think not.
- THEY'RE GEMINIS!!! YOU CANNOT TRUST THEM!!! PERIOD!!!

Sagittarius

SEASON

14
Banana Split-and-Run

How can Morgan be a Gemini?! She's so COOL and she saved my notebook! But maybe her freckles were distracting me from her true and twisted Gemini nature? It's very, very unfortunate. Meanwhile, I'm beginning to think that joining the circus would be easier than breaking up with Jamie. Although if Zanna's correct, joining the circus shouldn't be too hard for me: I have clown blood positively pummeling through my veins.

I arrive at Queen's on Wednesday morning, flustered as a scribble. So when Imaran Kalmati goes, "Good *meow*-ning, Wildcat!" I almost don't notice he's speaking to me.

I stop in my tragic tracks. I'm just outside my homeroom, and Imaran is loitering by the lockers with some Lad Friends of Kieran Wakely-Brown's.

I don't know Imaran well, but I know he once lied on a dating app that he was twenty-seven. He has real stubble and only got found out when he tried chatting up Queen's food tech teacher, Miss Rice (or Spicey Ricey, as we all called her afterward).

"Um, hello?" I reply, glancing over my shoulder, but there's no one there. Imaran is definitely talking to me. I glance between the Lad Friends. "Are you . . . okay?"

"Oh, I'm fine," says Imaran. "Wildcat."

Then all the Lad Friends rumble with rumbly laughter. I frown at them and walk on, deciding I'll just leave them to it. After all, I have much bigger salmon to salt than worrying about some new Lad Friend in-joke.

"Christ on a bike!" Siobhan exclaims at lunch. "Where's Kenna? That CLODPOLE is supposed to be lending me her mascara."

"Maybe she's sitting with someone else?" Alison suggests.

"Don't be absurd!" Siobhan snaps. "Kenna doesn't have other friends!"

Alison returns to her lunch tray, her cheeks pink, and I scan the cafeteria for Kenna. That's when I see Jamie standing by the garbage bins with Lucas. Fiddlesticks! I bow my head, but that boy is like a bloodhound when it comes to me. He sniffs right round and spots me, his face lighting up like a birthday cake. Gooseberries galore, what now?!

"Y-you know," I stammer, "I should go! I have a thing . . ."

"You haven't finished your sandwich," Zanna points out unhelpfully.

"That's because I'm dieting!"

"You?" Habiba frowns, dropping her spoon into her low-fat yogurt. "Dieting? Yesterday you bought three desserts!"

"It was two desserts!" I protest. "The banana doesn't count."

"It was a banana split!" says Habiba, and I'm just about ready to burst into flames. I don't have time for this nonsense—Jamie is coming! Frisbee-hurling my sandwich toward the garbage, I push back my chair, then there's the most enormous crash. I let out a scream of surprise.

Behind me, Millie Butcher trips right over, lunch tray and all.

The sound of shattering plates silences the whole cafeteria. Broccoli and gravy drown the floor, and broken crockery scatters round my feet. I gawp across the table just in time to see Siobhan retracting her foot, eyes wide as, well, unbroken plates.

What the frog-in-frocks just happened?!

Before I can say or do anything, two cafeteria workers have descended on the scene like seagulls. One helps Millie to her feet. "Are you hurt? That was quite the tumble!"

Millie's lips are trembling. "I tripped," she murmurs. "I'm really sorry."

"Don't worry, my love!" The cafeteria worker leads her away. "We'll get you cleaned up. Come, you've had a nasty shock . . ." Another seagull approaches with a CAUTION: SLIPPERY SURFACE sign—as if the fifty square feet of gravy isn't giveaway enough.

The chatter in the cafeteria rises again as everyone babbles about what they saw, where they were looking, when Millie Butcher plunged to the floor. A table full of Kieran Wakely-Brown's Lad Friends ogles the scene and one of them calls, "Nice one, Wildcat!"

"What?!" I gaze around the cafeteria, but everyone's looking right at me.

"Why is everyone calling you Wildcat?!" demands Siobhan, but before I can tell her I'm absolutely fusion-confusion on that one, too, Habiba butt-squats in.

"That was fitspirational, Siobhan. You totally tripped her

up!" She flicks back a curtain of sleek, dark hair. "All those reflex exercises in netball have clearly paid off . . ."

"What?" Alison's eyes widen, and she goggles at Siobhan. "Siobhan, did you?"

"Chill out, Alison!" Siobhan bites into her apple, tossing back her hair. "It was just banter. Anyway, Millie probably thought it was Cat's chair leg." Siobhan flashes me a smirk. "Thanks for that."

"What?!" I exclaim. "But I didn't mean . . . !"

I don't know what to say. I catch Alison's eye, but she just frowns into her panini like an ostrich in the sand. I know she doesn't like confrontation, but really?! A dangerous thought flashes through my mind. Should *I* confront our esteemed Queen Bee?

"You shouldn't have done that, Siobhan," Zanna says, looking genuinely shooketh to her black Baltic boots. "That was mean. Like, seriously. There's a line—"

"Look," says Siobhan as the gang goes quiet. I think we're all a little speechless-apricots actually. "I didn't think she'd actually fall."

I want to back Zanna up, but then I remember what was going on before Millie's fall: JAMIE! He's already waving in my peripheral vision. I'm protected by a moat of gravy and warning signs, but I'm also *trapped* by the gravy myself!

"Cat?" he calls. "Hey, Cat!"

Not a moment to lose. I am Batman! I leap over the puddle of gravy.

Only, I don't leap *over* the gravy. I fall short and land right in it.

There's another crash as I fall, bringing the sign down with me, and the cafeteria freezes. Again. Gooseberries. I feel a warm, slimy wetness seep into my back, then just as I'm about to die from horror and disgustingness, Jamie's face looms over me. I'm ready to scream!

"Damn, Cat!" he says. "What did you do that for?!"

For the love of Aphrodite! Does he think I did this intentionally?! But before I can even lose my temper, the seagull cafeteria workers rush to my rescue, helping me to my feet. "I did put a sign right there!" one of them says, and I wheeze my apologies, eyeing up my escape route.

"Let's sit you down," the cafeteria worker says.

But I shake my head. "No need! I have to get going!"

"Cat, you're covered in gravy!" Alison interjects, but I'm already speedboating away. Jamie's still holding his lunch tray, tangled up behind the cafeteria workers. It's just the time I need to slip out and once more avoid the Dreaded Conversation of Doom.

I think the fact that I'd rather swim through floor gravy than talk to my boyfriend might be the gayest wake-up call of my Amazing Aquarius Life so far. Unfortunately, Jamie probably isn't smart enough to piece that together, so I'm still going to have to talk to him.

Once the gravy dries, my skirt is encased in a brown crust, and I get some very odd looks. Eventually, I sneak into the English block. Perhaps I can get to my locker and change into my PE uniform? But just as I'm cat-burglaring my way to my locker, the boys' bathroom door swings open and I bump right into Rich Elizabeth.

Her eyes widen in surprise. She shoves the door shut, but not before I see who was about to follow her out: Kieran Wakely-Brown! I blink between Elizabeth and the bathroom door. What could they possibly be up to in there? Comparing vast fortunes? Inspecting the pipes?

But Rich Elizabeth gathers herself fast. Her face settles into a sequined smirk, and she folds her willowy arms. She's a lot taller than me. I suppose she can afford to be: longer trousers and . . . all that.

"Really, Wildcat?" she says. "You're going to judge me? *You* are?"

"Well, I'm not a plumber, so it really wouldn't be my place . . . !" Then I trail off, startled as a starling. Kieran's Lad Friends christening me with a new nickname is oddballs enough, but Rich Elizabeth is the first girl to call me that. "Elizabeth," I ask carefully, "why is everybody calling me Wildcat?"

Rich Elizabeth giggles expensively, then stops. "Oh, goshingtons," she says. "You really don't know? Well, it's because of Jamie, of course! He told Kieran all about your wild night of passion. Honestly, Cat, I never knew you were such a saucy minx!"

A saucy WHAT?! I feel the blood leave my head. Then I feel the blood leave my shoulders, knees and toes, knees and toes, as well. I'm practically exsanguinated where I stand.

"Wh-what?!" I stutter. "At Siobhan's party? But nothing happened!"

Rich Elizabeth observes me down her nose. "That's not what Kieran says, chicka."

I'm so speechless, I don't have any words to speak. I stare into space until it gets creepy, and Elizabeth has to slide her way around me to leave. She clip-clops down the corridor in her horsey-saucy über-pricey heeled shoes, and I try to process everything she just said. Then Kieran sneaks out of the bathroom after her, but I'm still too stunned to react.

A wild night of passion? Me?! With JAMIE?!

Someone hand me Siobhan's laundry basket! I feel like throwing up all over again.

Group Chat: The Gang

Lizzie, 1:05 p.m.:
OMG guys have u heard the goss on Cat? It's always the quiet ones...

Cat, 1:06 p.m.:
???

I'm literally right here!

Lizzie, 1:07 p.m.:
OMG, wrong chat!!! Sorry baby xx

Zanna, 1:10 p.m.:
Since when has Cat been "quiet"?

15
Boys Will Be Boys (Unfortunately)

Everyone carries on calling me Wildcat all through the afternoon, and the next day even Loudmouth Jasmine McGregor hoots with laughter when I walk past her and her Foghorn Friends. If Jasmine McGregor knows, then I truly am bamboozled. Even Siobhan can't protect me from the biggest pair of vocal cords in Lambley Common!

I go to the library to hide and wallow in a beanbag. Then I clock Miss Bull glaring at me, miserable old milk bottle that she is (who wears beige at age thirty-five?!), so I grab the nearest book and open it so she won't throw me out. Just my luck though—the book turns out to be *101 Things to Know about Smallpox*, and I have to read it for the rest of break. By the time I'm finished, I'm feeling a billion times more nauseous than when I arrived.

Then I have math, which is boring as bread. First, because

it's math—duh!—but also because I am in the lower track with only Kenna for company. I don't mind sitting with Kenna. Without her mouthpiece (Siobhan), it's quite peaceful. But it does mean I sometimes end up listening to the lesson—shock and horror galore. Kieran Wakely-Brown and his Lad Friends all chortle the moment I walk in though. It seems everyone in the world (and maybe on Jupiter as well) knows about the Wildcat fiasco.

I just want to forget the entire cringe-montage, to be honest, so for the first time in my life, I try to concentrate on what Mr. Tucker is saying. (Something about algebra, which is very tragic indeed.) Anything is better than thinking about my current predicament.

Then something hits me in the eye! I squeal out loud. It's a ball of paper, and it bounces off my forehead, landing on my desk like a snowball. Across the room, Kieran Wakely-Brown and his Lad Friends are sniggering like snails. I glower at them, rubbing my eye.

"Excuse me, Cat." Mr. Tucker frowns away. I may have squealed quite loudly. "Is something distracting you?"

"Um . . ." The last thing I am is a snitch, and I certainly don't want Mr. Tucker elbowing around like teachers always do, making everything worse. I hide the paper ball in my hands. "I was just thinking about how smallpox can lead to blindness in up to one-third of cases."

His eyebrows shoot right up at that. "I beg your pardon?" he blusters, and everyone is giggling more and more, like ghouls in a graveyard.

"Um, nothing," I mumble. "Sorry. I'm not distracted at all."

Mr. Tucker glares at me, then shakes his head and turns back to the board. Kenna makes a rude-looking gesture at Kieran that I'm not actually sure is sign language. Glaring at the Lad Friends, I unfold the note under the table.

SHE DOESN'T WEAR A COLLAR, SO WE CALL HER WILDCAT. STROKE HER LIKE A KITTEN AND YOU'LL GET HER ON HER BACK!

I read the note twice over before I understand what it really means. Suddenly, I'm feeling rather clammy in my crannies. Either I've got smallpox (early symptoms do include fever and nausea), or I'm actually quite upset!

It's just a stupid poem. There's no need to overreact.

But then all the boys are purring and yapping and, suddenly, tiny dots speckle my vision. It's not nice when everyone is giggling at you. This must be how Millie felt when Siobhan said she ate like a piggy and everyone oinked at her in the corridors. I knew I shouldn't have laughed along! Karma is real and, also, what if I do have smallpox, the first case in England since 1978?! I actually want to cry . . .

"Cat?" asks Mr. Tucker. "Are you crying?"

And that's when I realize that yes, I am. I am weeping like a Pisces in the middle of math. It doesn't get much worse than that. Tearfully, I rush out of the classroom before Mr. Tucker and all his teachery blustering can stop me.

It's unlikely that I'm dying from smallpox, but either way, I'm in tricky trouble. I walked out of class! Only girls like Brooke the Crook do that, and detentions are a walk in the park for her.

She's been arrested nine times for shoplifting. (Or so the rumors say.)

But how was I supposed to learn algebra with Kieran catapulting couplets at me? My life is turning into a very unpoetic mess, which is sad news for my poetic ambitions. Outside in the drizzly cold, I find a bike rack and sit down. I sigh into the weepy gray sky.

Everyone is calling me Wildcat, and even Alison Bridgewater probably thinks I took part in sinful and horrifying shenanigans with Jamie. I always thought love was supposed to be pretty and flowery and, well, preferably between two enchantingly gorgeous princesses. Perhaps that's unrealistic. But I never expected it could get as messy and horrendous as this. I honestly don't think my predicament could get any worse . . .

"Well, well, well, Cathleen Phillips."

My heart drops. Hastily wiping my eyes, I look up and see Mrs. Warren observing me from behind her spectacles.

"Um, Miss, I can explain!"

But Mrs. Warren holds up a finger of silence. "How about you come with me to my classroom," she says, sinister as a snowman in high summer, "and we have a conversation about why you're sitting in a bicycle shed when you should be sitting in class?"

"Is that absolutely necessary?" I ask, but from the way Mrs. Warren harrumphs and twitches her eyebrows, I assume it probably is.

Mrs. Warren doesn't say a word the whole way to her classroom. Maybe she's going to expel me! Can homeroom teachers do that in the middle of a normal school day?! She sits in a chair that looks as ancient and tweedy as she does and nods me to a seat. Silently, I sit down.

I expect her to dive right into butchering my bacon, but instead she opens the bottom drawer of her desk and pulls out a miniature kettle, already filled with water. I watch in awe as she plugs it into the wall and flicks the switch. Then she takes two small mugs from the same drawer, adds the tea bags, and sits in silence until the kettle has finished boiling.

I don't think I've ever seen such a frightening sight in all my Aquarius Life!

"You'll be glad to know, Cathleen," Mrs. Warren says, pushing a cup toward me, "I've not asked you here to scold you. I will be turning a blind eye, just this once."

If I were drinking the tea, I'd probably spit it everywhere. I gape at her like a gibbon. What the fallopian tube would persuade her not to punish me?! "You . . . what? Really?"

Mrs. Warren sips her tea. "I've had my eye on you since our detention together, Cathleen. Recently, you've seemed a little out of sorts. Would that be the case?"

She holds my gaze, her lips pursed into a thin line. That's when I realize that—oh, gooseberries—this is about the wrist writing! I open my mouth, but no sound escapes. Oh, humiliation of humiliations! Why would she bring up that? Right then, I burst into tears.

NO! Stop this at once! I absolutely cannot cry in front of Mrs. Warren! Yet here I am, doing just that: a truly code-red situation. There are tears running down my cheeks, and I am sniffing loudly, so there's no way it isn't obvious I'm crying. Mission failed miserably.

Matter-of-factly, Mrs. Warren opens her top drawer, and I see a box of tissues, the perfect size of the drawer, slotted inside. She pulls one out and hands it to me as I sniffle pathetically.

"I don't like boys like I'm supposed to," I weep. What in the name of Boudica's bronze leg hair am I doing?! I'm suddenly oversharing like a Leo on cocktails! "I haven't told anyone except Zanna, and I've even got a boyfriend, and I have to break up with him, but I don't know how, and everyone is calling me Wildcat because of something I did at a party, but I didn't even do anything!" I gulp shamefully. "It's all gone really wrong."

Incredible. Of all the people in the world to come out to, I've chosen Mrs. Warren.

There's a long dust-bowl silence. I blow my nose tragically. After a considered pause, Mrs. Warren takes another sip of tea. "I don't have children, Cathleen . . ."

I sniff, confused. "Um. Sorry?"

"But my sister does. In Ireland. Two boys. Now, my younger nephew . . . he told us he was gay when he was fifteen. My sister—she's a Catholic—she had her concerns, but I told her to love him all she could at home, because school was going to be hell for the boy. I know schools, after all. I've seen many a child flushed down the toilet in my time."

I realize I've been holding my breath the whole time Mrs. Warren's been speaking, and if I release it now, it'll be the loudest guffaw ever. So I keep holding it in like a puffer fish.

"But I was wrong," Mrs. Warren continues. "Nobody cared at his school. These are different times, Cathleen. There were bullies, some silly comments, but it was nothing like I'd expected. He even found a youth support group . . . I'd recommend it.

They were good people. Very colorful. Though I've never been one for wearing rainbow myself."

I blink. "Um . . . you, Miss? Wow, I'd . . . never have guessed!"

Mrs. Warren doesn't smile. "You'll find your way, just as he did, and many others before the both of you. Do you need another tissue? That one looks quite grotesque."

I drop the tissue into the garbage bin and nod for another. I dab my cheeks. Then I reach into my bag and pull out my compact mirror. My mascara has run, so I dampen the tissue with my tears and clear it up. *Sehr tragique* indeed.

"Well, enough of that. I have a staff meeting to attend." Mrs. Warren stands, so I stand, too, narrowly avoiding knocking over my teacup. "Perhaps you should go home early today. I can write a note to your math teacher to explain you were with me."

"Mr. Tucker."

"I know who he is, Cathleen."

"Oh. Yes. Sorry." I gawk at my shoes, suddenly very sheepish. "Um, thanks," I mumble. "For not giving me a detention. And all that."

Mrs. Warren doesn't look at me. Perhaps she's finding this heartwarming interaction as cringe-fest hot-cross buns as I am. "You're quite welcome," she says. "Anyway, off with you now. I have a second cup of tea to enjoy."

I don't need telling twice! I'm out of the door quicker than a rabbit without life insurance, speed-walking all the way to the school gates. Oddly, I feel slightly better though: not an emotion I'm used to after conversations with Mrs. Warren.

The world really has turned completely topsy-turvy.

16

I Come in Peas

As I head home early from school (a fortunate turn of events indeed), I find myself passing Morgan Delaney's blue front door, and once more I'm temporarily overcome with visions of Morgan gallivanting into the river. A truly dreamboat moment.

But I must remember: she's a Gemini! Even if she is rather swoonful . . .

Just as I'm about to carry on home, the door opens and a blond, older version of Morgan hops down the steps and into the matching blue hatchback in the driveway. She beetles out of Marylebone Close and down the main road. I'm not Sherbet Holmes, but I can safely assume that's Morgan's mum, and since Morgan should be in school, Morgan's house must now be empty. A useful piece of knowledge to possess, should I be a burglar.

I'm not a burglar, but I *am* nosy. So, since I have time to kill, I cross the road.

Unlike the iPhone Box, Morgan's house is quite ordinary:

two windows, a door, walls that aren't completely transparent, that sort of thing, which means it's trickier to snoop. I hover in the driveway, then sneaky-sneak to the nearest window.

Inside is a living room with a big aubergine-colored sofa. Not much to go on there, so I continue my sneaking round the side of the house, where a wooden fence separates the street from the backyard. Woe alas, perhaps I am jealous of Rich Elizabeth's lanky limbs after all, because the fence is too high to peek over. Unless . . .

Checking over my shoulder, I slide out my phone and switch to camera. Perhaps I *am* Sherbet Holmes! With my arm stretched up, I can angle the phone and peep right into the yard. I scoot the phone around, but the sun catches the screen, so I can't quite see clearly. I stand on my tiptoes, adjust my grip, and that's when the phone slips out of my hand.

Gooseberries, gooseberries, gooseberries! My phone is in Morgan's backyard! Why do actions always have consequences?! I hop from one foot to the other, nervy-nerving, then dart to the front of the house again. I'm sure there was a gate. Perhaps I can sneak in?! But when I find the gate, I find there's also (rather sensibly, I suppose) a padlock.

This is a very sticky predicament: a fly-in-a-Venus-flytrap-level disaster. If Morgan finds my phone in her yard, she's going to think I'm creepy as creamed leeks!

Then I notice a loose brick in the corner of the drive. It must have come from the patio, and the sun is shining directly upon it, so perhaps Aphrodite is giving me a sign!

She's right, I decide. There's only one thing to be done. I pick up the brick and angle it at the padlock. Then I hesitate. Will this really work? Times like this, one truly wishes to be Brooke the Crook: I doubt she flounders about with bricks like this. She'd probably just pick the lock! But I'm not Brooke the Crook. I have to smash the padlock. Oh, gosh.

I take a deep breath. "One . . . Two . . . Three . . ."

"Cat?!" says Morgan, and I drop the brick right onto my big toe.

· ★ · ✦ · ★ ·

Well, now I look very clownish indeed. One bandage and a bag of frozen peas later, I find myself on Morgan Delaney's aubergine sofa and in rather a lot of pain. Morgan (who, it would seem, is skipping school, too; all very dashing and reckless) reappears and drops my phone onto the sofa next to me. I quietly slide it into my handbag.

"Um, thank you," I say, scared to properly look her in the eye. "Sorry about that. It's just that your fence was a little tall to look over from the street, and . . ."

"Well, that's sort of the point, isn't it?" Morgan replies, so cucumber calm, I'm not sure if she's judging me horribly or not. She sits down next to me, and finally I dare to sneak a peek. Her face gives nothing away.

"Are you mad?" I ask sheepishly, and Morgan snorts a laugh.

"Are *you* mad? If you wanted to see the yard that badly, you could have just knocked on the door." She nods to the bag of frozen peas spread across my foot. "How's the toe?"

"Um . . ." I glance down. "Probably a bit more two-dimensional than before?"

"There's a bike pump in the garden shed if you want to blow it back up," Morgan says, then she smirks. "But maybe you already know that."

Gooseberries galore, this is embarrassing. Since I can't even meet Morgan's eye without my organs wanting to escape my body and scuttle away, I grab my bag and jump to my feet. "Well, I should probably go! Thank you for the peas and not pressing charges and all that; I've taken up more than enough of your time though—"

"Cat, hang on," Morgan cuts in, and I stop babbling. "I'll stop teasing, okay? Even if you make it . . . astonishingly easy." Morgan smiles and I notice that scattering of freckles across her nose again. They're very aesthetically pleasing. I feel another blush coming on. "You can stay for a bit," Morgan says. "Like, if you want."

I stare at Morgan, still far too flustered to keep my cool (if it ever existed in the first place), but I realize that I do want to stay, for some reason I can't quite put my broken toe on. So I sit back down and shove my foot back under the bag of peas. Not ideal.

"So, how come you were—" Morgan begins, but at the exact same second, I blurt out, "Do you have any siblings?" Then I beam hopefully, hands clasped to my knees. Anything to stop her from asking why I was snooping around her house like a slapstick stalker!

"I have a twin actually," Morgan says. "Her name is Arya and she still lives in Bristol. She goes to this fancy theater school, so she stayed with my grandma."

"Oh, that's so interesting!" I keep beaming. I need more questions before Morgan tries quizzing me again, so I plow on like a truly boring conversationalist. "Do you look alike? I mean, if you're twins. Who's older?"

Morgan doesn't seem to mind the questions, thank Sappho. "She's older, and yes, we look exactly the same. I think she has a nicer nose. If we're being picky."

I think Morgan has a nice nose. Siobhan commented on her nose, in fact.

"I think you have a nice nose," I say, brain-to-mouth filter switched off as usual. I flush crimson. "Um, I mean, as far as noses go. Well, Siobhan said you had a nose anyway. A *nice* nose, I mean, and . . . I agreed."

Morgan narrows her eyes. "Siobhan complimented me? I thought she hated my guts."

"Siobhan doesn't hate you," I say, then I blink at Morgan, and we both burst out laughing. "Okay," I giggle. "She might hate you a bit. But don't take it personally! Siobhan would fight the Virgin Mary if she could. She's just like that."

Our laughter fades and Morgan tilts her head at me.

"I can't figure you out," she says, as if I'm deep and mysterious. I wish! I think a cabbage in a cabbage patch possesses more mystery than me. "You're best friends with all those popular, pretty girls, but you're actually all right. I usually hate girls like you." She licks her lips. "No offense."

I swallow down my odd, fluttering flickers of, um, whatever I'm feeling. What *am* I feeling? Morgan is just so honest and direct. It's actually kind of . . . hot.

Wait—did I just think that? Kind of hot?! Also, I haven't said anything in five entire seconds. I open my mouth—always a mistake. "Um, no offense taken! Although Zanna isn't that popular. Don't tell her I said that! Kenna is pretty though, and Alison Bridgewater is . . ."

131

I pause. Morgan is watching me, eyebrows raised. I am definitely talking like a waterfall, but she seems amused.

"ALisOn BrIdgeWatEr?" she echoes me, in a faux-British twitter, and I flush crimson. I should definitely not talk about Alison Bridgewater.

"Alison is . . . fine! She's cute. I mean, not *cute*, but . . . she's my friend, you know? And a Pisces. We all need one Pisces friend! And Alison is, well . . . Alison Bridgewater."

That was about as smooth as Dad's beardy face. Have I totally outed myself?! But Morgan just smiles that not-quite-smile of hers, then says, "It's okay. No need to get into a counterclockwise spin about it. You can say she's cute if you think that."

I laugh hastily. "Well, I don't. I mean, she's fine! She's Alison."

"You've mentioned that."

We both fall silent again. I'm definitely blushing, which is über-unfortunate, but luckily Morgan doesn't point it out. Eventually, she says, "Do you want to watch a movie?" and I nod at once. Anything to stop myself from speaking more.

Morgan chooses *The Devil Wears Prada*, and we sit side by side on the aubergine sofa. It seems odd to sit so far apart, so I shuffle closer, then I notice her pinkie finger is lickably close to mine.

Morgan looks over. "You good?"

"Yes!" I squeal, and carefully don't look at her for the rest of the film.

Except I do look at her. I look several times. A few times, she even looks back, too. It's very, very . . . hot. Meryl Streep me down.

· ★ · ✦ · ★ ·

When the movie has finished, I notice I have a wagonload of red-faced texts from Mum. I reply that I'm obviously completely okay, and that I don't think there *are* any serial killers in Kent, but she still wants me home, so I tell Morgan I have to leave.

Morgan watches me put my shoes on. Since my toe has swollen to onion-size proportions, this isn't actually very easy to do.

"Um, thanks for having me," I say, tugging at my shoe.

"Didn't have much choice, did I?" Morgan smirks. Then, just as I'm opening the door . . . "Cat?" Morgan looks at her feet. "Do you want to go to a gig next week? I have tickets for this thing in London because the band members are . . . um, friends from Bristol. It's sort of alt, soft rock . . . Should be pretty cool."

I should probably tell her that if it's cool, I'm the last person she should go with, but I find myself nodding. "Um, I'd love to! Definitely! You know someone in the band?"

Then the strangest thing happens. Morgan blushes. I think she knows she's blushing, too, because she rolls her eyes. "Don't judge me, okay? But I actually had a massive crush on the singer back in Bristol and, er . . . Well, it taught me a lot. It's all cool now though."

I know all about the pantalooning awkwardness of crushes, so this is a discovery indeed: a kink in Morgan Delaney's glittering Irish armor. I nudge her with my toe, smirky-smirking. "You crushed on a singer? Is he, like, super-duper yummy?"

"Yeah, she's pretty cool," Morgan says, nodding. "But like I said, I'm over it now." She hasty-laughs, rubbing her elbow. "So, will you come?"

Then she meets my eye, just as I'm about to inhale all of Lambley Common. *She.* Did Morgan just say *she's* pretty cool?

Or did she say *he's*?! I blink a number of times. I grip my bag. The flock of swallows that represents my ability to speak migrates to South Africa.

"Um, cool!" I blurt out. "Well, that's wonderful. I need to go, but, um, message me the deets! You know, the details. Like, *deets*, you know?" I laugh like a nervous ukulele. "I should go. Bish, bash, bosh, and all that jazz, or . . . ultra-soft rock, or whatever! Goodbye!"

Then I walk off down Marylebone Close, more clownishly than I've ever walked anywhere before. Morgan probably thinks I'm off to join the circus. But my head is spinning like I've been drinking Kenna's Chichester cranberry juice all over again. I'm sure that Morgan said *she*.

Morgan is like me. Morgan likes girls.

MENTAL LIST I DEFINITELY HAVE NOT MADE ABOUT MORGAN DELANEY

- She's Irish. Her accent is actually rather dreamy-licious. Ahem.
- She has über-cool GREEN glasses. GREEN!
- She takes music class and crushes on singers, so perhaps she likes music?
- She has a twin, but hopefully Arya is the evil one.
- Morgan LIKES GIRLS. If I liked Morgan, this would be useful, as I, too, am a girl.
- Of course, I can't like Morgan like *that* because I like Alison Bridgewater.
- And because she's a GEMINI! Absolutely criminal.
- DID I JUST AGREE TO GO TO A GIG WITH A GEMINI? This could be the most self-destructive act of my life! And yes, I am including the time I tried rock-climbing. Thank GOODNESS there was no one in that tent. Well, except Luna.

17

The Old Bowl and Chin

Siobhan throws one. Siobhan throws two. Siobhan throws *three* potted cacti at Kieran Wakely-Brown, and it looks like she's still got another few in her bag! Kieran ducks and one whizzes millimeters from his head and explodes against the tree trunk behind him.

"Where did she get them?" I ask.

"I think they're from the main office," Zanna says, grimacing. "She must have grabbed them on her way in."

The entire homeroom is crowded against the window, gasping with each near miss. But then Siobhan has Kieran pinned against the tree and—WHAM!—a cactus finally hits its mark. The homeroom group hisses in secondhand pain, and Siobhan stomps over to where he's cowering, a particularly bristly-looking cactus wielded in her grasp like a mace.

"Not the boys!" I hear Kieran cry. Then, a moment later, "AAAAARGH!"

"Should we . . . Should we stop her?" Alison murmurs.

But Zanna shakes her head. "It would only fuel her more."

We all wince as Kieran collapses, eyes squeezed shut, hands clutched firmly to his . . . Well, you get the idea. Siobhan turns on her heel and marches toward the English block. Everybody flees to their seats, and Siobhan crashes into the room moments later, glaring at every boy in the class. I expect her to go straight to her desk, but instead she comes to mine.

Under the table, Zanna grips my hand in fear.

"Well, that's Kieran sorted out," Siobhan announces. "No one will be calling you Wildcat anymore. As soon as Elizabeth wimped out and explained, Kieran was cactus fodder."

I stare at her. "Wait. You dumped Kieran . . . for me?!"

Siobhan blinks at me like I'm dumb as a doorbell. "DUH! As if I'd let some blister-licking BOY spread LIES about my BEST FRIEND! Oh, and I sorted Jamie out, too."

I'm so tossed to the four winds that Siobhan dumped Kieran Wakely-Brown and both his beautiful forearms for MY sake, that I almost miss that last part. I look up, eyes wide.

"You *sorted out* Jamie?" I ask. "What do you mean? Is he . . . alive?"

Siobhan goggles at me. "Of course he's alive! What sort of psychopath do you think I am?!" Outside the window, Kieran lets out a pained groan. Aphrodit-EEK . . . "But he's not your boyfriend anymore. I dumped him for you at the school gates, so you're welcome."

I gasp out loud. So loud, in fact, that the whole room turns yellow. I dive across the table and drag Siobhan into the hugest polar-bear hug I can, which isn't easy, over a desk and a Slavic companion. Zanna shifts helpfully to one side.

"Oh, Siobhan!" I cry. "Thank you! Thank you, thank you, thank you! I've been trying to break up with Jamie all week! I love you so much! I love you so, so much!"

"Christ on a bike, Cat, will you calm down?!" Siobhan grabs me by the shoulders and shoves me back into my chair. "Get ahold of yourself, woman! I just did what any strong-minded, influential, universally admired natural leader would do. It's fine."

Then Siobhan stalks over to her desk, where Alison asks cautiously if she's sure she's okay, and Siobhan blusters that of course she is—why wouldn't she be?! I gaze out the window, into the sunny blue sky, and try to soak up each sweet drop of this moment.

Siobhan's takeover of my life seems too good to be true! All through English, the air feels lighter, cleaner, fresher . . . It could just be that they finally fixed the air-conditioning, but it could also be that I'm free. Free of Jamie and his terrible tunes, free of pretending!

Then again, Jamie isn't known for his ability to catch a hint, so when I walk to the picnic tables, I'm holding my breath, half expecting to find Jamie moping around with a new nightmarish melody to win back my heart. So when I see Luna and Niamh sitting there with MY friends, I practically faint on the spot! I choke on phlegm and hack up the grossest goblin-cough ever, right in front of Alison Bridgewater.

"Gosh, Cat!" she simpers, moth-wing eyelashes fluttering in concern. "Are you all right?"

"Fine," I croak. I glare at my sister. "What are YOU doing here?"

"Chatting with Siobhan, obviously," replies Luna, beaming across the table like some sort of vegan Sunday School teacher. "We're both Scorpios, so we have a lot in common."

"Find your own Scorpio!" I begin furiously, but Siobhan loudly clears her throat.

"Well, since we've barely seen you this past week," she snaps, "we're considering whether to replace you with the next best thing. This is basically a job interview."

Ah. There's a chance she's annoyed about my constant absences: she doesn't like it when one of the gang makes other plans. In sixth grade, we were friends with a girl called Marianne Weatherly, but she made other plans one break time, and we've quite literally never seen her since. I think Siobhan may have made her switch schools. And countries.

"I was only hiding because of Jamie," I grumble, looking at my feet. "And that's sorted out now." I pause, then pointedly look at Siobhan. "Thanks to *you*, Siobhan . . ."

With Siobhan, Alison, and Kenna on one side of the table, and Luna, Niamh, and Zanna on the other, there's nowhere for me to sit. But Siobhan can never resist a groveling compliment.

"It's fine," she says. "We can be free women together. Or whatever." Then she nods curtly to Luna and Niamh. "All right, you two. I've made my point. You can go."

Luna lets out a laugh. Then Niamh nudges her and gently shakes her head. Luna's eyes widen, then Siobhan clears her throat, and the two of them scramble to their feet. "We have quilting to do anyway," Luna tells me pointedly, then they both scuttle away.

"Where's Habiba?" I ask, taking my rightful seat, and Siobhan scoffs.

"Habiba's in the library thinking about what she did," she says. "Showing up with the same earrings I'm wearing today! She's lucky I haven't blocked her on Instagram."

"In fairness," interjects Alison quietly, "I don't see how she can have *known*—"

"I post a selfie EVERY MORNING, Alison!" Siobhan snaps. "Habiba should have checked!" Alison falls silent, and Siobhan folds her arms. Then, quite shockingly indeed, she says, "Sorry. The whole Kieran situation means I'm a little touchy. I know I'm usually super tranquil, but today I'm just not in the mood."

"Don't worry!" I nudge her. Sulking can't dampen my mood today. Not now that I'll never have to hear Jamie singing "Cathleen" again! "Being single is wonderful! You're free of the old bowl and chin!"

"Don't be an idiot!" gasps Siobhan. "Why would you want to advertise that no one wants you?! URGH! I should never have dumped Chidi. I got so angry he wouldn't invite Stormzy to my cousin's baptism, I totally forgot how hot he was."

"Not like you to be blinded by anger, Siobhan," Zanna says.

Siobhan's nostrils flare again, so I hasty-laugh and say, "But wasn't he also a Gemini, Siobhan?! Remember my motto! You should never trust a Gemini. They're all two-faced! It's basically scientifically proven."

"Fact," agrees Siobhan. "My mum's a Gemini, and she's utterly demonic."

Kenna frowns. "Doesn't your mum volunteer at a food bank?"

Siobhan glares at her. "Yes, and? It's not like she cooks the food herself!"

Kenna must have a death wish because she actually opens her mouth to reply, but luckily before she can, Siobhan perks up again.

"Christ on an ACTUAL bike! Is that Morgan Delaney walking with Millie the Micronaut?! That's the final straw. I knew she was a total chowder brain, but this confirms everything. She's clearly determined to be Queen McFreak of Lost Causes."

I goblin-cough again. I'd slightly hoped that with all the boyfriend drama, Siobhan might have forgotten how much she dislikes Morgan Delaney. Or else how can I ever tell the gang I'm going to a gig with her? Also, shouldn't it be O'Freak? But, just my luck, there she is with Millie Butcher, walking toward the art studios. Although now that I think about it . . . there's not actually anything wrong with that, is there?

I sit up proudly. "Well, maybe you misjudged her, Siobhan. I think Morgan's okay." Everyone goes silent. You could hear a pixie sneeze. Although that might just be Siobhan's eyeballs rupturing—because she looks fire-drill furious. I gulp, my moment of bravery wavering like a handkerchief. "Um, although she's a Gemini as well, so maybe, um—"

"I think what Cat *means*," interrupts Zanna, "is that it's nice Morgan doesn't want anyone to feel left out." There's a pause. We all give Zanna a warning glance. "Like, if she wants to be Queen of the Weirdos, who cares? You guys are hardly in the same friendship market anyway, Siobhan."

Siobhan gives Zanna an "I'll deal with you later" glower. Then she sits back, watching Morgan and Millie like a cobra in school uniform. I dreamy-flashback to sitting with Morgan on her aubergine sofa and bite my bottom lip. Then I look at the tabletop and hope no one will notice me nervy-nerving. Alison slowly opens her scrapbook.

Siobhan sniffs, and Alison freezes mid-page-turn.

"Excuse you, Cat," says Siobhan slowly. "How do you know Morgan's star sign?"

My lungs crumple like shrink-wrapped salmon. How am I supposed to answer that?! Luckily, I'm saved by Lip Gloss Lizzie, who comes lipping over just in time, wanting to know all about Siobhan's breakup.

"Tell me everything, babe!" she coos, flexing her nude acrylics. "Especially the worst parts. I couldn't believe it when I found out he cheated on you with Elizabeth!"

Ah. So perhaps they weren't just plumbing together in the boy's bathroom after all.

Kenna, who's polishing her reading glasses, snaps them right in half. Alison gasps. Siobhan's entire body goes finger-in-a-plug-socket rigid. We all stare at Lip Gloss Lizzie in horror, whose lips begin trembling in fright.

"Oh . . ." she murmurs. "I thought she'd talked to you . . . Did you not . . . ?"

Siobhan rises to her feet like an entire apocalypse. "HE—DID—WHAT?!"

Safe to say, Morgan's star sign doesn't come up again. And we all learn that throwing an entire picnic table is easier than you might think. But nothing can throw *me* off this morning.

Jamie is gone and I am looking forward to Morgan's gig! Not that those things are connected. It may still be soul-bonding Scorpio Season, but it's not a date. It's not strawberry picking. Even so, Siobhan cannot find out, or else she'll tie me by my ankles to a ceiling fan.

And that looked very uncomfortable when she did it to Jasmine McGregor last year.

Chat Thread: Zanna Szczechowska

Zanna, 6:40 p.m.:
Clown, I'm bored. Distract me. Call?

Cat, 6:46 p.m.:
Sorry Zan-Zan, I'm going OUT!!! xx

Zanna, 6:46 p.m.:
Oh coolios. Where you off to?

Cat, 6:47 p.m.:
London!!! WITH MORGAN!!! DON'T TELL SIOBHAN xx

Zanna, 6:47 p.m.:
You're with Morgan Delaney???

Cat, 6:49 p.m.:
The very same . . . Zanna . . . She is über-liciously COOL

Zanna, 6:50 p.m.:
But you hate Geminis??

Don't do anything stupid like fall in love with her

Cat, 6:51 p.m.:
Why would I do that???

Zanna, 6:51 p.m.:
You really want me to answer that?

18
Homicidal Housewife

Sagittarius Season—the season of openness, generosity, and enthusiasm—is here! Which might explain why Mum is so shockingly relaxed about me gallivanting to London with a girl she's never met. Or maybe after Kate-Bush-panicking the other day, she's had time to reflect and realize that if I actually got murdered, she could cut back on the food bills? It could be that I've told her we're being "chaperoned" by Ruth, Morgan's crushable singer friend . . . which isn't completely untrue. Ruth will be there. It's her gig!

Luna is with Niamh, making kaftans from recycled materials, so Mum says she and Dad will have "a saucy lasagna night" together. Then she does this creepy jive over to Dad, who joins in creepy-jiving and says, "Sounds delicious!"

Delicious as my bruised big toe, I should think, unless Mum's had cooking lessons!

I ransack my wardrobe for a "soft alt rock" outfit. Since I have no clue what any of that means, this proves challenging, but eventually I craft a suitably divine-feminine-energy ensemble: black jeans, a glittery silver tank top, and a choker. Then I grab my leather jacket and head to Lambley Common Station, which is a slab of concrete with no shelter, so naturally it's raining when I get there. I have to use my jacket as an umbrella!

Then I drop my change everywhere while trying to use the ticket machine, and with miraculous timing, Morgan arrives just as I'm scrabbling about like a rat in a ratbag. I only glance up at first, then I register what I'm actually seeing, and I'm slapped into salmon-level speechlessness.

Morgan just looks so . . . well, good. Gooseberries.

Black leather pants, belted with a chain. Her shoes have enormous block platforms, and her top seems to be constructed entirely from buckles and key rings. She's added neon-green extensions to her hair, and albatross wings of eyeliner scream from behind her green-rimmed glasses.

Morgan tilts her head, frowning down at me. The rain seems to have stopped raining just for her. "What are you doing squatting in the gutter?"

"Um, nothing!" I scramble to my feet. "Just my laces, you know?"

Morgan glances at my feet, and I remember I'm wearing heeled boots that don't *have* laces. Luckily, Morgan possesses the ability to let all clownishness wash over her, so she buys our tickets and we reach the platform with no more laughable moments. It's only a matter of time though. I'd give it ten seconds max before I'm once more juggling away my dignity.

It's very Freezy Fridays. I hop from one foot to the other. It'll be December in a few days, and Mum told me this jacket wouldn't be warm enough. It's so irritating when she's right.

"So, your ex-crush!" I say, rubbing my cold hands. "Is she, like, a singer full-time?"

Morgan curls a lock of green round one finger. Her nails are painted moon silver, very über-licious indeed. "She's still mostly singing in bars. There's an EP on iTunes though. It's called *Homicidal Housewife* and . . ." she trails off. "Why are you hopping?"

"Sorry." I stop hopping. I dread to think what sort of music would warrant the title *Homicidal Housewife*, but I swallow down my bubbling pomegranate of terror. "Singing in bars is still super cool though! You might say, the bar's set high . . ."

Morgan frowns at me. "What?"

I panic silently. What indeed?! Luckily, the train arrives right then, so I'm able to strut on board with true divine feminine energy.

Just as I'm sitting down, Morgan says, "I love your jacket, by the way."

I smuggy-smile. "Well, good. I wore it specially."

Morgan bites her lip, observing me for a few heart-sweltering seconds. I wish, I wish, I wish I could tell what she's thinking. I've never met anyone so murky and mysterious! Then her smirk returns, and she says, "Wore it specially, huh? I'm flattered."

It's actually a very über-licious moment.

Crazy scenes in London. We're in Shoreditch and there's graffiti everywhere, all very colorful and exciting. I see glass skyscrapers over the rooftops, but also crumbly brick buildings and restaurants tucked into the arches of railway bridges. I suppose it's to be expected seeing as we're now in Cool Cubes Central, aka East London.

Morgan explains that we'll have to wear special wristbands at the venue so that no one serves us alcohol and that Ruth is making sure we get spots right at the front. Siobhan would be fuming if she knew Morgan had so many connections! It's almost worth telling her, just to see if she'll actually burst a blood vessel. But I grimace, remembering the conversation at the picnic tables: "Queen McFreak of Lost Causes" . . . My friends can never discover that I'm hanging out with Morgan Delaney. Siobhan would have my kneecaps for castanets!

When we find these rusty-looking garage doors (the venue, apparently), Morgan even knows the bouncer. "Hey, Lacey!" she says. "Me and my friend have guest tickets."

Lacey has a shaved head and tattoos of skulls on her shoulders. I'm slightly scared to meet her eye. I feel like I'd end up as a piñata at my own funeral if I crossed her. She gives us the wristbands (which glow in the dark, ooh-la-la!) and lets us in.

Inside, it's all brick walls and green glass bottles towering about artistically. There's a stage in the center and lots of edgy-edge gig-going types, drinking and dancing and looking generally effortless, absolutely at ease. Someone jostles my shoulder, and I tug at my wristband nervously, feeling a little out of place.

Then I notice two women sitting at the bar.

Of course, seeing two women together is not unusual. But the *way* they're sitting—so close and giving each other gooey glances over their cocktails—keeps my eyes on them. They're in glittery miniskirts and fishnet tights, lacing together their fingers and laughing. Then one leans forward and kisses the other on the cheek, stroking aside her wavy blond hair, and suddenly my heart's twittering and I'm overcome with the urge to write Elsa-Rapunzel fan-fic. Very gay-panic indeed.

"Cat, stop checking out the lipstick lesbians," Morgan says, barging into my poetic moment like a rusty bread knife. "I've found Ruth. Come and meet her."

Then, before I can say "Elsa's bright blue bra," Morgan takes my hand and drags me through the crowd toward the stage. *My hand.* I suddenly get a rush of Alison-like tingling. It's very suspicious and silly, but I can't deny the tingles. Gemini-ness aside, it is rather gorgeous holding her hand.

As people move aside, I spot a girl with shoulder-length, pastel-pink hair and the most glitter-licious makeup I've ever seen. She's in a circle of slouching hipsters, and I'm just staring at her in awe when I realize *she's* who Morgan is approaching! When Ruth spots us, her face lights up. She has one of those teeth-baring smiles I both love and hate oh so very much. Aphrodite be praised.

"Morgan, my baby-girl!" she coos. "You look astonishing!"

They hug and Morgan turns to me. "Ruth, this is my friend Cat."

I'm rather dumbstruck, so I step forward silently like a fair maiden being presented at court: all hail Queen Ruth, gorgeous, flawless, pink-haired Empress of All Things Holy and Lesbian. I'm just readying to do a genuine curtsy, Aphrodite help me, when Ruth hugs me. Her hair smells like pink ice cream . . . strawberries galore!

"So nice to meet you, babe!" she says. "Hey, has anyone told you that you look *so* like Madonna in *Desperately Seeking Susan*? Aren't you the cutest!"

Morgan elbows me. "I literally forced her to get a jacket."

"Obsessed," Ruth says as I go all dopey-antelopey. Then a shady guy in sunglasses taps her shoulder and whispers in Ruth's ear. Ruth beams at us. "Okay, you two, I'm on in five. Catch you later!" Before I can locate my tongue to say goodbye, she touches my arm. "Really do *love* your look," she says, then she's gone.

"Um . . ." I glance at Morgan, who seems to be awaiting my feedback. "She's cool!"

Morgan smirks. "You look like you've been taken out with Cupid's sawn-off shotgun," she says, and before I can reply that I haven't the faintest idea what she means, the stage lights up like a spiritual experience. We're jostled like bowling pins as the crowd wakes up.

"HOW ARE WE FEELING TONIGHT, Y'ALL?!" Ruth yells into the mic, and that just proves it: any non-American who possesses the audacity to say "y'all" is definitely a demigoddess. The crowd belly-bellows back, and Ruth's band explodes to life. Drums and guitars and lots of unnecessary mist dazzles across my vision. Morgan whoops, more enthusiastic than I've ever seen her before, and Ruth spins her mic in her heavily ringed hand, tossing back her pink hair and parting her cherry-red lips to sing.

"HOMICIDAL HOUSEWIFE!
STARING AT THE KITCHEN KNIFE!
DO YOU WANT TO CHANGE YOUR DUMB LIFE?!
OR ARE YOU JUST A HOUSEWIFE?"

Okay, so it's not Shakespeare. But Shakespeare would probably pee his Tudory tights if he were with us tonight: Ruth would eat him as an appetizer! Morgan shrieks at the stage, and Ruth points right at us and winks, and suddenly I've grabbed Morgan's hand and we're fist-pumping together like, er, professional fist-pumpers. We're exceptionally good at it, too.

Two songs later ("Burning Buckingham Palace" and "Margaret Atwood's Chain Saw Revenge"), Ruth swaggers over to the lead guitarist, who's windmilling away dressed like a manga cartoon, and kisses her right on the lips. The crowd roars, and Ruth explodes into another verse, and I look at Morgan giddily. She smiles back radiantly, and the screams fade away. It's just the two of us.

Well, it's not, obviously. Duh—this is a concert! But I keep holding Morgan's hand and whooping at the stage, drunk on the music, the lights, and the questionable lyrics . . . For the rest of the evening, I'm motion-in-the-ocean happy, which means I am highly, highly happy and also very musically refined indeed.

Cat and Morgan's Napkin Song

THEY CALL HER MORGAN AND THEY ARE GREEN
WITH ENVY AT EVERYTHING THIS QUEEN HAS SEEN
FROM KISSING A STRANGER IN BUDAPEST

"No way is that true!"

"It's completely true."

"Why were you in Budapest?"

"Because I'm really cool."

"Okay . . . that does add up."

TO SPENDING A WHOLE WEEK UNDER HOUSE ARREST.

"Now you're just being ridiculous, Morgan."

"No, I'm not. I was grounded by my mum."

"Oh . . . How come?"

"Because I'm really cool and she couldn't handle it."

"Okay . . . I can believe that actually."

THEY CALL HER CAT BUT SHE DON'T GO "MEOW"
CUZ SHE'S TEARING UP THE TOWN LIKE
    BOOM-BOOM-POW!
SHE'S PRETTY IN PINK BUT I HAPPEN TO THINK

SHE COULD WEAR ANY COLOR AND THEY'D STILL
   WINK-WINK!

"That just sounds like you're calling me pretty."

"Maybe I am."

"Ahaha . . . AHAHAHAHAAAAAAAA."

AHAHAHAAAAAAAAAAAAAAAAAAAAAAAAAAAAAAAAAA
AAAAAAAAAAAAAAAAAAAAAAAAAAAAAAAAAUAKFIEDJD
HPKSBNGFNW

"Cat . . . ? Are you okay?"

"Yes?"

· ⋆ · ✦ · ⋆ ·

19

Seven Sapphic Sisters

I'm wondering if I've perhaps swallowed a caterpillar, because all the way back to Lambley Common, my stomach feels like it's full of flapping butterflies. Me and Morgan can't stop giggling like goons over our Ruth-inspired lyrics, and by the time we're back at the station, my throat is sore from laughing. We go a bit silent salamanders on the walk home though.

Eventually, I say, "Thank you. I had an amazing time."

Morgan smiles, then taps my hand. A strangely intimate tap, I feel like, but a tap is just a tap, not a whole bathtub! I probably need to stop flanneling.

"Don't sweat it," she says. "I'm glad you came."

Whoops. There go the butterflies in my stomach again.

We're almost at Beech View Lane, which is very upsetting. I don't want the night to end. I glance at the park we're passing and, like she can read my mind, Morgan stops walking.

"Hey," she says. "Want to go in the park? It looks super creepy."

I goggle between Morgan and the murky darkness. There

aren't even streetlights in the park, and if there are (as Mum constantly imagines) any serial killers skulking around, a deserted park in the middle of the night would be the perfect spot to find them.

"Um, er," I stammer. "Is that a good idea?"

"What are you afraid of?" Morgan asks. "Come on! It'll be fun. Anyway, look: the moon's full. We might bump into a vampire, or a werewolf, if we're lucky."

"Do we have the same definition of lucky?" I ask.

But Morgan is already edging toward the gates, and I'm not about to be a wet-wipe wimp, so I follow her in. Everything goes very silent salamanders again. The playground looks like a killer clown's backyard at this time of night, but we head onto the grass, where trees are scattered about like . . . well, trees in a park, and it's a bit less scary then.

Morgan sticks her hands into the pockets of her loose black coat.

"I like nature," she says, and somewhere nearby Luna swoons. "Need to get out here more, to be honest. I always get perspective when I'm close to the trees."

"Yes . . ." I say, not sure I can compete with such a philosophical musing. "I mean, same!" I glance at her from the side. "Do you still have a crush on Ruth?" I pause awkwardly. Perhaps not the smoothest change of topic. "Sorry, you don't have to say . . ."

But Morgan waves a hand. "It's fine. I told you, I'm over it." Her dark lips curve into a smile. "Ruth ran my school's A Capella Club. I'd always hang around after, pretending to dust the keyboards or something to talk to her, so in the end, she caught on. She brought me this book, *Carol*, which is a lesbian romance and basically was her not-too-subtle way of telling me she understood. She looked after me. Like a lesbian mum, you know?"

"That's nice of her," I say quietly. I've never thought about it before; girls with the same thoughts and feelings, passing down their gay wisdom through the generations. Perhaps my life wouldn't have slithered down such an unfortunate Jamie-shaped hole if I'd had that.

"Well, I guess she was my Alison Bridgewater," Morgan says, and I almost swallow my tongue. In fact, I do swallow my tongue! I hack up the ugliest cough and have to fan myself with my hands. "You totally have a crush on her, right?"

"Why would you think that?!" I croak.

"Because of that reaction, for one," Morgan says. "Anyway, I've spotted you watching her at the picnic tables. Your gay-panic is next level when she's around."

Gooseberries! If Morgan can tell, can anyone else?! Is my secret not really a secret at all? I cross my arms, suddenly noticing the cold. "Well, I wouldn't quite call it a crush . . ."

"Oh, no," says Morgan. "You're not in love with her, are you?"

"NO?!" I splutter at once. But then I don't know what to say. I mean, what's a crush and what's love? I've only really felt it for her: the warm tingles, the torturous daydreaming . . . Is that love? "I just really like her," I mumble, meek as a Virgo. "That's all."

We stroll side by side through the trees, my mind skittering like a bee's nest. I've told my secret to someone who isn't Zanna. Is Morgan going to tell anyone? Does she think I'm totally ridiculous now? I watch her closely, but she's giving nothing away.

"So you're a star girl, huh?" Morgan asks.

I think about my *Star Bible*, and how I once did an entire semester of stand-up paddle-boarding classes because my horoscope told me I was "losing touch with my athletic spirit." Although I think my athletic spirit intentionally lost my number.

"You could say that," I reply, then I giggle. Morgan glances over curiously, and I explain. "Sorry. This is going to sound very strange . . . but I actually have a motto that you should never trust a Gemini, and here I am with one, in a park in the dead of night."

Morgan raises her eyebrows. "Oh, really? Is that why you went all freaky in the parking lot?" She throws back her hair and cackles. "You're so funny. Why don't you trust us?"

"It's no laughing matter, Morgan!" I protest, although I'm actually laughing myself as well. "I have a cousin, Lilac, who's a Gemini. She does ice-skating and my mum thinks she's absolutely perfect, but she's literally the most evil person alive!"

"And you think that means I am, too?" Morgan asks amusedly. "I didn't realize my entire moral compass was written in the stars. That's actually quite handy. Does this mean I can steal chocolate from toddlers and say my horoscope made me do it?"

"Well, they don't completely make us who we are!" I explain. "They just give us a push in a certain direction . . . At least, they do if we let them! We live on a planet where the ocean comes in and out with the moon, so . . . why can't we be connected to the stars, too?"

Morgan narrows her eyes. "I actually really like that. It's poetic."

I'm not entirely sure she's serious, so I narrow-eye her right back.

"Truly?"

"Truly."

Morgan's eyeliner has smudged, maybe from all the dancing, but her green extensions are like glow sticks. Morgan in her after-party shine. She's really rather beautiful.

"You're all right, Cat." She sighs, and I blush, then look into the sky. But I think there's starfruit in my eyes because I just want to keep on admiring her! Very suspicious feelings in my happy gay heart. "You're lovely. Just stop crushing on your straight friends."

I focus very hard on the moon, which is like . . . well, the moon. Silver and magnetic. It's putting me in the glowiest, dopiest mood. "What do you mean, 'lovely'?"

Morgan laughs. "What do I mean?"

"Well, do you mean my personality, my appearance . . ."

"I mean all of you, you compliment-seeking weirdo."

A heartbeat pause. I realize we're standing shoulder to shoulder, so close I can feel her warmth. Her eyes shine at me through the dark, mysterious and smirky as ever, and I'm suddenly very moonstruck and awake.

"You're lovely, too, Morgan," I say. Then I kiss her.

Oh my, Aphrodite! I am kissing Morgan Delaney, and her lips are soft and sweet and feather-light and butter-smooth. I think this all at once, and I really feel the stars, and the moon as well, glittering above our heads, silhouetting us on a silver horizon.

Then I open my eyes and hers are still open. Oh, gooseberries. I pull away. Maybe I should have asked if it was okay to kiss her. Did I just assault someone?!

"That was nice," Morgan says, and my panic steadies.

I hold my seahorses. The police have not been called. "Was it okay?"

Morgan tries not to laugh. "Well, I thought so, yeah."

Her glasses are wonky and that's probably my fault, so I reach out and straighten them. Then I gaze into the sky again. "That was my first kiss," I mumble. "With a girl."

"Did you like it?" Morgan asks, a bit gooey-giggly. "Rate it out of ten."

My heart is still spinning like Saturn on a Saturday night, so that's probably a good sign. "Um, definitely a strong seven and a half?"

Morgan steps closer. I let her slide her fingers into mine.

"I'm sure I can give you at least a nine," she whispers, and I gulp and try not to faint. I squeeze her hand, dizzy and happy and wonderstruck. I could happily stay inside this moment for the rest of my life, and possibly longer. But before I can kiss her again, Morgan points to the stars. "I always like the Seven Sisters. Right there. You see them?"

I follow her point. "I always wonder if there are really seven."

Morgan snorts a laugh. "Yes, Cat, there are. Seven stars, seven sisters."

I giggle. "Do you think one of them is gay?"

Morgan cackles. We're still holding hands.

"I think all of them are gay," she says. "Seven sapphic sisters. And all of them are probably Geminis as well."

I'm still trembling like an anxious trapeze artist. Did I really just have my first kiss?!

I know I've kissed Jamie. Technically or . . . biologically. But was it really a kiss? It never made my heart spin or my lips spar-kle. I never wanted to bury my face into his hair, his neck, just to soak up his scent. I kind of want to do all these things now. But does Morgan? I hope she's not just being Sagittarius Season experimental. I want this to stay perfect.

"So, I love that you love the stars," says Morgan carefully. "But do you think it'll be possible to come back down to earth long enough to try for that nine out of ten?"

I giggle giddily. "I think it almost definitely will be possible."

"Oh, only almost?" says Morgan, giving me that smirking smile of Aphrodite, eyes glittering, and my legs go seaweed limp with excitement. A lesbian crush. I've never been so happy about Siobhan being right!

Tenderly, we brush fingertips, and my butterflies spring dutifully into action. Morgan pulls me toward her and kisses me again, for a lot longer this time. She even slides her hand into my back pocket! It's very saucy lasagna; I'm too daffodil-dizzy and smooched up to even breathe . . . Divine, divine feminine energy galore.

Our kiss is perfectly poetic, and not just because the moon is mooning away and the stars are dizzy-dallying, but because I am wide awake in this gorgeous, giddy moment, kissing Morgan Delaney and being kissed right back. It's the most romantic moment of my wild and messy life so far.

IT'S OKAY TO LIKE A GEMINI IF—

- ~~They write a SONG with you?~~
- ~~They kiss you under a star-speckled sky??~~
- ~~They kiss you REALLY, REALLY WELL under a star-speckled sky???~~
- ~~They kiss you REALLY, AMAZINGLY BEAUTIFULLY under a star-speckled sky and then walk you ALL THE WAY HOME and say, "Sweet dreams . . . Not too sweet though, or there's nothing to look forward to."~~
- ~~WHO SAYS THAT????~~
- It's okay to like a Gemini if the Gemini is Morgan Delaney.

20

The Tragic Bangs

School is utterly useless to me now. I barely take in a word all morning. It's the second-to-last week before Christmas break and, in younger years, this would mean movies and games and no real lessons, but in the chain gang that is ninth grade, you get no such luxury.

Zanna keeps nudging me like she thinks I'm asleep, probably because I keep smiling and staring out windows, looking at the sky, the clouds, reliving my first real kiss over and over again. I get funny looks all day, like I'm wearing a tutu or something.

(I'm not, just to be clear. Wearing a tutu to school is something I'd never do.)

I've told no one about the kiss, not even Zanna. I don't want to share it yet; it's my memory. If only I could put it in a jar . . . I'd store it on a shelf and take it out every day and open the jar just a crack to smell the scent of the moment inside . . . It would keep me going through my very darkest days, like when Mum tries to cook a "family roast" on Sundays.

I'll never get tired of my first real kiss. I need to write poetry again, just to express myself, release the emotions! Who knew the effects of kissing could last so long? One kiss and I'm giddy for days! If it's like this every time, how will I ever get married, hold down a job, live a wholesome life? I'm amazed everyone isn't stumbling about blindly all the time, drunk on the beauty of kissing someone so wonderfully as I kissed Morgan Delaney . . .

"Cat, what the actual brain clot do you keep grinning about?" Siobhan car-crashes into my thoughts, and I wipe the smile off my face. I mean, she's right: I have been grinning a lot today. Yesterday as well. And last night. And in the car with Mum. And mid-zone-out, while Luna talks gibberish. But really, can you blame me?! I've been KISSED!

"I'm not smiling!" I protest. "I don't know what you mean."

"You look like that woman on the front of the raisin boxes," Siobhan replies. "Gazing into the freaking sun. If I didn't know better, I'd say you'd necked someone for the first time."

That gets me highly nervy-nervous. Around the picnic table, Kenna and Habiba instantly look curious, like curious cockatoos. Gooseberries galore, does Siobhan have to be so dangerously perceptive?! Where's Zanna when you need a smooth change of subject? She did say, but I think I spaced out . . . playing *Animal Crossing* or singing Polish hymns, I would think.

"Oh, leave her alone!" Alison coos, stroking my shoulder. "Let her smile about anything she wants. Maybe it's because it's almost Christmas!"

No one looks very convinced by that.

"Christmas is for babbling babies and blubbering biscuit bakers," Siobhan retorts. "It's a dreadful holiday." Then she sits up a little. "Almost as dreadful as that! What has Millie the Micronaut done to her hair?"

We all look over. Millie is on her way to the art studios, and she appears to have bangs. Siobhan clearly thinks this is the funniest excuse for a giggle-fest since Miss Ward, the French teacher, wore a bra we could see through her blouse.

"Hey, Millie!" Siobhan calls, and Millie stops walking. I suppress the urge to shout at her to pick up the pace and run. "What happened? Is that a pudding-bowl haircut?!"

Habiba and Kenna giggle while Alison and I stay nervously silent. We watch like ducks, waiting for Millie's next move, and that's when the Triple M's show up: Morgan, Maja, and Marcus, goth-gobbling toward the art studios like turkeys with beak piercings.

I resist the urge to squawk like a claustrophobic chicken. I haven't seen Morgan since the park, and we haven't talked at all about what we are, or what we'll say to each other in school, under the hawk eyes of Siobhan! But before I can invent a *romantique* master plan, Siobhan's off again, like an Aries on a mission.

"That really is the most tragic haircut I've ever seen! You poor thing!" Siobhan breezes over to take a look. "The hairdresser should have given you better advice, Silly Millie. He's butchered your look—oh, no offense. But bangs make round faces look chubby, you know? I'm not trying to be mean! It just looks a little heavy on you. Like a mop."

For a moment, I slightly zoom outside myself and (sadly) not because I'm having a spiritual experience. I'm used to Siobhan making outrageous jokes—she once told our English teacher, Miss Jamison, that her new blond highlights were "a catcall waiting to happen"! But saying those things to Millie . . . it's unkind. Siobhan is punching down. And not just because Millie is a full foot-and-three-big-toes shorter.

Millie clearly isn't amused, either. Squaring her shoulders, she looks Siobhan right in the eye. "You're a cow, Siobhan. Get a life."

Kenna gasps. Habiba drops her energy bar in alarm. Millie, answering back! This is new territory. We watch Siobhan, waiting for her to flare up. But she just laughs, like she's thrilled. "I'm trying to help you, Mills! You should be grateful. I usually only give to charity once a year. If I gave any more, I might also not be able to afford a decent haircut."

"I've got to go to class," Millie snaps, then she reaches into her blazer and slides out her phone. My heart rate almost has a chance to slow down.

But Siobhan pounces. "OMG, is that a CELL PHONE?!" she shouts as loud as she can. Habiba hyena-howls again. Siobhan glances over, grinning like the laughter's her fuel. "That's not allowed, Mills! Someone call Mrs. Warren!"

"Shut up, Siobhan!" Millie keeps turning away, but Siobhan jumps around her, surrounding Millie single-handedly. She'd make an excellent sheepdog.

That's when Morgan seems to notice the kerfuffle. She taps Maja's shoulder and nods in our direction. I begin sweating nervously. I should say something, but I'm pie-glazing paralyzed! Especially when the Triple M's start walking toward us.

"Who are you texting?" Siobhan raves on. "A boyfriend? A lesbian admirer?"

I look up sharply. Then Millie's shouting and Siobhan has snatched the phone! She's dangling it above Millie's head, which, due to Millie's magnificently minute height, means Millie doesn't stand a chance. She jumps for it, but Siobhan is having great fun, dodging her.

"Hey, Siobhan!" calls Morgan, marching over, and I can hardly watch. It's like a gas explosion sparking up before my Aquarius eyes! "Give her back her phone right now."

"I just want to know who you're messaging!" Siobhan crows, ignoring Morgan and avoiding another desperate lunge from Millie. Siobhan studies the screen as I panic speechlessly. "Who is Ross? OOH-LA-LA! Is that an anime character or something?!"

"Give it back!" Millie screams, and Siobhan looks down her nose.

"Go fetch, doggy," she says, then she throws it over her head.

My mouth falls open. That's an iPhone! I watch in horrified slow motion as it narrowly misses the grass and hits the concrete path. A chunk flies off the back! Millie rushes after it, whimpering, and that's when Morgan grabs Siobhan's shoulders and forces her to take notice.

"Did you just throw her phone?" Morgan demands.

Siobhan studies Morgan with a furrow in her brow like she's genuinely amazed Morgan has the audacity to challenge her. "I'm sorry? Are you involved in this conversation?"

"It's broken!" retorts Morgan. "Look what you've done!"

Siobhan rolls her eyes. "Chill out, Mogs. Sorry, what actually is your name? Actually, never mind. You're not relevant to my life."

Habiba half giggles, but even she's fading. Kenna's gone trembly. We're all watching Millie crouching on the path, picking up shards of her phone screen. I mean, it *is* pitiful. I'd go and help if I wasn't worried Siobhan would make blueberry jam of my bone marrow. Even Siobhan must feel something in her stony Scorpio soul! But Siobhan isn't looking.

"You're going to have to pay for that," Morgan says, taking a threatening step closer.

I widen my eyes, but Siobhan stands her ground, placing her hands on her hips and tossing back her hair. "Get out of my face. I can smell your breath and it's not pretty."

Well, that's not true! But Morgan steps back anyway.

"You're gonna get in trouble for that," she says, then she gestures at us. "Everyone saw you lob that phone."

"Oh, really?" Siobhan turns. "Habiba? Did you see me throw that phone?"

Habiba hesitates. "No, babe . . . Looked like she dropped it to me."

Morgan's eyes pass over Alison, then Kenna, then they finish on me. Everyone is watching. I open my mouth, but then I catch Alison's eye. I could swear she gives the tiniest shake of her head. And I close my mouth. Morgan just narrows her eyes at me, looking disappointed as a disappointing spring roll, then glares back at Siobhan.

"Well, I shouldn't be surprised. Barbie Basics always stick together."

Then she strides over to Millie and crouches down with her, patting her on the back. Millie's cheeks look scarlet, like she's almost crying. I watch Millie, how Morgan whispers to her, and suddenly I'm almost crying myself—a truly tragic turn of events.

Because I should have said something. But I didn't. And it's too late now.

Chat Thread: Morgan Delaney

Cat, 10:10 p.m.:
You ok? You looked uber annoyed earlier lol xx

Morgan, 10:13 p.m.:
Weren't you?

Cat, 10:14 p.m.:
I mean, Siobhan took it too far!!

Morgan, 10:14 p.m.:
Don't you think you could have told her that?

Cat, 10:15 p.m.:
It's not as easy as that!! I'm not as brave as you xx

Morgan, 10:15 p.m.:
I don't believe that. You could be all that and more
I'm not gonna pretend, Cat. I thought it was lousy of you. You just watched it happen. Do you think that makes you any better than Siobhan?? Just bc you didn't throw the phone yourself doesn't mean you weren't responsible. She did it but you enabled her

Cat, 10:17 p.m.:
Siobhan's been my friend for YEARS tho, Morgan
It's rlly hard to call out a friend!!!!
And you know Siobhan?? I can't just stand up and stop her

Morgan, 10:18 p.m.:
But that's the thing. You CAN. And I thought you were the type of person who would. Guess I was wrong. Gtg sleep anyway, night

21

A Hiccup in the Stanza of My Life

I'm breathing through my hands and counting to five. I got to school ten minutes ago, and as soon as I stepped through the front gates, the hiccups began. I've been hiccuping ever since and can't seem to stop! Every ten seconds, another one comes.

"Something's changed." We're in homeroom waiting for Mrs. Warren, and Zanna is observing me. She tilts her glasses down. "What have you not told me, my useless blond friend?"

Smooth liar that I am, I blush at once. "Nothing." Then I hiccup.

"You were gazing into the distance and smiling all of yesterday," Zanna says. "Now you look depressed. Like Wednesday Addams at Disneyland."

I scowl because I *am* depressed. Morgan hates me (she may actually be right, too), and winter feels cold and wintery again. But I didn't tell Zanna about the kiss! So where do I even begin?!

I hiccup again. "I've got the hiccups, Zanna," I say. "I'm not depressed."

Zanna nods. "I definitely believe you. In fact, I think religions have been founded on less belief than I have for you at this moment."

A hiccup cuts off my reply. Then the bell rings, and while the bell is still ringing, in strides Mrs. Warren. She does this every day. Not a moment early or late. She literally enters during the ring. Maybe she waits in the hallway beforehand? Or she knows to the exact second how long it takes to walk here from anywhere on school grounds. Frightening stuff.

"Good morning, ninth graders," she says. I hiccup. "Silence, please." She runs through the roll call, me hiccuping every ten seconds, then folds it shut. "Now, Siobhan, Alison, Habiba, and Cathleen Phillips. You're wanted in Mr. Drew's office right away. Off you go."

There's a ripple of "ooooooh" round the class, and I gaze with googly eyes at Siobhan, Habiba, and Alison. But they look just as puzzled as me! Mr. Drew, the vice principal?!

"I believe I specified 'right away,' girls," Mrs. Warren says, and we scramble to our feet, grabbing our bags and filing out of the room in silence. Except for me. I hiccup twice.

"Siobhan, do you . . ." I hiccup. "Do you know what this is about . . . ?"

Siobhan scowls, automatically leading the way down the hall. "Of course not!" she snaps. "Do I look like a psychic?! And stop . . . doing that. Whatever it is. You sound like an old seagull with one lung missing. Get a grip!"

Mr. Drew's office is by the main office, a once-cacti-heavy zone whose windowsills have been mysteriously robbed of their succulent glory. Then we turn an eerily underdecorated corner and see Kenna waiting outside Mr. Drew's door, trembling all over.

"Oh, Siobhan!" Kenna wheezes, practically collapsing into Siobhan's arms. "Thank goodness you're here! I was all by myself and I didn't know why and—"

"What a performance!" Siobhan mutters, clapping one hand over Kenna's squealing mouth. "Mr. Dog-Doo is clearly trying to intimidate us, calling our weakest link in first."

Alison is very nervy-nervous, lacing her fingers in and out, in and out repeatedly, like she's knitting a sweater. Habiba rolls her eyes though. "I don't think he's quite that tactical, Siobhan. Anyway, Mr. Drew loves me. Netball captain, remember? And I totes cured those raging sixth graders . . ." She smugly holds her fingers in a peace sign.

Furiously, Siobhan smacks her fingers out of the sky. "Will you wake up from your Instagram coma?! My dad is a psycho-therapist, Habiba! He knows how people work. This is all just a front. Whatever he throws at us, we aren't going to crack! Even if it's waterboarding—and it could be! This is senior staff."

Then Mr. Drew's door swings open. I hiccup again, then my eyes pop-a-doodle-doo! Out of the room comes Morgan Delaney. She hurries past, avoiding my eyes, then Marcus comes out with Maja, and a moment after that, Millie Butcher, hiding behind her bangs.

"Come in, girls," says Mr. Drew, and I gulp.

Mr. Drew is brisk and northern. We file into his office like tuna fish and line up before his desk. I hiccup again. He takes his time, shuffling papers about, then taking a sip from a red mug saying WORLD'S BEST DAD on the side—doubtless a gift from his brisk northern children. Then he clears his throat.

"Right, girls, so here we are," he begins, which I'd have thought was obvious. "Given that you saw who was just here, perhaps you already know what this is about." He pauses, but no one speaks. I hiccup. Mr. Drew frowns. "Are you all right, Cathleen?"

"Just, um, hiccups, sir." I try to hold my breath. Just to be helpful.

"When I think of our ninth graders," Mr. Drew plows on, "I think of upstanding members of the school community, setting a good example. So, imagine how disappointed I was to hear that you girls targeted and bullied a fellow student yesterday."

Next to me, Alison whimpers. Siobhan remains uncharacteristically silent. Habiba's peace-sign fingers droop in shame and Kenna sniffs sadly, but no one says a word. Except for me—hiccuping once more. I think I'm about to burp. Gooseberries! What did I eat this morning?! I try to swallow it down as Mr. Drew northerns on.

"The consensus is that you girls intentionally damaged Millie's phone. It goes without saying that a phone is a very expensive piece of property—"

"We didn't mean to break it!" Kenna blurts, and Mr. Drew stops.

Siobhan bristles. And I'm sorry, "we"?! *I* didn't break the phone! Then again, Morgan's texts are still swimming round my head like angry piranhas. I fight back the air bubble that is forcing its way up my throat. I definitely can't hiccup now!

Kenna's brown eyes tremble. "It just . . . got broken!"

Mr. Drew sits back in his chair. "So, you admit that your actions yesterday resulted in Millie Butcher's phone being broken?"

There's a rustling as we all shifty-shuffle. Then Kenna nods; Alison, too. Habiba is so still, she could be a mannequin. Then I notice that's not Habiba: it's one of those creepy skeletons they keep in science classrooms. What in the name of Piccadilly Circus does Mr. Drew have a skeleton in his office for?! Habiba is nodding, too, like a sad, deflated netball. In the depths of my throat, an air bubble swells. Oh, gooseberries, DON'T BURP!

"Right," Mr. Drew says. "Well, firstly, you're going to have to pay for the damage. I've spoken to Millie's mother, who told me Millie was deeply upset by yesterday's events. I'm disappointed, girls, in all of you. I have yet to decide exactly what level of punishment—"

"It wasn't them."

Mr. Drew stops short. Then one by one, our heads turn to Siobhan.

"I threw the phone," Siobhan says rigidly. "It was me. I aimed for the grass, but I missed. Which is shameful, actually, as I'm sensational at netball . . . But it was me, not them. I took it too far. And I shouldn't have done it."

The silence hums. Siobhan, owning up? I'm mind-bazooka-ed!

"Right," Mr. Drew says. "Thank you for your honesty, Siobhan. I'm sure your friends will appreciate it. How about we let them go and have a bit of a chat by ourselves?"

Siobhan nods, drumming her fingers angsty-angsty on her leg. I don't blame her—"a bit of a chat" with Mr. Drew sounds more frightening than a Tudor execution! Actually, I doubt there's much difference between them.

Mr. Drew nods to the door. "But, girls," he says. "I don't want to hear any of your names come out of Millie Butcher's mouth again. Do I make myself clear?"

"Yes, sir," the others chorus, and I open my mouth.

That's when it comes. The burp I've been holding in for five full minutes. The sound seems to echo, vibrating my throat, and I stand, arms spread wide like I'm singing the opera.

Finally, it ends. I clear my throat, glancing apologetically at Siobhan. If she wasn't looking before, she's looking now, and her eyes are so wide, she looks very disturbed indeed. Mr. Drew just sits there, stunned.

Carefully, I raise a hand to my mouth. "Loud and clear, sir," I croak.

"It's not fair!" I babble at lunch. "Everyone burps! Even girls!"

We're in the cafeteria and Siobhan still hasn't reappeared. Perhaps Mr. Drew did execute her! Meanwhile, Habiba has just blessed the entire table with a full account of my hiccup-induced burping. Including Lip Gloss Lizzie and her glossiest, most popular girlfriends.

"That's so funny," says Lizzie's boyfriend, Gloss-Guzzling Lawrence, who's here with some Lad Friends and lots of floppy blond hair.

"So," agrees Lip Gloss Lizzie. "Probably the funniest thing since you told Mr. Derry he was the love of your life, actually."

I let out an exasperated gasp. "I didn't tell him he was the love of my life! I told him he was truly beautiful, which is completely different . . . I didn't mean to say it to him anyway!"

"Who did you mean to say it to, then?" Alison asks, and I flannel internally.

Zanna clicks her tongue. Thank Sappho for Zanna, changing the subject at just the right moment. "Siobhan's parents are going to kill her. I wish there was some way we could watch—" I elbow her. "I mean help."

"We'll have to throw her a hashtag-able party," says Habiba. "For saving our butts."

"Siobhan probs won't be free to host any parties for a while though." Lip Gloss Lizzie sighs, as if the inconvenience to her social life is the saddest thing about this, and not that Millie was so upset that she told her mum, which is what's guilt-guillotining me.

Alison coughs. "I mean, it was completely her. It would have been totally unfair if we'd gotten detention as well!"

Kenna shrugs. "I don't know that it was *all* her fault, Alison—"

"It was!" Alison glances round the table, her brown eyes dewy and beautiful in their distress. But also . . . dare I say it? A little ignorant . . . ? "We never said anything to Millie! We shouldn't all get detention because Siobhan broke Millie's phone—"

"But we should have said something," I cut in. I guiltily examine my half-eaten pizza. "We didn't do it, but we let Siobhan do it. That's wrong, too."

Alison looks into her food and my heart twists. I want her to smile again. Alison isn't a bully. For her, it must be the worst thing in the world to be called one. But (unusually for me, I'll admit) I think I'm right. And oddly, bizarrely, and strangely . . . I might have just lost a little respect for Alison Bridgewater. It's the most peculiar realization of my gay, gay life.

Then over Alison's shoulder, I see Morgan. She's sitting with the now-Quadruple M's, who seem to have opened their ranks to Millie full-time. Suddenly, I'm standing. I beeline for Morgan, ignoring my friends' puzzled frowns. Maja spots me, and I think she must say so, because they all stop talking right away. I hover awkwardly by the table.

"Um . . . Millie?" I swallow. "Sorry about your phone. I should have said something. And not just yesterday. All the days, when . . . people said things. Or Siobhan, rather. I should have told her not to. I'm, um . . . I'm sorry."

Silence. Well, this is awkward alligators. But I've said my piece, so I slowly back away. I can't repair her phone or emotional scars after all. But then Millie says, "Thanks, Cat."

I stop retreating. "Oh. You're welcome! And, um, your bangs look really nice by the way! Bang-tastic, in fact. Like Zooey Deschanel but, well, blond!"

Millie lights up. "I love Zooey Deschanel!"

"Who doesn't?! Um, I'll go finish eating, then." I turn away.

"Cat?" I hear, and I whirl round again. Morgan is finally looking at me and—oh, my giddy, gay heart—she's . . . smiling? Just a little. "Just do better. You're not like that."

I nod profiterole-profusely. "Yes! I mean, no, I'm not, and yes, I will, and um . . ." I take a deep, steadying breath. Must! Not! Malfunction! "I'll talk to you later?"

Morgan picks up her wrap. Then, in the smallest way possible, she nods. I want to pick up a plate and throw it like a Frisbee, I'm so relieved. But I think I really would get a detention for that, so I'm just happy and excited on the inside instead.

Chat Thread: Siobhan Collingdale

Cat, 4:00 p.m.:
HEYYYYYYYYYYYYYYYYYYY

I know u must be sad, but here is a horoscope to cheer u up!!! Despite what has happened, EVERYTHING IS PEACHY-PERFECT! It's Sagittarius Season, so for a Scorpio like you, it's the perfect time to make strong financial decisions and take your goals to the next level. Try doing homework upstairs! And sticking coins to the ceiling when you're sleeping will bring good luck, so make sure you have blue tack!! :) xox

Siobhan, 4:10 p.m.:
I'M GOING TO BE DOING *EVERYTHING* UPSTAIRS YOU UTTER FLUTTER-MUFFIN, I'VE BEEN SUSPENDED AND MY DERANGED MOTHER IS GROUNDING ME FOR A MONTH!! SHE'S TAKING MY PHONE AS SOON AS I SEND THIS, I'M PRACTICALLY IN JAIL!!! HOW IS ANYTHING "PEACHY"?!! ARE YOU STUPID?!!!!!

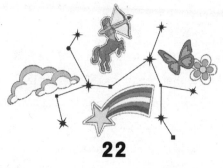

22
Gucci Good and on Top of the World

Siobhan's suspension is tragic news for the gang. How will we buzz to the best of our ability without our Queen Bee? But Siobhan says nothing in the world will change her mother's mind, not even offering up Lip Gloss Lizzie for a free (and "much-needed") makeup lesson.

Of course, the moment Siobhan is out of the picture, Loud-mouth Jasmine McGregor and her Foghorn Friends don't waste a second asserting their newfound power. Kenna goes missing for an entire afternoon before Mrs. Warren finds her locked in a stationery cupboard. Then in PE, Jasmine and Cadence Cooke weaponize the portable tennis-ball launcher—it's absolute chaos! Zanna, Alison, and Lip Gloss Lizzie go down in a firestorm of neon green, and Habiba only escapes by scaling a nearby tree.

Then I make the gravest of grave mistakes. The gang has been sticking together—strength in numbers and all that—but on Thursday, I walk to art alone. Just when I'm taking a shortcut through a dangerously empty hallway, I hear "WOOF, WOOF, CAT!" and I whirl round to see Jasmine McGregor and three Foghornians!

And one of them has DUCT TAPE.

Without even a duck-related pun to offer as truce, I race down the hall, pursued by a brigade of hooting hooligans. I skid round the corner toward the auditorium—perhaps I'll be safe if I can infiltrate the sixth grade assembly! And that's when I collide with Morgan.

"Morgan!" I gasp, blinking in surprise. "What are you doing here?!"

"Skipping English, because I hate *Of Mice and Men*," says Morgan nonchalantly. Then she frowns as hunting cries echo. "What are you doing here?"

"Jasmine is terrorizing me!" I squeal. "Without Siobhan, none of us are safe!"

Morgan narrows her eyes, then she grabs my hand. "You don't need Siobhan. Follow me." We rush round another corner, skidding to a halt by the PE locker rooms. Morgan reaches into her blazer and—

"Is that a key?!" I squeak, and Morgan smirks.

"Miss Graham dropped it right in front of me." She unlocks the door and beckons me in. "Trust me. It's a really good hiding place." Then she shuts the door behind us, and we wait, silent as statues with stage fright. Outside, Jasmine and her friends hoot by.

We escaped! I sigh with relief, then collapse onto the bench. Then I smile at Morgan, very smirky-smirky indeed.

"Did you just save me?" I ask. "That was very knight-in-shining-*amore* of you, Morgan. Very romantic actually."

"Get over yourself," she mutters. "You already know I like you."

Nothing could get me so flanneling and useless as that. I giddy-giggle and Morgan rolls her eyes. Then I skim across the bench in a way I hope is "suave" and hop to my feet in front of her. We eye each other for a hot, *hot* second, then carefully, delicately, I kiss her cheek.

"Urgh," says Morgan. Not ideal. But then she adds, "I'm so screwed," and links her fingers into mine, just like at the park. She pulls me toward her, kisses me again. I try to kiss her back without letting my atoms break apart and bluster away to the four corners of the earth. It's harder than it sounds. Then she runs a hand down my waist, and I practically catch fire.

I don't, thank Aphrodite. That would be most inconvenient.

Suddenly, TEACHER voices. But Morgan grabs my wrist again and tugs me toward the gym. "Quick," she hisses. "If we get to the athletic fields, we can sneak out."

I think if she suggested we fly to Kentucky, I'd do it, so we scamper across the gym like scampery skippers (which in fact, we are), then out into the fields. Then we're running across the soccer field, still hand in hand, giggling like clownish fools.

"Morgan!" I gasp. "Where are we going?!"

"I told you," Morgan replies as we reach the riverbank. "There's a gate back here and a footpath. It's cute. And it's off school grounds, too."

We stalk through the reeds with me glancing furtively around, half expecting Mrs. Warren to rise like the Irish Loch

Ness monster from the river. Luckily, she does not. I keep Morgan's hand clasped in mine until we find the disused gate. It's shrouded mysteriously in brambles, like a portal to, well, the footpath. But Morgan finds a stick and whacks down the nettles to carve out a path: all very heroic and dashing. She creaks open the gate.

"Coming?" She tilts her head at me like she always does, and the butterflies start flap-flap-flapping away again. Soon, we're on the gravelly footpath, following the river. Then Morgan says, "So, life's tough without your Queen Bee, huh? I can't say I'm sorry she got suspended. No offense, but she seems like a real Regina George."

I hasty-laugh. But I don't actually think Morgan is joking, so I put back on my serious face, which Zanna calls my "dead fish face." "Yes . . . Siobhan's crossed a few lines recently. Well, lots of lines. It's all very . . . um . . . scribbly. But she's not always like that! She's loyal and, um . . . really good at hosting parties!"

Morgan scoffs. "Loyal? She's even awful to Kenna! Like, her actual best friend?"

"She doesn't mean it though . . ." I begin. Then I pause. "Well, she does. But you don't know everything, Morgan! Like, did you know Kenna is dyslexic? And nobody knew until seventh grade, when she got really overwhelmed and stopped coming to school completely! Siobhan went round and literally dragged her back in footie pajamas. Then she helped her talk to Mrs. Warren and get the right help . . ." I hesitate. "She also started her 'Books Are for Losers Anyway' campaign, but Miss Bull didn't let that take off . . ."

I'm not sure Morgan's entirely convinced. "I'll have to see

where we stand after Christmas. I just hate bullying, Cat, and Siobhan was really punching down. It's wrong."

"Yes," I agree. "And you were right, Morgan. I'm sorry I enabled. But I did tell the gang that we can't say 'Millie the Micronaut' anymore! Hopefully that will, um . . . help." Morgan smiles, so fingers crossed I've done something right. "So . . ." I say, expertly changing the topic. "Going anywhere for the holidays?"

"Ireland." Morgan rolls her eyes. "I'm not keen, but we have to visit grandparents . . . It'll be drama this year, with my dad having left, but Mum says it has to be done."

Morgan hasn't mentioned her dad leaving before, but I remain chili-chill and composed. "You have lots of family, then?" I ask, demonstrating my oodles of maturity.

"Irish Catholics usually have lots of family," she says. "And they'll definitely ask if there's some special boy in my life, as usual."

I gasp. "What will you tell them?"

"Maybe I'll tell them there's a special girl instead. That'll shake things up."

I giggle stupidly, then wonder if she's actually serious. Is she asking me to be her girlfriend? We've reached a low stone wall by the river. If Morgan is expecting me to answer, or hoping that I will, she gives nothing away. Which is good because I'm just opening and closing my mouth like a kipper. Morgan hops up onto the wall.

"Careful!" I hold out a hand.

"It's not a big drop," Morgan says amusedly, then she reaches out her hand. After a slight hesitation, I take it and approach the Edge. Morgan is right: it's not a big drop, though the river is shallow and those stones do look pretty pointy. There are some ducks, too, and I consider saying, "What's a duck's favorite snack? Quackers and cheese," which would be exceptionally hilarious but . . . hmm, maybe not cool enough for Morgan . . .

"What are you thinking about?" Morgan asks.

"Quackers and cheese," I blurt out. Wait! That's not right! I blink at Morgan. "Um, I mean . . ." I grapple. I'm thinking about her, obviously, and us skipping about rainbowily, like real raisin-box ladies. But I don't want to SAY that! "Definitely not about ducks," I confirm.

Morgan nods slowly. Then she bursts out cackling. "Wow. You're so weird." She tries to stop laughing but starts again, then I laugh, too. My eyes drift to her lips. They look glossy, sweet with balm. The kind her hair might get stuck in . . . Or my hair if I were closer.

I shift closer. Our toes touch. "So . . ." I ponder. "What are *you* thinking about?"

The water is trickling away merrily in the background, and it's all very poetic, very romantic, a sign from the stars that soul-bonding is occurring! But Morgan seems to hesitate. She shrugs. "Honestly? I'm kind of thinking about Alison."

I blink at her in surprise. "Alison Bridgewater?" I try to gather myself. "Well, I understand. She's pretty and a Pisces, which is always a win, but, Morgan, I don't think she's into girls like we are—"

"Cat?!" Morgan gives me a look. "Obviously, I don't mean like that. I've just been thinking, you know, about you . . . And I like you." She pauses. I slightly want to swoon but manage not to. "But I know you like Alison. So, I'm just wondering . . . well, how much?"

Now it's my turn to turn goatish. I gulp, trying to think of the right words, how to explain to Morgan how I really feel.

"I've never liked anyone other than Alison Bridgewater," I begin. "Until I met you. So, I think it's more that . . . I don't know how *not* to like her? Even though I really do like you, Morgan! And I wouldn't want to be here with anybody else. I just still have some Alison to, er . . . work through?" I'm saying totally the wrong words. I look at my shoes. "Sorry. That doesn't make much sense."

"It makes sense," says Morgan. "But if I can ask . . . What headspace does that leave for, like, anyone else? If you're still working through things?"

Morgan looks up, and I take in her eyes, her nose, her freckles. How she jumped into a river for me, how she'd probably do that again. And loving someone: it's different when they're right in front of you. Not like watching through a window anymore. I kiss her gently.

"Enough," I say, and it's absolutely the truth. "It leaves enough."

We kiss LOTS after that. So much, I estimate I could give Nine*teen* Rules of Necking, should I have to. I could get used to kissing this frequently. Her lips are just so soft . . . Really, it's exceptionally clownish I ever thought I could have a boyfriend. How could Jamie ever compete with this? I take my hand off the wall to brush Morgan's peachy-soft cheek. I'm in my element . . . ! Then I hear scrabbling sounds. There's a dog sniffing at my shoes.

"Gooseberries!" I exclaim, breal

then the dog jumps. It's yapping and n

know, so I lean back and then—SAPI

desperately grab at the stonework. Mor

And I slide right off the wall.

There's a panicked flapping as the d

realize I'm lying spread eagle in the river,

clothes, running through the curls of my

sky: wintery and ice-cube white. It's not wa

Gooseberries indeed.

Morgan leans over the wall, one hand clas

along with an elderly lady, the rabid dog und

beret pulled snugly over her ears. It works for

"Christ on a cracker," Morgan says. "Are you

I lift up one hand and spread my fingertips.

patter onto my nose. Then I realize I'm laughing

but I don't actually care. I just made out with Mc

are tingling, so either the pneumonia's kicking in a

in dreamboat heaven!

I've surfboarded across the stars to my very sa

wholesome Gemin-ending. I'M NOT GOING TO DIE A

I'm feeling Gucci good and on top of the world. Tl

doesn't wash away with a little water.

I'm in a ludicrously soggy-snoggy mood. It's the best mood ever.

I'm humming "Twinkle, Twinkle, Little Star" as I turn onto Beech View Lane. That's how soggy-snoggy I am. But then I spot Luna. She's slouched on the edge of a planter with her head bowed, half buried in an evergreen hedge. If I didn't know already that she's my pacifist sister, I'd think she were some sort of lurking murderer! Or possibly a depressed gardener.

"Luna?" I call, and Luna looks up, then quickly looks down again. Her cheeks are red and blotchy. I walk right up to her. *Drip, drip, squelch.* I'm getting a bit chilly. A trickle of water is actually running down my spine as I speak. "Are you crying?"

"No," says Luna.

"Looks like you are."

"Well, I'm not," she insists, tears running down her cheeks.

"Luna, you're literally crying right now! What's wrong?" I cross my arms with a squelch. "Are they out of vegan sausages at the health food store or something?"

"Don't make fun of me!"

I hesitate, then sit next to her. "What's going on, then?"

Luna sniffs a couple of times. Her lashes are droopy as dying flowers. It's not like Luna to cry. She's normally too outraged, and she thinks tissues are bad for the environment anyway. She also once told me that if you meditate twice a day, nothing can break your spirit, so she must be upset-umbrellas galore to be publicly weeping like this.

"I've been talking to a guy . . ." she begins, then she frowns. "Are you wet?"

187

I ignore her question. "Awww, Luna! A guy! But that's great!"

"Whatever," she mutters. "He's, like, a trans guy. You know? Female-to-male?"

I roll my eyes. "I know what trans means, Luna. I'm not Mum."

She still manages to frown judgmentally. "Well, he's trans, and everybody at school found out. The boys are all calling me a lesbian now, then someone wrote 'mommy muncher' on the back of my chair in science . . ."

She pauses to cry some more. Gosh, boys really are vermin at twelve. I mean, at any age, but twelve especially. I nod supportively. "And is that why you're upset? Because they called you a lesbian?" I swallow down my gay-panic. "Terrible people, lesbians, I agree! Just criminals in dungarees really—"

"What? No!" Luna wipes her eyes on her sleeve. "I'm not homophobic! But now Dorian's trying to be all heroic. He says he won't be part of my life anymore because no one's going to understand and it's going to be too difficult for me. And Niamh is upset, too . . ."

DORIAN?! Trust Luna to find someone who's picked a name as scholarly and mythological as hers! But I'm more worried about Niamh. If Luna's lost her best friend, she'll have way more time to bother ME—a highly Risk-Ian-McKellen situation!

"And what happened with Niamh . . . ?" I ask nervously.

Luna sighs. "I canceled plans with her to hang out with Dorian this weekend, and she said it was anti-feminist of me. But she's the one who ate chicken last week, so if anyone's a fraud . . ." Luna glances at me again. "Cat, why *are* you soaking wet?!"

"Let's focus on you." I shake my hair back, showering us both with cold water. "Niamh is probably just stressed because Siobhan is home 24/7! Like, can you imagine?" Luna grimaces, then nods. I really am a true healer of souls. "Anyway, arguments happen," I continue wisdomfully. "I argued with my friends all the time when I was in eighth grade!"

Luna says, "I'm in seventh grade."

"And in seventh grade as well. Ahem. As for Dorian . . . just remind him that you're Luna Anaïs Celeste, and you don't need anybody looking out for you! Tell him you don't care what other people think. You don't even have to lie! Tell him you only wear secondhand clothes and he'll understand everything—"

"What's wrong with wearing secondhand clothes?!" Luna protests.

"Um. Nothing." I smile quickly, trying to forget the mental image of Luna's cork crop top. She calls it "recycling"; I call it a grave, grave mistake. "Just do something dramatic! Win his trust. Like, write him a poem! Would he like that?"

Luna sniffs again. "He probably would actually. He's really spiritually in tune, Cat. He's over at LCA, in the year above me, and he's on the debate team. He's done a TED Talk before, so he's really smart! And he wants to get plastic out of the ocean."

I grimace. "Don't we all?"

Luna side-eyes me. "I know you think it's silly, but I think he's cute."

"I don't think it's silly! He sounds nice and . . . activisty. Which is perfect for you, isn't it? You can change the world together and . . . cute things like that."

Luna watches me, and I feel like we're seeing each other properly for the first time in months. And not just because Luna finally got contact lenses. I think ever since she changed from Lauren to Luna, our relationship has been different. Now though, she shuffles closer and puts her head on my shoulder. There's a pause.

"You really are wet, you know," Luna says.

"Yes. And it's freezing, so I should probably get inside." I ease her off. Gosh. My sister, Luna, having relationship drama. "Um . . ." I hesitate. "I'm a lesbian. Or whatever. So, you can give your graffitied chair to me. Not that I'm a mommy muncher. I mean, I'm not against women with children, it's just . . . I'm fourteen."

Okay, I did *not* expect to come out to Luna. Not during Sagittarius Season! Coming out should really be a Pisces Season event when everybody's weeping anyway. I wait for Luna to react. Maybe frown. Jump to her feet in her surprise. Instantly launch a nonprofit foundation called Gay Children in Need. Something like that.

Then she just says, "I know, idiot."

I leap up, goggly-eyeing her. "What? You *know*?!"

"I found your fan-fic page years ago," she says, rolling her eyes. "You married Elsa from *Frozen* to Rapunzel from *Tangled*. It was a fun story . . . or epic poem, I suppose you'd say. Although *epic* implies good, and really it was just long. You painfully over-used the words *swooning* and *gasping*, too. But I kind of guessed after that."

I sit back on the planter with a squelch, carefully not

swooning or gasping. I can't believe Luna read my fan fiction! It was, like, my biggest secret in the world when I was twelve. The story I wanted was never going to be a film. So I wrote it myself, in poetic verse, which was slightly a blessing and slightly a curse. Very tragic indeed.

Eventually, I elbow her. "You're so annoying."

Luna smiles smugly. "You're so annoying, too."

Chat Thread: Morgan Delaney

Morgan, 10:07 a.m.:
About to get on the ferry xx

Cat, 10:14 a.m.:
OMG DON'T DROWN XX

Morgan, 10:17 a.m.:
Tysm for putting THAT thought in my head xx

Cat, 10:17 a.m.:
:D xx

Cat, 11:41 a.m.:
You in Ireland yet? DID U DROWN?????

Morgan, 11:49 a.m.:
Luckily I did not. Miss u already haha xx

Cat, 11:51 a.m.:
Aww :) I miss you too my sweet Lepricorn xx

Morgan, 11:53 a.m.:
Leprechaun. Also, never call me that again

Xxx

24
Smoky and Mysterious (or Maybe Just Smoky)

It's gloomy scenes once Morgan has gone to Ireland. What am I supposed to do with myself now?! It's two weeks before she's back, and in the meantime, all the gang are either away or (in Siobhan's tragic case) grounded. Properly, properly gloomy scenes.

A horoscope might cheer me up. What can I expect for the remainder of Sagittarius Season? But it turns out to be more of a horror-scope. Apparently, a new romantic connection is right around the corner! Gooseberries! I don't want a "new romance" meteoring my Potential Thing with Morgan! I need to avoid this like Disney avoids Elsa's love life!

I close all my curtains and disconnect my computer from the internet. That should solve it. There can't be any "new romance" if I spend the holidays like a hermit! But after two phoneless hours, I discover that hermit life is actually brown-shoes boring.

Hmm . . . what now?

Right when I'm thinking the holidays couldn't get worse, Mum strides into my room like it's the middle of the day (which it is, but still) and announces that Auntie Rose, Uncle Hillary, and my posh-as-poodle cousins, Lilac and Harmony, are coming here for Christmas, because they still haven't visited the iPhone Box and "want the full tour."

"MUM!" I protest. "What tour?! We only have one room!" Lilac will never let that go—not when she resides in a 950-room palace. "And I don't want to share my room with Lilac! She's put spiders in my mouth when I'm sleeping before!"

"Oh, sweet Lilac!" sighs Mum as I gesticulate in disbelief. "I can't wait to hear all about her figure-skating exam! Passed with flying colors, Rose says!"

I groan. At least Harmony is fine, if you consider being a nine-year-old obsessed with circus acrobatics as "fine" (she once tried to trapeze her way out of a top-floor hotel room). But Lilac, the Gemini Empress of Everlasting Evil?! A truly tragic predicament.

When Mum strides out again, rambling about family hikes in the glorious countryside (I think I'd rather be lawn-mowered to death!), I end my hermit era and switch my phone back on, in search of a suitable distraction to bring back my will to live.

Unfortunately, the only distraction I can find is Zanna. We sit on video call, and she instructs me on how to straighten my hair (not easy, given that my hair is Hula-Hoops). I fill her in on all the Morgan-related gossip, and we gasp away like true gossaholics.

"To the left," Zanna guides me. "To the right. No, my right."

"Which way is that?!" I ask, and Zanna's grainy image squints.

"I think for you, it's right," Zanna says, and I begin moving the straightener. "Okay, wait. Sorry. I actually meant to the left."

"Whose left?!"

"Yours." Zanna pauses. "I think."

If she weren't precisely 997 miles away in some boring bungalow near Warsaw, I would probably murder my Sagittari-UNBELIEVABLE friend.

"Zanna," I explain calmly. "I know that you have never had a relationship before . . ."

"Well, in fairness, Cat, neither have . . ."

"But straightening my hair is really quite important," I say. "I'm making sure Morgan doesn't forget me while she's in Ireland! I need to stay relevant and exciting."

"I think you're confusing being in a relationship with being in *Vogue*," says Zanna. "But I'm still happy for you. Does this mean you're over Alison now?"

I pause my straightening. "Well. Yes. I suppose it does."

"Only it looks like you've got her Christmas card on the wall behind you," Zanna says, and my eyes widen. "I know it's from her because she gave me the same one."

"Don't be ridiculous!" I drop the straightener and jump to my feet, marching to the wall and tearing Alison's card down. "I put all my Christmas cards on the wall."

"You didn't put up mine."

I frown at the phone, still propped up by my mirror. "You didn't give me a card, Zanna."

"Oh," says Zanna. "That's valid."

Before I can accuse her of being an even worse friend than I previously thought, Mum calls that lunch is ready (Aphrodite only knows what she's conjured up today), so I swipe Zanna off the floor and head downstairs.

Still on the lookout for dangerous new romance, of course.

Outside the tranquility of my bedroom, the iPhone Box is all sad and festive. Yesterday, we trudged off to some tragic farm to buy a Christmas tree, which is now lurking leafily (well, needly) by the sofa, giving me allergies.

Mum idiotically decided we had to decorate the tree "as a family," but mostly Luna just hung a bunch of crystals and pine cones everywhere, which Mum said looked "a little hippie-dippy." She wanted these cringe-fest baubles we painted smiley faces on ten years ago when *I* could barely hold a paintbrush, but Luna said she was "dampening the energy of this entire consumerist holiday." Mum should know by now that doing anything "as a family" is a terrible idea.

I'd buy a plastic glittery white tree personally and shower it with icicles like in *Frozen*, but no one ever listens to my ideas. Oh, well. At least Luna's happy: she's been ecstatic since Dorian got all loved-up from her poem. I really am an amazing sister and life coach.

"Cat," says Zanna when I tell her this. "If you became a life coach, I think average life expectancy would drop by at least a decade nationwide."

I glower at the phone. "Well, thank you for helping me straighten my hair. It looks very *iconique*. But I have to go and be smoky and mysterious with my family now."

"Smoky and what?!" Zanna snorts a laugh. "You just look

Swedish, to be honest. Oh, wait though, did you remember to—"

I've had enough of Zanna's nonsense for one morning, so I hang up the phone, cutting her off midsentence. That will teach her. Besides, she couldn't look Swedish if she tried! I brace myself for lunch at the island counter, *Bible to the Stars* clutched to my chest.

Mum's prepared home-baked stuffed rolls, so to cover up the taste, I bury mine in cheese. I think she's actually burned the rolls though, because there's a very smoky smell hovering about. Even Luna wrinkles her nose when she comes down. She's been in her room all morning, wrapping presents in dried seaweed. It's best not to think about it.

Luna grimaces at the stuffed rolls. "I'll have to eat quickly. Dorian will be here soon!"

Dorian is taking Luna on a date to a Christmas market in Sevenoaks. Luna's prepared an entire gift bag for him. If it weren't so deeply, deeply sickening that Luna has a boyfriend, it would be rather cute. She's tied her hair into Harley Quinn pigtails and her lips are painted dark red, apparently using "crushed forest berries" for lipstick.

She floats around the kitchen preparing smashed avocado while I eat my roll with cheese like a normal person. Mum joins us at the island counter with a roll of her own.

"Funny time of year to be having a barbecue," she comments, sniffing the air.

Trust Mum to blame her disastrous cooking on the neighbors! I'm about to say this out loud, but Luna is already huffing away at the mere mention of the word *barbecue*.

"Barbecues are barbaric, Mum," she snaps.

"Yes, I suppose so," sighs Mum. "Lauren, can I try some of your green paste?"

"*Smashed avocado*, Mum," Luna says. "And no. You just called me Lauren."

They start off on another world war, and I take a deep, calming breath. I suspect I'll need to take many deep, calming breaths over the holiday. Then I smell smoke again. There's also an accompanying sound: like crinkling tinfoil or Bubble Wrap popping. I frown over my shoulder at the hippie-dippy Christmas tree, and the whole room is shrouded in mist!

"Mum," I say, interrupting the squabbling. "Are there still rolls in the oven?!"

Mum glares at me, still red-faced from shouting at Luna that of course she's never butchered a pig herself. "What is it now, Cathleen?" she demands, then her eyes widen and she leaps to her feet. "Gosh! Why is there smoke all over the living room?!"

Luna gasps. "Is it a spirit?"

Mum scoffs. "Luna, don't be ridiculous! I've told you before, there's no such—"

Then we hear glass shattering. More crackling. It sounds like a terrible percussion band is rehearsing upstairs. We all dash into the front of the house, food forgotten, and the whole upstairs landing is clogged with smoke! My jaw drops. Beyond my bedroom door, I can see . . . FLAMES?!

"OH MY GOODNESS!" shrieks Mum, gesticulating at us like a windmill. "QUICKLY, GIRLS—OUTSIDE! RIGHT NOW, CAT, STOP GAWPING!"

We run for our lives. Well, I grab my *Bible to the Stars* first. Mum's already on the phone, babbling about firefighters, and we all tumble out onto the driveway. We stand in a row, watching the flames dance about behind the windows like crazed sock puppets.

Since the front of the house is basically one big window, I can see my bedroom door from here, and the smoke—billowing about just like Mum. This is possibly the most dramatic moment of my life! So I take out my phone and switch to Instagram Live.

Then one of the front windows shatters. Mum screams and leaps in front of us. I almost protest: Can't she tell she's blocking my view?! But then glass is raining onto the driveway, and I forget the livestream. We rush to the road. Sirens are already blaring in the distance.

"How is this happening?!" Luna wails, and I comb my hands through my hair, nervously computing the damage. My laptop is in there! My books, my clothes . . . ! My school uniform, though that's no loss. Oh, gooseberries, MY LEATHER JACKET! Has my divine feminine energy gone up in smoke?! No—wait! I think I left the jacket in the hallway.

I sigh with relief, curling a strand of hair round my finger.

Then my eyes widen. I look at my finger. I look at my hair.

At my unnaturally straight hair.

Oh no . . .

Chat Thread: Zanna Szczechowska

Zanna, 12:39 p.m.:
Hey, did u remember to turn off the straightener?

I tried to ask but u hung up lol

Cat, 1:25 p.m.:
[Cat has sent an image to the chat]

Zanna, 1:34 p.m.:
Omg

Please. Please tell me you're joking

Cat, 1:47 p.m.:
:/

Zanna, 1:49 p.m.:
Omg

Omg

Omgggg

25
Evil Cousin Lilac's Pretentious Risotto

"Well, this is just brilliant!" splutters Mum for about the seven hundredth time since we started driving. "No clothes, no toiletries . . . Oh gosh, we haven't even got the Christmas presents! I had that gorgeous necklace for Rose . . ."

She's been mongoose-manic since the firefighter showed her the hair straightener, which was blackened and half-melted, charred sections of the duvet still clinging to it like a love-starved Piscean.

"Did someone forget to switch this off?" he said, holding it up for the whole world to see.

Then Dorian showed up with his parents to find us skittering about the driveway, and Luna had to cancel their date. She hasn't looked at me since. And as if I haven't been punished enough, Mum phoned Auntie Rose, who (after much dithering and dramatics) said we had to come to London at once. My heart sank so low, there's a strong chance it's now being kicked about by Australian soccer players. The entire holiday with Lilac?! I'd rather risk the flames!

"When are we allowed back home?" Luna grumbles.

"I don't know, darling," Mum bristles.

"How am I supposed to freshen my aura?" Luna beavers on. "I left my sage in my room. I literally have nothing except for my phone!"

"For heaven's sake, Luna, neither do any of us!" Mum snaps. "At least we have somewhere to go. Thank goodness for my sister, or else we'd be sleeping in your father's office!"

I lean my head against the window and watch the countryside fade into the smoggy-gray smog of South London. It could be worse. We could be going to Birmingham. At least Kew Gardens is round the corner from my aunt's house. The whole area is gravel drives, expensive trees, and bungalow-size bay windows. Uncle Hillary is some sort of CEO and Auntie Rose is a private counselor, so they're Rich Elizabeth–level rich.

But absolutely nothing is worth having to spend time with Lilac Victoria West.

We're exactly the same age, which Mum and Auntie Rose loved: we were going to be cousins AND best friends. Then came Lilac's Fifth Birthday Party, with its theme of "Princesses at the Ball." It was Gemini Season. I wore my pink Rapunzel dress, and Lilac waltzed up in a handmade gown of white lace, then had the audacity to call my costume "grubby and distasteful." Which is quite linguistically advanced for a five-year-old.

It probably was grubby, to be honest. I'd been wearing it for weeks—Mum had resorted to bribing me with chocolate squares just to take it off and have a bath. But it was still a very rude thing to say, so I "accidentally" spilled Ribena on Lilac's white dress.

It's been war ever since.

We pull into the crescent-shaped driveway of the Wests' mansion. The door opens before Mum's even switched off the engine, and Auntie Rose collapses down the front steps, fussing and wailing as if WE had caught fire, not just our see-through house.

"Oh, Heather!" she cries, flinging her arms around Mum. "Tell me everything! What a terrible thing! Dinner is ready; come in right away! When is David arriving?"

Where Mum is slim and blond, Auntie Rose is shaped like a teapot and has dark wavy hair like Luna's. In fact, she looks like Queen Victoria . . . But I'm not allowed to say that anymore due to an "insensitive" birthday card I once made. I suppose it was a little unflattering that I drew Queen Victoria aged eighty-one.

Mum and Auntie Rose carry on wailing. I sullenly follow them up the steps into the ballroom-scale "porch," which is decked out in wood paneling and red carpet like some kind of medieval castle. Luna continues to ignore me.

"Good evening, Cathleen," I hear, and I judder to a halt, already shivering.

Lilac's feline blue eyes glint through the evening haze. She has the family blond hair, but unlike mine, hers is straightened to perfection, and she probably didn't burn her house down to achieve this. She exclusively wears white, like some sort of murderous nurse.

"It's delightful to see you," she purrs. "How's life in—oh,

where is it? Lambley *Common*? Ghastly shame about your house, although at least you finally have an excuse to upgrade your wardrobe . . ."

URGH! I clench my jaw. Lilac's Downton Abbey drawl already has me wanting to stick my head into a blender. Although that would probably please her enormously. "Shouldn't you be laying out cutlery?" I ask sweetly. "We are *guests*."

"Cat's right, darling!" Rose calls from the kitchen. "Come help Mummy!"

I smirk at Lilac, whose smile has faltered. "Run along, *dear*," I say, and she stalks off.

Luna appears by my shoulder. "Have you guys started fighting already? For Thunberg's sake, Cat! Can't you two just get along? I'm friends with Harmony!"

"Harmony's not a literal demon," I retort. "Anyway, why are you defending Lilac?! She probably wishes we'd roasted to death in the fire! And she's a Gemini."

Luna sniffs. "Well, you share a star sign with Rosa Parks, but I don't see anyone calling you the mother of the civil rights movement."

I splutter in protest. "I'm fourteen!"

"So was Rosa Parks," says Luna. "At some point."

I'm about to get very annoyed indeed. But then I spot my straightened hair in the gold-plated mirror and remember our tragic circumstances and what Luna is missing . . . because of me. Lightly, I elbow her. "Hey, um . . . I'm sorry you missed your date with Dorian."

Luna studies me, probably calculating how much annoyance

she can justify. Then she sighs and adopts her peak-zen face. "It's okay. At least a fire will cleanse the house. I've been certain for ages that there's a ghost in my room."

I laugh but Luna glares at me pointedly, and I realize she's actually dead serious.

The evening drags on. Gooseberries, how could I not have turned off that stupid straightener?! Why did I turn it on at all?! I like my curly hair! I glower into my bowl.

We're currently imprisoned in Auntie Rose's gigantic wood-paneled dining room, and Lilac has prepared some pretentious truffle mushroom risotto that Mum is absolutely gushing over. Lilac is lapping it up, beaming around with a golden saintlike glow.

"It's all about the herbs really," she's drawling on. "My personal favorite is marjoram, although I do enjoy that exotic tang from standard oregano as well."

She says oregano like "oreg-AH-no." I'm slowly becoming homicidal.

"It's *so* important to know how to cook," Lilac simpers, then she swivels her evil little Gemin-eyes onto me. "Otherwise, you grow up to be completely helpless, like some people I know." She daintily nibbles rice off her fork like a stupid rabbit.

"Well, I think that's just wonderful!" Mum gasps. "Then again, Rose always was the cook in the family! I never got the gene, so poor Cat never stood a chance."

I choke on a broccoli stalk. Why is Mum picking on me?! Luna is sitting right at this same (enormous) table, and nobody's calling her out! Also, Harmony is wearing a top hat and a bow tie, which absolutely no one has commented on. Has the entire planet split with reality?!

"I can cook!" I protest, dropping my fork. "I can make, er, sandwiches!"

Lilac titters. "And can you achieve that without setting fire to anything?"

"Mum!" I exclaim, gawping about the table. "Didn't you hear that?!"

"Let's not joke about fires, darling," Auntie Rose chuckles. "Your cousins have had a highly stressful day! Look how Cat hasn't even brushed her hair . . ."

Lilac smirks, then turns to Mum. "Sorry, Heather," she says, as if using Mum's first name is going to hide her serial killer personality. "I forgot myself. I want you to know that if you need any makeup or toiletries, you only have to ask. I'm quite happy to share."

"Oh, Lilac, you're such a sweetheart!" says Mum as I stare in disbelief. "You'll save me from having to go shopping tomorrow without my face on!"

"Obviously, the same goes for you, Cathleen," Lilac coos. "I have so many limited-edition eyeshadows. Foundation, too, if you'd like to cover that zit on your cheek."

I'm just about ready to throw my risotto over her smug, blond head, but then the door opens and Dad and Uncle Hillary stride in, looking all manlike and hearty.

"Evening all!" Uncle Hillary chimes, running a hand through his gunmetal-gray hair. I always think Uncle Hillary looks like a Bond villain, which is not impossible, seeing as he spawned Lilac. And he's a Scorpio as well.

"You took your time!" Rose says, glancing at the pompous grandfather clock in the corner. "I almost thought you'd forgotten us and gone to the pub!"

Dad and Uncle Hillary exchange quick glances.

"Of course not, darling," Uncle Hillary says. "David and I had to board up the broken window in Lambley."

"What did the insurers say?" Mum asks.

Dad scratches his head. "Well, it's a funny thing," he says, but it's not. It won't be. "The fire alarm didn't go off. Apparently, there were no batteries inside! If the alarm had worked, we could've stopped the fire a lot sooner. Not sure where we stand on insurance now."

"Well, why were there no batteries?" Mum frowns and my stomach suddenly tumbles. Oh, gooseberries. This is bad. "They ran out and you never replaced them? David, honestly!"

"Um," I interrupt. "I took the batteries. For my flashlight."

The whole room goes silent. Except for an odd squeaking. I frown, then I notice that Harmony's produced a blue balloon, which she's tying into the shape of a dog. Really? Now?!

"Oh, Cat." Mum looks about as jolly as an Easter Island statue. Then her lip wobbles. Her eyes turn all weepy and watery and, oh my Cancer Rising, she's CRYING. "You're a liability, Cat, you really are!" Then she claps a hand to her mouth and rushes out of the room.

I sit in stunned silence. I have made my mum cry. I'm officially the worst person who has ever lived, after Lilac.

"That went well," Lilac says, and with that, my self-control evaporates. I take my fork and hurl a great steaming dollop of pretentious risotto right into Lilac's smug, blond face.

Only, I don't. I miss and catch Auntie Rose in the eye.

Gooseberries.

Auntie Rose was very forgiving about the risotto incident. She said the vision in her left eye was "always a little on the blurry side anyway" and that I didn't have to worry. But I'm sure Lilac is already plotting my demise and, to make matters worse, Harmony announced she's now singing opera, which Luna positively leapt on. Now the two of them are in Harmony's room, "practicing" together at the top of their lungs.

This is going to be an even longer Christmas than I first anticipated.

I'm lying on the vast king-size bed in the second guest bedroom, staring at the ceiling (which is about a hundred miles away, given how lofty the rooms are), when my phone rings. I'm expecting it to be Morgan, since she still hasn't replied to my messages about my house being on fire, so I'm seriously shocked-satsumas when I see Alison Bridgewater's name on my screen.

"Cat!" Alison gasps when I (slightly too quickly) answer. "Is it true that your house caught fire? I saw the pictures on Instagram and had to call to make sure you're all okay!"

I flounder a bit because Alison's *voice* . . . It's just so angelic. "Um, it's true! Not to worry though . . . These things happen! To, er, some people. Well, to me."

"Where are you staying?" Alison asks, and I grimace.

"London, with my cousins. Alison, when I tell you my cousin is evil—"

But before I can explain how truly demonic Lilac is, Alison gasps. "But, Cat, I'm in London, too! My grandma lives in Ealing! Aren't your cousins in Hampstead?"

I cough. "Well, almost . . . Kew actually, but close!"

"Oh, amazing!" Alison gasps. "Do you want to meet up tomorrow?! Honestly, Cat, I'd love to see you. I'm dying here! Every day is just my mum and grandma being nostalgic for Ghana and speaking Akan together . . . which isn't great since I only speak English!"

Alison plows on about this exhibition she wants to see, do I want to come, and I murmur along—"er, yes, um, for sure!"—but my heart is already spinning like the legs of the Road Runner. Alison. Me. London. Together. Like one of my pre-Morgan gay-dreams! But real.

WHY FALLING IN LOVE WITH A PISCES IS A TERRIBLE IDEA

- They cry all the time for no reason over absolutely everything.
- They'd probably cry just from reading the title of this list!!!
- They're so useless but get away with it because they're "creatives."
- They fall in love with anyone who smiles at them, so you'll never be special.
- They're so dreamy and beautiful . . . Wait . . . WRONG LIST!
- Apparently loads of them think feet are sexy. How freaky is that?
- They have gorgeous souls, like a tiny glowing jellyfish in a gold-infused turquoise bowl spun from the most delicate, fragile Venetian glass . . . WAIT, THAT'S NOT A BAD THING, EITHER. AAARGH.

26

Aphrodite's Sacred Goose

I'm late for meeting Alison Bridgewater, and it's entirely Lilac's fault. I was ready on time, so I went downstairs (which is about a two-hour journey in that house) and grabbed my boots. But as soon as I slid my foot in, there was a horrific crunch, and my foot went all cold and wet. I took my foot back out again only to see that my boots had been filled with snails! Worse, the snails were now crushed and smeared over my toes. Lilac appeared at the top of the stairs, cackling demonically and lacing her fingers together in that way evil geniuses do.

"Oh, Cathleen!" she said. "To think, that's your *only* pair of shoes, too."

Anyway, long story short, it took half an hour to capture my cousin and tie her hair to the banister. By the time I left in Lilac's white designer boots, Lilac shrieking at me to free her as I shut the door, I was über-late and had to jog to the Tube station—truly desperate times.

Luckily, Alison is easy to find on the steps of the Victoria and Albert Museum, because she's wearing a mustard-yellow coat, cream-colored gloves, knee-high boots, and a white beret. She looks very Gaga-gorgeous . . . and Lady Gaga is GUCCI gorgeous indeed.

"Babe!" she coos, flinging her arms round me. I almost lose my balance on the steps and get a face-full of her hair as well. Not that I'm complaining. "I've missed you so much! How are you?"

"Well . . ." I falter. Alison is gripping my hands, brown eyes brimming with dewy concern. It's difficult to think of complete words. "My house caught fire. And my mum is mad at me because I kind of left my straightener on and . . . that's what caused it."

Alison's smile doesn't fade, but it does freeze a bit. She's probably thinking I'm the dumbest doorknob she's ever met.

"Oh gosh," she says eventually. "That's . . . not good!"

"No," I agree, and we both laugh awkwardly.

I suppose I'm waiting for her to say something a little more than "that's not good," but she doesn't, so we head into the museum. Alison has a membership, so she can see exhibitions for free and bring a guest. I feel very Donatella Importanté as she flashes her card.

"I hope you'll like this exhibition," Alison says. "It's textiles, felt-weaving, that sort of thing. We can't tell Siobhan though because there may be corduroy . . ."

Alison keeps on explaining, but I get slightly distracted by a gleaming marble statue of three rather naked ladies, all snuggy-hugging each other. We're in the large gallery before the exhibition rooms, and most of the hunks of rock in sight are about as boring as Botticelli's big toe, but the three ladies make me stop in my lesbian tracks.

A little too much actually. Alison turns around and notices.

"Cat? What are you looking at?"

I flush crimson. "Me? Oh, um, nothing! Just this interesting statue. Quite, er, nicely made, right? Decent use of marble, um . . ."

Alison looks at the sign. "*The Three Graces.* They're the daughters of Jupiter."

I drag my eyes away. "Wait. They're *sisters*?!"

Alison giggles, then nudges my elbow. "Yes, Cat! Why? You almost seem disappointed. What did you think three naked women were doing, nuzzling together like that?"

I don't like where this conversation is going, and I like even less that it's going anywhere with Alison Bridgewater, so I hastily swivel on my heel and carry on toward the exhibition. Well. I might sneak a photo of *The Three Graces* first. I can always pretend they're not sisters.

"He's kind of hot," Alison says, nodding to another statue of some muscled, beardy man who appears to be murdering a cherub. "He reminds me of Winston Duke from *Black Panther.* Gosh, Winston looks gorgeous in that movie. Have you seen it?"

"Yeah, totally!" I wheeze. "He's a real, er, dreamboat."

Alison looks a little like she doesn't believe me but, luckily, before she can interrogate me further, we arrive at the exhibition, which is all rather bizarre. Everything's in this shadowy gray room and mainly consists of strange mounds of colored felt labeled with outlandish titles like *The Weight of Women's Worries* and *My Puppy's Patterned Tire Tracks.*

Alison links arms with me. "Powerful stuff, right?"

I nod profusely. "Yes. Very, um, moving. Makes you think."

"What are you thinking about?" Alison asks.

We pause before an orange-reddish mound, and I gulp back my gay-panic. Truthfully, I'm not thinking about much, because I'm WAY too aware of her hand on my arm. "Looks like a fruit bowl," I blurt. "Um, with oranges in it."

"Oh, right, yes!" Alison glances between me and the sculpture, nodding earnestly, but I think she's a little confused. Especially since the piece is titled *Flames of Sorrow—One Lone Man's Personal Hell*. Gooseberries, this is going to be a difficult day.

Alison continues to distract and panic me round the whole exhibition. While most visitors appreciate the textiles, I note that:

- In Room A, Alison touches my arm twice.
- In Room B, Alison touches my arm twice more.
- In Room C, Alison only touches my arm once, but she steps on my foot by mistake as well, so it half counts. Possibly.

There's a cool sculpture in Room C, electric white and shaped like a twist of DNA, a streak of vivid green running through the middle. Morgan would think it was awesome. I point it out to Alison, but she only tilts her dreamy head and frowns.

"It's all right, I suppose," she says. "Come on, let's go."

Oh, well. I take a picture for Morgan, then hurry after Alison.

After the exhibition, we wander round these glass cabinets full of grimy-looking bowls and broken old crockery (historical artifacts). Alison takes out a notepad and sketches some of them: very artistic and wonderful. Then, because I'm a touch bored, I begin humming with a very still face until the security guard starts frowning and scratching his ears.

"*Hmmmmmmmmmmmmm,*" I go, getting progressively louder, until the guard looks properly disturbed. I really am very hilarious and brilliant.

Alison tries to suppress her giggling but can't quite manage. The security guard glares at us, then starts marching over, so we skedaddle into the next room. "You are the worst!" Alison gasps. "You're going to get us kicked out, if you're not careful."

Our eyes meet, mid-giggle-fest, and that's when my heart plays up again, an absolute violin quartet of fluttery nervousness. I'm staring right into her soft brown eyes, and they're very, very beautiful, so I hastily look away, into the nearest glass case.

Then I see *Figurine of Aphrodite* and that catches my attention at once. She's tiny, only mug-size, and faded orange, like she's made from terra-cotta. She's sitting on a large bird, with scarves wrapped around her head, and topless as all ancient Greeks must have been.

I say to Alison, "Look! It's Aphrodite, the Goddess of Love."

Alison leans down to look. "It says she's sitting on a goose! They're a symbol of hers. Isn't that the strangest thing? What have geese got to do with love?"

"Well, a lot, I would think," I tell her. "If Aphrodite uses them as footstools."

Me and Alison look at each other, then burst out laughing. In fact, we probably sound a lot like Aphrodite's Sacred Goose. Then the security guard comes stomping through, blustering about us being far too loud, and it's time to escape again, giggling as we go.

We grab hot chocolates after the museum, then Alison insists we get on a random bus, "just to drift around and see where it takes us." All very bohemian. We see the Christmas lights from the top deck and sip our hot chocolates artistically. Like real bohemianists.

We're also sitting knee to knee. Which I'm totally relaxed about, because I have an almost-girlfriend, and I don't fancy Alison anymore. Do I? I swallow a gulp of hot chocolate, but it's way too hot, and I end up dribbling it into my hand! Alison (who's luckily checking her phone at this precise moment) looks up. "You okay?"

"Yes," I cough, quickly wiping my hand on my jeans.

Alison leans her head against the window. "It's so romantic, isn't it? Watching the city pass by . . . All that life, Cat, all those people. But my grandma says that London is probably the loneliest city in the world. She says there's lots of sadness here. Isn't that so sad?"

I'm sweating nervously by now, although it might just be that the hot chocolate is burning my hand. Gooseberries galore. Are these cups made of tissue paper?!

"Um," I say, trying hard to think poetically as my hands begin smoking. "I guess not everyone has found their goose yet, have they?"

Alison giggles. Honestly, it's amazing how she isn't in love with me, given how much I make her smile. "You're so right. I know I can't wait to find mine." Then she raises her hot chocolate and taps it against mine. I continue to sweat horrendously. "To finding our sacred geese."

"In Aphrodite we trust," I agree, and tap my cup right back.

Aphrodite is playing games, dropping me in situations like this! Alison keeps sharing beautiful, poetic thoughts all round London, totally buttering me in Pisces-Aquarius dream-creams, and I try to keep quiet and remember that I have Morgan, even if she isn't right here, right now, like Alison.

But gooseberries indeed, it's very confusing.

I kissed Morgan, and I loved it so much. But now I am here with Alison Bridgewater, the same Alison Bridgewater I've dreamed about for two entire years, and everything feels scarily red-rose romantic. I'm in an Alison snow globe, and someone won't stop shaking me.

Chat Thread: Morgan Delaney

Morgan, 10:21 p.m.:
Heyaaa . . . So am I seeing this correctly? You set fire to your house?
Sorry I didn't reply for ages. I'm on a farm and there's literally NO signal

Cat, 10:57 p.m.:
Do not worry at all my green-haired goose!!!!
Yes. House. I MIGHT have caused a bit of drama

Morgan, 11:11 p.m.:
Oh my gawwwd
Well do you wanna call soon? We can catch up
I miss you lots btw. What you been up to? X

Cat, 11:28 p.m.:
Alison's in London, I've been hanging with her!!!
Yes let's call!!!! I miss you tooooo xxx

Morgan, 11:29 p.m.:
Why am I a goose btw?? What does that mean???

Cat, 11:39 p.m.:
OH SORRY LOL
Just a JOKE from my ACTIVITIES of the day
I'll explain when we call!!!!

Morgan, 11:40 p.m.:
Cool . . . Can't wait xx
Gtg, parent, urgh. Speak soon xx

Cat, 11:45 p.m.:
Yes!!! Soon :) xx

218

Capricorn

SEASON

27

A Very Dangerous Christmas Snow Globe

On Christmas Eve, Auntie Rose and Uncle Hillary are hosting a posh-poodle party, and Lilac is inviting all her tragic friends. We spend all day hanging sad decorations around the house, Luna prancing about with genuine holly in her hair, and Harmony dressing as a mime for no particular reason. I just want to call Morgan, since we are supposed to be a Thing, but every time I try to escape, Auntie Rose sheepdogs me back onto decoration duty.

"Such a shame you don't have *anything* to wear tonight," Lilac drawls, slithering over. Risky, since I'm currently up a stepladder, trying to throw tinsel over the chandelier in the hallway. Lilac places her foot dangerously on the bottom rung. "Everyone's going to be here in their finest, and you'll have no choice but to wear those desperate jeans as usual."

Auntie Rose bustles through from the kitchen, and Lilac quickly retracts her foot. "I know, Lilac!" Auntie Rose chimes.

"Why don't you give Cat some of *your* clothes? You have so much you never wear, and your cousin has lost everything!"

That wipes the smirk right off Lilac's evil face.

"Mum!" she whines. "That's not true!"

But I pounce, beaming like a bauble. "That's so generous of you, Lilac! Thanks!"

Lilac darts her ghoulish eyes between me and Auntie Rose. She can't say anything too evil and she knows it. It's a sweet, sweet moment of victory.

"Whatever," she hisses. "I'm sure I'll have something you can squeeze into. I have a whole garbage bag of clothes I'm donating, so you can check there. They're all for charity anyway."

Auntie Rose chuckles heartily. Honestly, a mother's love really must be unconditional. If I gave birth to Lilac, I think I'd have my womb bleached.

"Oh, Cat?" Auntie Rose says, just as she's heading back to the kitchen. "Why don't you invite that friend of yours? What was her name—Alison? That way, you'll have someone here you know!"

"It's very late notice," Lilac cuts in. "We probably don't have enough room."

"Oh, Lilac!" Auntie Rose sighs. "We can make room! It's Christmas!"

Then she rustles away laughing merrily to herself, and Lilac skulks off upstairs, muttering under her breath in whatever banshee snake-tongued language she secretly speaks. She's probably going to put some sort of curse on me, but I have bigger turtles to tickle. Alison Bridgewater might be here tonight! Suddenly, decorating seems a lot more important.

Lilac's poodle friends are all as ghastly as I predicted. I spend some valuable time thinking up appropriate nicknames: Botched Bryony, Floppy Fiona, and Sour-Faced Sanjivani. But the biggest plot twist of all is that Lilac has a boyfriend! The concept alone is horrifying enough to make me want to stab myself repeatedly with one of Auntie Rose's gold-plated salad forks. I christen him Has-to-Be-Hypnotized Henry, then head to the Tube station to fetch Alison. She didn't take much persuading to come. Apparently, her grandma wanted to take her to church tonight, which is very sad scenes indeed for Christmas Eve.

"Wow," breathes Alison as we walk back. "This is such a beautiful area!"

I hum in half agreement. "Shame my cousin lives here though."

Alison giggles. "Oh, babe. She can't be that bad! Not if she's related to you."

We reach the crescent-shaped drive, and Alison gazes around looking starstruck. I suppose it is quite big and impressive. The lights around the doorway bathe the drive in a golden glow and catch Alison's cheeks. For a moment, I'm distracted by an aching, deeply poetic longing, very floundering and goosed up indeed. Then Lilac answers the door, and the flowers in my heart instantly wither.

"Good evening," she drawls, deliberately blocking our entry. She icily regards Alison. "Merry Christmas and all that. I see you've brought your baggage with you."

I step forward, already preparing my fists. "Sorry, what?!"

"Calm down, Kit-Kat," purrs Lilac. "I only meant your friend has a handbag. Make sure you put it upstairs out of the way."

222

Alison silently nods and my cousin prowls off. "Ask Cat if you need anything," she calls over her shoulder. "I'll be busy."

Alison blinks. "Well, that wasn't uncomfortable at all."

"Told you," I reply, and Alison giggles.

Inside, the party is already in full swing-a-ling-ding. Uncle Hillary and Auntie Rose's friends are all drinking expensive red wine and posh-laughing, like *haw-haw-haw*. The Christmas tree dominates the living room: huge and pompous, imported from Norway for no particular reason (Luna almost died over the carbon footprint) and covered in lavish decorations, all handpicked from various National Trust properties around the country.

Alison slides her coat off and I gulp. She's in a shoulderless red dress, and I can see her collarbones, which suddenly seems like the faintiest thing in the world. Since when have collarbones been so beautiful?! I hang her coat with mine in the closet. I took ages choosing what to wear from Lilac's garbage bags, but eventually found a fitted white dress from French Connection. Lilac looked particularly scathing when I walked down the stairs wearing it.

"You look lovely!" said Dad, beaming proudly.

"I'm surprised it fits you," Lilac muttered. "You have way bigger hips than me."

"Yes," I agreed. "And a bigger personality, too!"

Dad actually laughed, so Lilac's now ignoring him.

I shuffle to Alison, who's gazing around like she's at the Golden Gates of Heaven.

"You see that weird guy by the salads?" I whisper. "That's Lilac's boyfriend. I've decided to call him Has-to-Be-Hypnotized Henry."

That gets Alison very giggly. More so once we've stolen some of Uncle Hillary's red wine. We then go about discovering the names of all the guests and dreaming up their nicknames.

"Laughs-Too-Loud Lavender," I suggest.

"Oh!" squeals Alison. "How about Hairy-Nosed Hugo?!" She claps her hand to her mouth like she's just said the rudest thing in the world. I thought that was fairly tame, personally. "Look what you've turned me into, Cat! You're such a bad influence."

I grin. "Well, you'd literally be in church if it wasn't for me, so . . ."

We posh-laugh a lot about that, which only makes us laugh more. Then we invent some prayers. "Holy Father in Heaven," I say, and Alison raises her wineglass in approval. "Lady Gaga be your name. King Kong's tum is full of rum, and Buddha thinks you're lame!"

Just as we're about to collapse from the weight of my masterful clownery, Harmony taps the side of a glass with a spoon and announces that she and Luna are going to perform an operatic number for the guests. Mum instantly pours herself a fresh glass of wine.

"Are we sure about this?" I hear Dad mutter.

"Just keep smiling, David," says Mum, grinding her teeth.

Harmony is still dressed as a mime, but then the curtains from the dining room are flourished aside, and there's Luna in a white tuxedo. I almost spit my drink. Her hair is in a topknot, and she looks like an onion. It's hysterical!

We watch solemnly as Luna takes a seat at the grand piano. Harmony spreads her arms and takes a deep breath. I think everyone else in the room takes a deep breath, too. Absolutely terrifying moment. Then Harmony sings. And to my utter shock and amazement (and I think to everyone else's as well), she's actually good. It's an absolute Christmas miracle.

·★·✦·★·

Bored of Lilac's harpy friends flicking their forked tongues at us, Alison and me go upstairs to my room. I turn on my softest lamp, because I know all too well that Alison Bridgewater doesn't like overhead lights, and we collapse onto my bed.

"This has been fun," Alison murmurs. "I'm so glad you invited me."

Perhaps we've snuck a glass of wine too many, but everyone and everything suddenly seems perfectly far away. The planet is entirely empty apart from Alison and me, lying side by side on the queen-size bed, just like in one of my dreams.

But this isn't one of my dreams. Aphrodite is testing me tonight.

I study Alison closely. Her hair is cloudy. Her eyelashes are long and dark. I want to tell her she's gorgeous, but I know I shouldn't.

"I'm glad you're here," I say, spaced out as a haiku.

Alison smiles, then rolls onto her side. We're facing each other, so close that our noses could touch, if I inched forward just a little.

"Cat," she whispers sleepily. "What dreams do you have for the new year?"

I gulp. "Um . . ." Gooseberriesgooseberriesgooseberriesgalore. My chest is swelling up like a goose. All I can see is Alison's face, Alison's eyes, Alison's hair. "I'm not sure. What about you?"

Alison smiles right into my soul, and every flower that's ever died comes back to life.

"I want to find love," she says, petal-softly. "Not just a boy-friend, like Siobhan's natural cleanse . . . I want real love. The kind that makes you question everything, or inspires you to be your best, most perfect self. I want someone to love me so much, they feel dizzy, and I want to feel the same back. Do you think that's crazy?"

I gulp. "I think that's beautiful."

This close, I can see Alison's eyes are not completely brown. There are little flecks of gold in them. Maybe it's just the lamp-light, but either way, she's heavenly; she's divine. Gooseberries. I love her so much. I just do, and I can't even help it. I lick my lips. I can taste wine, beads of fruity saliva. I can smell her scent: cherries and strawberries.

"Alison," I murmur. "Can I tell you something?"

My heart should be in my throat right now, but it's not. I'm suddenly not scared anymore, not even a little. I'm entirely in Alison's snow globe, and it's safe and warm and twilight dreamy.

"What is it?" she asks.

I glance from her lips to her eyes.

I take a breath. "Alison, I'm actually in love—"

An explosion rips through the moment like machine-gun fire. WHAT?! We roll right off the bed and jump to our feet, then goggle at each other in alarm, suddenly wide awake and very confused indeed. Sappho strike me down. What did I just almost do?!

There's another bang and we rush to the window. Fireworks! Outside, the sky glistens gold and red and pink. Since this place is more palace than house, there's a small balcony outside, and I open the window and take Alison's hand, leading her out among the flowerpots.

226

Of course, as soon as we're outside, the fireworks stop. The sky stays black. We gaze into it. Then I notice something—or rather, lots of somethings: small and silver and glittery.

"Look!" I point, and Alison follows my finger.

"Stars," she whispers, shivering a little from the cold.

"Freaking stars," I repeat. "Aren't they so beautiful?"

"The most beautiful thing in the world," she replies, and I gaze at her. *No,* I want to say. *That's you.* But then Alison slides her phone out and swipes to the camera. "Take a picture with me? Kiss my cheek or something cute."

I stare at her cheek as she holds up the camera. I've never kissed Alison before. Not on the cheek, not anywhere. But slowly, carefully, I touch my lips to her skin and breathe her in. I hear the snap of the camera, but the sound is distant, somewhere in the background.

"Perfect," she says.

"Yes," I reply.

But I think she's just talking about the photo, and I'm talking about this whole entire moment and us, under these stars, in this vast, vast universe, together.

Alison giggles, swiping through the photos. "I love you so much, Cat."

I smile sleepily, chin still resting on her shoulder. "I love you, too."

But I mean it a little bit more than she does. I think I may be the biggest goose on Aphrodite's entire goose farm. And just to be crystal clear: that's a massively big goose.

Group Chat: The Gang

[Habiba sent a post by @alisonbw.xox to the chat]

Habiba, 10:45 a.m.:
You guys are SOOO CUTE! #GOALS!!!

Lizzie, 10:55 a.m.:
Omg … Cuteness … !!! Cat ur lips look so perf xx

Zanna, 10:59 a.m.:
Aww. You guys could TOTALLY be a couple.

Cat, 11:00 a.m.:
HAHAHA ZANNA VERY FUNNY

Lizzie, 11:01 a.m.:
She's not wrong tho … Aww be my gay besties?? xx

Alison, 11:01 a.m.:
LOL! Guysssss, you are too sweet!!!

Love u Cat!! Still have ur lipstick on my cheek ;) xo

Zanna, 11:02 a.m.:
Good grief

Cat, 11:02 a.m.:
HAHA SHE'S JOKING ZANNA LMAOO ILY2 ALISON

Alison, 11:02 a.m.:
I'm actually serious, what brand did u use??

28

The Albatross in the Room

On Christmas morning, I manage to sneak downstairs, shovel some coal from the living room fireplace into Lilac's stocking, then take all the labels off her gifts under the tree so that she'll have no clue which ones to open. A truly masterful master plan!

Tragically, Lilac still figures out which gifts are hers. Worse still, she gives me a card in an envelope full of loose glitter, so I open it up and instantly get showered with tiny gold flakes, which get absolutely everywhere. I have to change my entire outfit!

So as things stand, Lilac and I are even, and the war is far from won.

Uncle Hillary gets Lilac a MacBook with an accompanying case. The joke is apparently that the case is *lilac* in color, but I think it looks more lavender personally, and I state this loudly.

"Luckily, you're not the designer!" Mum says briskly.

Well, she's no fun. But then she is a banker. Also, I think she's still annoyed that I burned the house down, because she gives me socks. I'm almost sent into a coma! What is this sad, sad world coming to? I wouldn't even buy Satan socks for Christmas.

Or his daughter, Lilac.

Of course, the albatross in the room is that I haven't spoken to Morgan in almost an entire week! She says she's going to call me in the afternoon on Christmas Day, which is very Christmassy, Missmassy (because I miss Morgan muchly), and romantic.

But Morgan truly is in the epicenter of emptiness (rural Ireland). She can't get any signal, so we have to postpone. Then when I'm waiting for her call on Boxing Day, sloth-lounging in the hammock in my cousin's house-size conservatory, Luna suddenly bellows from upstairs, making good use of her operatically fine-tuned lungs.

"CAT, COME UPSTAIRS QUICK! I FOUND A PHOTO OF LILAC DRESSED AS A PIECE OF BROCCOLI!"

Now, this I have to see! Abandoning my phone, I race toward the stairs. I hear Lilac gasping from the living room, and she appears at the bottom of the stairs behind me. "DON'T YOU DARE!" she shrieks like a banshee with lemon in its eyes.

But I skedaddle upstairs anyway, Lilac hot on my huckleberry fins, then ninja-dive round the corner into Harmony's bedroom, slamming the door shut behind me. Lilac hammers on it like a siege tower, but I slide the bolt across. Harmony has all the family photo albums open on the floor, and Luna's holding up the offending photo with a massive victory grin. I take one look and almost have an asthma attack.

"OPEN THIS DOOR!" Lilac demands.

"Wow, Lilac," I call back as Lilac hammers uselessly. "I love

230

your costume! In fact, you might say I'm *green* with envy . . ."

Then Luna, Harmony, and I fall about laughing like hilariously funny people.

But although humiliating Lilac is always a win-alicious win, by the time I retrieve my phone from the hammock, I've lost my chance to speak to Morgan, which is tragic as a Taurus. She's texted, saying we'll have to reschedule because there's still no signal at the farm.

I also have a text from Alison (swoon). She wants to know if I can show her Kew Gardens before she goes home at the end of this week. Of course, I tell her I can.

I feel prickly though. Almost guilty. In fact, I do feel guilty, because Morgan is trapped on some sad Irish farm and I'm here, parading around London with Alison! But I haven't done anything wrong . . . have I? Although missing Morgan's call isn't ideal.

That's when I remember the horoscope. Because what if this is the romance around the corner?! Alison Bridgewater, the ULTIMATE test. It's actually very Squeaky McSneaky. It is dreamy, living my Astral Alison Aspirations for a week. But it's still not real, like Planet Morgan . . . I still have to fly my starship home. I eat a lot of mince pies after that, mainly because if I'm eating, I can't get too distracted thinking about Alison Bridgewater.

But if my Aquarius Life has taught me anything (and it mostly has not, Zanna tells me), it's that it's actually monumentally tricky not to get distracted by Alison Bridgewater.

· ★ · ✦ · ★ ·

I am once more sitting before a mirror, putting on my clown paint for Alison. Well, obviously I do my makeup for me first . . .

231

But then, do I? Or is that just an Insta-feminist lie I tell myself so as not to headbutt a wall with despair?

I'm totally making myself look pretty because I'm meeting Alison in an hour.

Gooseberries galore. Do I really know what I'm doing, or am I like an Aries trying to be vulnerable (lost)? The last time I saw Alison, I almost confessed true love. That would have thrown a real chain saw into all the works and quirks. That firework truly must have been Aphrodite trying to save my backside. But will she save me twice?

I pause my clown-painting. Then I pace: out of my room and across the oak-floored corridor and into the playroom, which contained a whole indoor castle once upon a time. I remember the castle because Lilac pushed me off one of the turrets. But Lilac uses the room as a study now, or possibly a torture chamber. I slump into the desk chair and purposefully shuffle the papers on the tabletop in case Lilac is using them.

Then my phone rings and—OMG (oh my groceries)—it's Morgan! Has the twenty-first century finally reached rural Ireland?! I answer quickly, hands fuzzy with anticipation. "Morgan?"

"Cat." She doesn't bother saying hello. There's a lot of windy blustering, too, like she's on a hill somewhere. "Um, how are you?"

"I'm good!" I'm actually quite nervy-nervous though. "Um, how are you?"

Another pause, like she's hesitating. I pull the phone closer to my ear. "Yeah, you look like you've been having a great time," she says. "From Alison's Instagram anyway."

"Ah . . . you saw that?"

"Our Wi-Fi's bad, hon, not nonexistent." She doesn't sound amused.

I nervously spin the desk chair. "Yes . . . Morgan, I'm sorry I missed your call. There was this broccoli costume, you see, and, um, I lost track of things . . ."

More blustery wind. Morgan says, "Well, I was late. I had to walk through three fields to get any signal, and then there was this mad cow in one of them—"

"Mrs. Warren is in Ireland, too?!" I say, which I think is rather hilarious, but Morgan doesn't laugh. Then it occurs to me that when someone's trudged through three fields and survived a mad cow just to call you, making a joke is possibly insensitive. I open my mouth again. "Um, so are you okay? What happened with, um . . . the cow?"

Morgan sniffs. "I'm fine, Cat. Well, I had to get a shot actually, but . . . Listen, that's not important. I just get the feeling you're not as over Alison as you said you were."

"What?" I sit up. "Morgan, no! I'm not in love with Alison! That's crazy!"

Some crackling. "Who said in love?" asks Morgan. "I didn't say that."

I laugh quickly. This has suddenly gotten über-intense.

"Morgan, you don't understand," I explain, trying to remain chili-bean chill. "I've just got Alison in my head because I'm meeting her this afternoon." Then my eyes widen. "Wait, that sounds . . . I didn't mean . . . !"

But Morgan just sighs. "You're kissing her on the cheek in her post from—when was it? Christmas Eve? And from the looks of it, that's not the only time you've spent together. If you're not in love with her, you're doing a pretty great job acting like you are."

"Friends kiss all the time!" I protest. "And we're, like, best friends! What do you want me to do?! Stand six feet from her at all times?! That's not reasonable, Morgan!"

But Morgan cuts me off. "You're talking nonsense, Cat."

I open my mouth, but . . . No, nothing. We're silent salamanders. All I can hear is Morgan's steady breathing on the end of the phone. Hearing her voice again reminds me of everything: the kisses, the freckles, the inability to exist normally in her presence.

But I think it might be too late for that. Morgan sounds angry.

"Look, I'm not saying you cheated," she says briskly. "I guess we're not even, like, really together. But I'm not just some rebound from your straight-girl crush, okay? I may not be the Amazing Alison Bridgewater, but I think I'm worth more than some third-wheel kissing buddy."

"Morgan, listen." I grip the phone in both hands. "You don't understand—"

"No, I do understand!" she snaps. "I've been there and it sucks. But you're living in a daydream. You and Alison are never going to happen."

I wipe away a tear. "I never said I thought anything was going to happen!"

"But you still want it to," Morgan retorts. "And I like you, Cat. Like, really. And I thought you felt the same, because I'm not just one of your daydream drawings, I'm a real person. And I know you like her, but I thought I had the edge by actually being there for you? But I guess no one's worth more than your fairy-tale romance with Alison Bridgewater. So, I'll see you round school, but I think we should call it a day on . . . whatever this is. I hope you can be happy; I really do."

Then she hangs up. Just like that.

The silence presses against my ear like a black hole. Did I just get dumped? It feels awful, not poetic in the slightest, just utterly, completely horrendous. I wouldn't recommend it even to Lilac. And I once told her that putting marmite in her hair would help it grow faster.

I sit and stare into tragic, empty space until Mum pops her head round the door and says she and Lilac have had "some wonderful mother-daughter time" making fennel pancakes together—do I want some? That definitely pushes me over the edge.

I cry my sad, sad tears of a clown, but I'm not even sure who I'm crying for. Alison, Morgan, or ME, abseiling once more toward my *An Aquarius Alone* book-deal future. No Libra Season happiness, no Morgan Delaney. I've goosed up everything as usual.

Chat Thread: Habiba Qadir

Habiba, 1:57 p.m.:
Babe, can I have a horoscope? I have a date today!! Remember I'm actually a Virgo, I only say I'm a Capricorn bc Siobhan wants to be the oldest . . . TYSM! xx

Cat, 2:45 p.m.:
EVERY SIGN IS GOING TO BE MISERABLE. DON'T EVEN BOTHER GOING OUTSIDE, THE WORLD IS CURSED, GOOD THING UR A VIRGO AND GOOD AT SUPPRESSING EMOTIONS, YOU'RE GOING TO NEED THAT TODAY.

Habiba, 2:49 p.m.:
Right . . . I'll text Lizzie! Thanks anyway babe!! xx
#BePositive!!!

29
Auld Lang Sinusitis

Getting dumped over breakfast is dismal, very out of keeping with the joyful jingling of Sagittarius Season. Breakups are only supposed to happen in crybaby Cancer Season! Is my entire *Star Bible* a lie?! I leaf through it for guidance, and that's when I see it's already Capricorn Season. I Capri-can't believe it! I was so distracted by Alison's snow globe that I totally forgot the Winter Solstice! No wonder everything's gone so counterclockwise.

Then again. I suppose it could possibly be my fault. Just a little bit.

I still have to go to Kew Gardens with Alison, which seems highly unfair, considering I've been concussed and traumatized all over again (emotionally speaking). When we get there, it's raining, so we go into the glass houses. Alison doesn't even seem to notice I'm seriously Gloomy Tuesdays. She's dressed up in her usual sunny colors, a fluffy pink coat and the same white beret, and prances about drawing flowers in her sketch pad.

"Gosh, Cat!" Alison sparkles. "Have you seen this orchid? Isn't it beautiful?"

I look around and get face-planted by a leaf. It's a wet leaf, too, so droplets of water go right up my nose! I step back, sneezing, and then one of the greenhouse humidifiers goes off right on top of me, spraying my hair with a damp, warm mist.

Alison chooses this exact moment to look up. She bursts out giggling. "Oh my gosh, your hair is enormous! Look." Then she takes a photograph before I can stop her and shows me. I look like Selma Bouvier from *The Simpsons*.

Alison obliviously goes about posting the photo, which gets a string of gleeful replies from Siobhan, Habiba, Lip Gloss Lizzie, and even Zanna, that Sagi-TREACHEROUS b-word (banana). We walk on, me glowering heavily, then I walk into another gigantic, soggy leaf.

Alison steps round me, eyes still on her phone. "I need to talk to you about something, by the way," she says, and my interest is temporarily caught. "It's about a guy!"

My interest once more boomerangs away. "What guy?"

Please don't say Alison has gone back to Private School Oscar! I may have to drown myself with the humidifier if she has, and I'd rather not, mainly because it would take ages. But Alison shows me her phone screen, and there's a picture of a different but equally boring dusty-blond Hemsworth type. URGH.

"His name is Casper," she rabbits on as I battle the urge to strangle myself with an endangered tropical vine. "He goes to school in Sevenoaks, but he's not studying a lot because he wants to focus on his music. Isn't that amazing?"

"Well, Jamie would think so," I mumble, kicking a fallen

238

leaf. The leaf actually turns out to be a butterfly, which flaps off looking wounded, and I get a very ghoulish glare from one of the gardeners.

"He's writing ten whole songs," Alison continues. "He wants to write about ten different musicians who died before their time. It's a really interesting concept!"

"He sounds like a riot," I say, then I walk into another wet leaf. Today really is not my day.

Once we've trudged through the rain to the cacti greenhouse, Alison assuring me that Casper is "so sensitive artistically, sort of like Shakespeare—not that Casper is Shakespeare, but he could be the next Shakespeare, couldn't he?" I slide my phone out and open Morgan's chat thread. My thumbs feel clumsy as clamshells, but I message her anyway.

Cat, 1:51 p.m.:
Please don't be mad. I miss u xx

She doesn't reply. I check every hour or so for the rest of the day, but she doesn't even open the message. Then I reread my message and realize it sounds a bit pathetic anyway.

"Well, this was cute," Alison says, once we've toured all the greenhouses. We're hovering in the gift shop, where Alison's bought this disappointing packet of seeds. It hasn't stopped drizzling, and Alison doesn't want to walk around outside because she's wearing new Taylor Swift–themed Converse. "I'd love to come back when it's not raining!"

I don't meet her eye. "Yes, we'll have to do that sometime."

"You've been weirdly quiet today," Alison points out. And

for a moment, I think she might actually be about to ask if I'm okay. Then she says, "You'll have to tell me what you think about Casper when you're feeling more chatty. Like, you agree he's cute, right?"

Seriously?! You'd think she doesn't care at all, the way she carries on.

"Yes, he's wonderful!" I agree, crossing my arms. "Should we go?"

Alison nods, and we almost start walking . . . Then she takes my arm. I turn and gaze into her brown and beautiful eyes. I'm surprisingly un-dizzy though. I'm looking at Alison Bridgewater and my feet are completely on the ground.

"Babe . . ." she says, glancing out into the rain. "Can I borrow your umbrella?"

Soaking wet, I wave goodbye to Alison at the station. Once her white beret has disappeared through the ticket barriers, I check my phone. But my screen is still Morgan-less and empty: very chamber-of-loneliness scenes. At least there's pathetic fallacy what with the drizzle! Perhaps I can write heartbreak poetry this evening . . . ?

Then a van drives right through a puddle in the gutter and sprays me with brown water. I decide that sometimes rain is not poetic after all. Sometimes rain is just wet.

Alison goes home the next day, so our days out stop. I wake up on the last day of this tragic, tragic year and find that my nose is stuffed up and my throat is sore. Because as if being heart-broken isn't enough, Aphrodite has now struck me down with the plague as well!

240

Well, it's probably not the plague. It's a cold. But it's still very uncomfortable.

Every cloud has a silver lining though. I manage to give my cold to everyone else, Lilac included! It's quite funny, watching her snot about with a box of tissues under one arm. Seeing as she's the same shade as Snow White, her sore nose stands out like a sore, er, well, nose. I make sure to sing "Rudolph the Red-Nosed Reindeer" LOTS.

On New Year's Eve, everyone is too stuffy to even sing "Auld Lang Syne," which is also a win, since Luna and Harmony were planning an operatic version. We all sloth about on the sofas, watching that boring performance they do round the London Eye every year. Luna is brewing her own herbal remedy over the fireplace. Which means lots of crushed leaves in a saucepan and smells more like it would send you to an early grave than cure you. Then I notice Lilac's fallen asleep, so I roll one of my used tissues into a ball and throw it at her.

"Ew!" Lilac shrieks, jumping awake. "Ew, Mum! Mum! Look what Cat just did!"

Auntie Rose, who's also snoozing, swats Lilac away like a mosquito. Which is what Lilac is, to be honest. "Oh, stop fussing, darling, Mummy's very sick."

"Cat," mumbles Mum, not even opening her eyes. "Stop pester . . ." Then I think she falls asleep again. Lilac glowers at me, then huddles up even tighter in her white silk kimono. As if that could EVER be cozy.

Then the door comes crashing open, and Uncle Hillary chokes on his snore, springing back to life in his rocking chair. Dad comes striding in, which is scarier than the entire plot of

The Shining, given that he's not even wearing pajamas under his robe.

"Dad!" I protest, shielding my eyes. "Are you trying to scar me for life?!"

"I have some good news, folks!" Dad says, waving his disgusting handkerchief.

"Is it that you're never going to use the word *folks* again?" I ask, closing my eyes. "Because that would be very good news indeed."

"No, Cat," says Dad. "It's not that."

"You're not renewing your marriage vows, are you?" asks Luna.

Dad frowns. "No, Luna. It's not that, either. It's about the house."

That makes me open my eyes. Even Mum returns from her slumbery grave, brushing back a strand of sweaty hair to look at Dad. The door of Auntie Rose's newspaper cabinet opens, and Harmony rolls out. I startle. What in Snufkin's name was she doing in there?!

"Just practicing my magic box escape performance," Harmony says quietly as everyone ogles her in alarm. "Sorry."

Dad clears his throat. "Well, Matt Szczechowska has been a lifesaver. He's found a great team of builders to clean up the mess, but it's going to take a month or so, since they're having to rebuild Cat's floor and the bathroom below."

As I smuggy-smile that MY Sagittarius Soul Sister's decorator dad has come in handy, Lilac widens her eyes in horror. "You're not staying here for an entire month, are you?!"

Dad chuckles. "No, we're not." Lilac visibly relaxes. "We're going to rent somewhere small in Lambley for a month or two so you girls can get back to school. The real estate agent's found us somewhere very affordable right on Queen's doorstep, so it's very convenient."

That sounds like a disastrous idea. What excuse will I have to be late on a daily basis if we're living next door?! But before I can put forward this extremely valid point, Mum starts wittering on about how nice the remodeled bathroom will be. Trust Mum to get excited about a new bathroom. Life must be very dull indeed after thirty-five.

"We're moving?!" Luna goggles at him. "But where?"

"We've found a lovely little cul-de-sac," Dad explains, then he pauses to blow his nose like a foghorn into his handkerchief. "It's called Marylebone Close."

WHAT?! My eyes shoot wide open, and I almost jump to my feet. Since I am on death's door with the plague itself, however, I don't do that. I just snuffle in horror like a very sick person, which is exactly what I am. We can't move onto Morgan's street! She'll think I'm a strawberry-picking stalker!

Mum and Dad carry on raving about bathrooms and how truly lucky we are to have found somewhere, and I stare into space, vaguely fantasizing about a black hole opening in front of me. I'm so troubled and horrified that when Lilac sneezes and bursts into an enormous nosebleed, I can't even laugh or appreciate it! And if anything's sad and tragic, it's that.

Chat Thread: Zanna Szczechowska

Cat, 5:15 p.m.:
Happy Birthday Zanna!!!!
You are the worst friend ever!

Zanna, 5:18 p.m.:
Um. YOU are the worst friend ever. My birthday was literally over a week ago.

Cat, 5:19 p.m.:
OKAY SO YOU NOTICED
BUT ZANNA
I only remember birthdays by the zodiac season and I MISSED that Capricorn Season had started!!! Your bday is literally the LAST day of Sagittarius Season, so it's actually too easy to miss ... You should have been born more considerately tbh

Zanna, 5:22 p.m.:
That could be the WORST excuse I've ever heard you use
And I'm including the time you said you got distracted by a picture of Jodie Comer before you could write me a birthday Instagram story

Cat, 5:24 p.m.:
Well she is VERY pretty
But so are youuu!! I LOVE YOU ZANNA!!!!!

Zanna, 5:25 p.m.:
Every year my dad bets ten quid on you forgetting unless I remind you and every year I lose. You're making me look really bad here ...

30
Headbutting Walls in Despair

I never thought I'd say these words, but I actually miss the iPhone Box. The house in Marylebone Close is poky and dark, with a faded green front door and dusty-looking lace curtains in the windows. The yard is a depressing square of grass.

"Lovely," Mum says when she sees it for the first time, lips pursed into a thin line. I scuff my heels awkwardly in the background. She doesn't comment on the house again.

The rooms are mostly empty. Mine has pale yellow walls, like milk left out in the sun, and comes with a bed, a desk, a wardrobe, and a wobbly chair. I put my *Bible to the Stars* on the chair, and that's my decorating *fini*. Mum drags us to Maidstone the very first day to buy new clothes because my wardrobe was mostly unsalvageable. By which I mean it was burned, not that I have terrible fashion sense, as Lilac suggested.

"I should be making you pay for all this," Mum mutters at the register.

"I'll pay you back, then!" I retort, scowling like a Scorpio. "Siobhan says her gardener is quitting, so I can just do that until I've paid for everything."

Mum goes silent for a long time while all the security tags are removed, then she puts her hand on my shoulder, which is highly unnerving. I look up in surprise and see she's giving me this weird, watery smile.

"Mistakes happen, love," she says. "The world's still turning."

Then she pulls me into a weepy hug. The lady at the register gives me a stare that's probably asking me if I'm a kidnapping victim, do I want her to call someone? I slowly shake my head, but it's a very unsettling experience. I have to detach Mum from me in the end.

"What's wrong?" I ask Mum. "I don't have to be a gardener . . ."

"Oh, gosh, it's not that!" Mum wipes her eyes. "It's just that I always feel so lucky when I'm reminded that I could have Siobhan as a daughter instead of you."

· * · ✦ · * ·

When we get home, Dad has a cardboard box for each of us on the kitchen table. He's written our names on the top in black felt-tip marker and drawn a smiley face on the side. I think he believes this looks cute, but actually I'm wondering if Dad has found new employment as a serial killer. Which would at least be a step up from a banker.

"What are these?" I ask, approaching my box suspiciously.

"A few of your things!" Dad says proudly. "Of course, the rest is still in storage . . ."

Luna starts squealing because Dad's got her amethyst necklace and her Navajo-woven carpet (sourced from an authentic Navajo weaver in Arizona, of course). I carefully remove the lid from my box. Right on top is my leather jacket. I gasp, then hug it right to me. It smells musty-mosaics, but it's not burned to a crisp!

"Happy?" he asks.

I drop the jacket and fling my arms around him. He chuckles and pats me on the back.

"Thank you," I say. Then I remember myself and shove him away. These may be desperate times, but that doesn't mean hugging your parents is acceptable.

Back in my shoebox room, I hug my jacket like it's a baby. I can't help but think that if I'd had it with me in London, maybe none of what happened would have happened. I sigh, falling back onto my bed, still clutching the jacket like it'll grow legs and run away if I let go. Unfortunately, my bed here is narrower than I'm used to, and I hit my head against the wall.

The whole house seems to vibrate, but maybe that's just my skull. I clutch my head, hissing in pain. Gooseberries galore! If concussion were an Olympic sport, I'd be a gold medalist by now.

"Are you okay?" Luna pokes her head through the door. "What was that bang?"

"I'm fine!" I mutter. "I just headbutted the wall."

"On purpose?" Luna asks, and I scowl at her, rubbing my head.

"No, of course not on purpose! What do you think I am? Some sort of idiot?"

"Well . . ." Luna begins, but I give her a *look* and she trails off. I wait for her to leave, but instead she hovers. Eventually, she steps into the room and sits on the bed next to me. "Cat," she asks slowly. "Was Morgan Delaney your girlfriend?"

I almost choke. How in the name of Brunhilda's *Büstenhalter* does Luna know about that? The shock cures my concussion on the spot. "Why would you think that?!"

Luna won't meet my eye. In fact, she looks rather sheepy. "Well, I didn't want to tell you this. But there's a chance that me and Harmony were practicing contortionism in that toy box in the playroom? And then you came in and we heard your entire conversation."

I stare at her like she's absolutely bizarre. Which she is. Then I groan and fall back on the bed. (More carefully this time: my head can't take another blow.)

"Then you already know everything," I grumble. "I don't know why you're asking."

Luna can't take a hint. She lies down, too. "Were you two, like . . . together then?"

"I don't know." I sigh. "We watched movies and kissed and talked. And we went to a really cool gig together in London. Just things like that."

Luna hesitates. "So, you mean you, um . . . dated?"

I open my eyes and blink at the off-white ceiling. Because now that she says it, I think that's exactly what me and Morgan did. Only, I was too thick to notice. FML (frittata my life).

"So, what happened?" Luna asks.

I sigh and roll toward her. "I goosed it up."

Luna frowns. "You what?"

"Goosed it up," I repeat. "You know. Like, I ruined it."

"That's not an expression," Luna says.

"Well, it is now!" I roll toward the ceiling again. "I blame Venus. It is meant to represent my romantic side. And did you know my Venus is in Aquarius as well, Luna? That's a lot of Aquarius for one person! Apparently, it means I get lost in fantasy land. But I never expected it to double-goose me like this."

Luna tuts. "Well, it's true that Aquarians are fundamentally very shallow."

I frown. "Is that what I said . . . ?"

"And that you're a catastrophically selfish group of people," she continues obliviously. "Like, are you being 'aloof' or are you just indifferent to everyone around you?"

I cough. "Well, hang on a moment, Luna . . ."

"But, Cat," says Luna. "Have you ever considered that not everything is written in the stars? Sometimes, maybe you should just follow your heart instead."

I stare, almost ready to throw another Jane Austen hardback at her. "Are you being serious?!" I splutter, propping myself up on two very frustrated elbows. "You were the one who told me to find love in the first place!"

"What?" says Luna infuriatingly. "No, I didn't!"

I gesticulate wildly. Which isn't easy when you're lying down. I probably look like a panicking sunbather. "You said if I didn't pair up by the end of Libra Season, I'd have to wait another whole year to find love! My life has been a disaster since then!"

"Your life was a disaster long before that," Luna says. "But actually, Cat, that's not what I said. I told you that other people

249

think that's what Libra Season is about. But they're misguided. Which isn't surprising, given their capitalist upbringings—"

"Can we stay on topic?!" I interrupt, and Luna scowls.

"Libra Season isn't about finding love," she explains patiently. "It's about finding balance. Which could be love, but it could be anything! For me, it was starting my quilting club with Niamh. It's given me real mental clarity."

I want to ask her if she's absolutely sure about that. Has she actually seen her paper-clip earrings in a mirror? But perhaps now isn't the time. Instead, I stare at the ceiling. Have I been living my entire life wrong?! It wouldn't be the first time. But a short-lived dream of being a Taylor Swift impersonator is hardly the same as misreading an entire universe of stars. Gooseberries galore! Am I actually a zodiac clown?!

"So, what do I do now?!" I ask despairingly.

Luna smirks. "Well, you can fix it, obviously. You *should* fix it. Like I fixed things with Dorian after we disagreed about a clause in the Gender Recognition Act Reform Bill."

I blink. "You had a fight with Dorian?" They've literally been going out for thirty seconds, so to think they've already had their first fight and made up is deeply amusing.

"He's a Leo, so he's fiery," says Luna. "But I fixed it! And so should you, if you like her. And no offense, Cat, but you seem to really like her."

"She's a Gemini, you know," I point out, and Luna raises an eyebrow.

"Life is about taking risks," she says in purest peak-zen tones. "That sometimes includes trusting Geminis. You never know. Her other signs might balance out her corruptive Gemini tendencies! It's not all about the sun. Maybe she's a Pisces Moon."

We both sigh wistfully at the prospect.

Eventually, I nudge my sister. "You know, you're actually rather wise," I tell her. Then I pause. "For a Scorpio anyway."

Luna jumps right onto my stomach, and I'm winded half to death! We roll around in the bedsheets, trying to squash each other until Mum comes barreling in because we're "shaking the entire house." Which is a very Virgo thing to worry about actually.

Luna telling me to "fix things" is all very well and good, but how?! School begins tomorrow. And although I'm no expert, I don't think I have time to find a parrot and train it to say "I'm sorry, Morgan" between now and then (which tragically is the only idea I've had so far).

Also, what about Alison?! She'll be at school as well. After that phone call with Morgan, I don't know *what* to think. What if Morgan's right and I'm hopelessly trapped in love with Alison Bridgewater forever? Perhaps I need hypnotherapy. I can wipe my mind of Alison and—boom!—I'll be cured. But how much does hypnotherapy actually cost . . . ?

I lie awake long into the night, dreaming up solutions. Well, until 11:35 p.m.

Then I hear a car gravelling about outside. Marylebone Close is a cul-de-sac, so either a truck filled with killer clowns is paying us a visit (one can but hope) or someone is arriving home from their Christmas in Ireland.

I roll out of bed and ninja my way to the window, peering

out into the street. I was right! Morgan's mum's car has just rolled up the driveway across the street. I watch as the doors open, and then there she is: Morgan Delaney, dragging her suitcase out of the trunk.

She's got a ponytail, and I think I must be rather sleep-deprived, because all at once, my heart melts. I watch the ponytail swing behind her as Morgan hops up the steps and unlocks the blue front door. Her mum follows her inside, and then the door shuts behind them.

I check the clock again: 11:37 p.m. Perhaps I should keep a journal of Morgan's movements! Then I can learn her routine. What makes Morgan tick. How I might win back her Irish Gemini heart. Then I catch sight of my wide eyes in the mirror and see that I look creepy, very restraining-order-licious indeed. Perhaps I should just go to sleep.

·*·✦·*·

Segment from "Bad Boys Cry" by Jamie Owusu

(partially inspired by "Big Girls Cry" by Sia)

Sitting here, thinking 'bout our breakup,

Which I caused through my bad behavior.

Can't believe I reinforced the patriarchy!

Bad boys cry when they hurt their ladies.

Bad boys cry when they hurt their ladies . . .

I'll make it up, I'll make it up, I'll make it up . . . (x3)

TO YOUUUUUUUUUUUUUUUUU . . . !

·*·✦·*·

31

Universally, Spiritually Unbalanced

8:55 a.m. I see a flick behind Morgan Delaney's curtain. Mind you, it might not be her curtain: I don't know which bedroom is Morgan's. Even so, it's one for the movement journal I'm not keeping. Luna pokes her head around my door, and I almost drop my binoculars.

"What are you doing?" she asks. "We need to leave, Cat. It's nearly nine o'clock."

"We can't leave now, Luna!" I protest. "I need to make sure we won't bump into Morgan on the doorstep. It would be very awkward for me."

"Everything's awkward for you," says Luna impatiently. "It's just who you are as a person. Can we please leave? Niamh is waiting for me with a large bag of crystals. Mine are still in the iPhone Box, but I need them to bring balance to my inner spiritual universe."

I wish someone would bring balance to *my* inner spiritual universe, but unfortunately I fall over twice just getting my shoes on. I ease open the front door and peer about to make sure the coast is clear. Then I tiptoe out onto the driveway.

I can't see Morgan: just lots of black garbage bins standing about like penguins. I grab Luna's wrist and hiss at her to move quickly! Then I drag her down the front steps like a mother on her way to day care. Luna snatches back her arm at the corner of the driveway.

"Will you stop yanking me?!" she snaps. "You're going to dislocate something!"

I'm just about to tell her that if she doesn't get a move on, I blooming well will dislocate something, and she won't like it one bit, when Morgan Delaney's blue front door opens and there she is, eyes on her phone, but just a few yards away. I could scream out loud!

"AAAARGH," I go, which I realize *is* screaming out loud, and Morgan's already looking round, so I do the only thing I can: jump behind the nearest garbage bin.

Luna gapes at me. "Cat, will you get up?! What are you doing?!"

I gesture at her. "Just . . . push the bin or something!"

I flap at Luna and she flaps at me, and then she grabs the bin and pushes it. The wheels squeak away, which hopefully will account for the scream (very ingenious of me indeed), and I shuffle along the pavement, practically Russian-dancing my way toward the main road.

"Cat," Luna hisses, trying hard not to move her lips. "She's looking at us. I can't wheel this garbage bin all the way to school! Just get up!"

"Just keep pushing!" I hiss back, and Luna speeds up. I'm unable to Russian-dance that quickly; in fact, I think I may be about to fall over, so I grab the bin to support myself. Of course, this knocks Luna's steering completely off course!

"Cat, watch out, there's another garbage bin!" she exclaims, just as the two bins collide, and then they fall over and spill garbage all over the road. It makes an almighty clatter-meringue of a noise. And worse, I'm left exposed, squatting in the middle of the pavement like a duck.

What now?! I dare to open one eye and see that Morgan is standing in the middle of the road, looking right at me, arms folded. Well, gooseberries indeed.

"G-good morning," I stutter, and she rolls her eyes. She doesn't look pleased to see me. "Um, wild weather we're having, right?" Don't say it. "It's really, um . . ." Do NOT say it. "It's really, you know. Binning it down." Said it. Simply could not resist.

Luna looks positively shell-shocked. Morgan tilts her head at me. "You really can't be serious even for a second, can you? What are you doing here? I need to get to school."

"Funny coincidence!" I babble, hopping to my feet. "I actually live, um, over there." I point at the green front door. "Just for a bit. Until the fire damage is fixed. If you remember the fire, which, you know, I sort of, um . . . caused."

Morgan stares at me. "You've got to be joking."

Well, that's hardly the most encouraging response. I shake my head and Morgan looks between me, Luna, and the house a few more times, before muttering something sweary under her breath and marching off in the direction of Queen's.

"I think that might have been the most awkward moment of my life," says Luna.

I glare at her. "YOUR life?! Are you serious?!"

We bicker like vicars all the way to school.

I'm very stressed when I arrive for homeroom, so I sit down next to Zanna to do some important relaxation. Which means sketching Rapunzel holding hands with Pocahontas. Then Zanna says, "Good grief. What in the name of Michelle Obama is she doing with that?"

I frown at my drawing. "That's a paddle, Zanna, because they're in a boat. Why is your mind always in the gutter?! Honestly, just because you watched *Shakespeare in Love*—"

"No," says Zanna. "Cat, look."

And I do. I look very annoyed. I also look up though and see Siobhan has just entered the classroom, which is always a red-carpet occasion on the first day back. But today she's holding the most enormous, most glittering golden balloon I've ever seen. Like she's got a small planet on a dog's lead. It's shaped like a unicorn.

"Clip-clop me down," I murmur. "What *is* that?!"

"It's atrocious," Zanna says. "That's what."

Everyone is staring like ducklings at Siobhan's balloon. But then Siobhan glides across the room toward *Millie*, the one person who hasn't frozen to gawk. She's too busy hiding in the corner, eyes as buried as pirate's gold in a magazine interview with Zooey Deschanel. It's like the whole class is holding its breath. Which is a lot of breath to hold actually.

"Um, Millie?" says Siobhan.

Millie freezes. Her knuckles whiten on her book. "Yes?" she mumbles, without looking up.

"This is for you," Siobhan says, and Millie finally glances up.

To say she looks horrified is an understatement. I think she'd rather watch seven sweater-knitting grandmas get cement-mixed to death than be here right now. Siobhan places the balloon, which is weighed down with a plastic horseshoe on the string, on Millie's desk. The balloon eclipses the sun, casting Millie into darkness. It's actually bigger than Millie herself! Which isn't difficult, but still.

"Um," says Millie, ogling the balloon. "What do you mean?"

"What am I speaking?! Esperanto?!" Siobhan snaps, then she bites her lip, visibly gathering herself. "I *mean*, I bought this for you, okay? To say sorry for breaking your phone. And calling your bangs tragic. And other things I may have said that hurt your feelings."

Millie stares at Siobhan in shock. "To say *what*?"

Siobhan bristles like a porcupine with chopsticks. "Sorry," she repeats. "I'm sorry, okay?! And I bought you this balloon as a token of my sorry-hood. Or whatever."

I meet Alison's eye. She only shrugs in disbelief. Over my shoulder, I can hear Zanna suppressing a laugh. Habiba raises her phone to take a picture.

"You didn't have to do that," says Millie slowly. "Like, *really*, you didn't."

"Well, I wanted to," says Siobhan, tossing back her hair. "I've been feeling, um, guilty. Which is actually very uncomfortable, Millie! I had to write about it in a diary, like some sort of Brontë freak show. I'm sorry I've been a bit barbaric with you and not included you in things. I suppose what I mean is . . . if you'd like to sit with us at lunch, you can."

Zanna can barely contain herself. I actually have to stomp on her foot to shut her up but end up stomping on my own foot instead! As I'm rubbing my throbbing toe, Millie clears her throat.

"Um, thank you, Siobhan," she says slowly. "I'll pass on lunch, if that's okay, but I appreciate your apology and, um . . . balloon."

"Right," says Siobhan. "Well, good." Then she marches over to her and Alison's desk and sits down without another word. The whole class is completely silent, gazing at the balloon in awe, like it's a gift from King Cuauhtémoc the Aztec himself. Then the bell rings and in strides Mrs. Warren.

"Good morning, ninth graders," she says, then she stops, a frown wrinkling her brow. Which might just be her normal face, actually. Slowly, she turns to Millie. "Millie Butcher," she says. "May I ask what you are doing with this golden monstrosity?"

"Um . . ." Millie goes all red and panicky. "Well, actually . . ."

"It's from me, Miss," says Siobhan, standing proudly. Zanna lets out a cough. She's enjoying this far too much. "It's an apology for my behavior over the past few weeks."

Mrs. Warren's frown deepens. "Just for the past few weeks! Well, well. How very fortunate Millie must feel. Sit down, Miss Collingdale. And tuck in your shirt, please."

For once, Siobhan doesn't argue. Truly, truly shocking scenes.

· ★ . ✦ · ★ ·

"I can't believe she didn't want to sit with us at lunch!" Siobhan gasps when we are standing about outside after homeroom.

"After everything Mr. Drew said about Millie not feeling welcome in our homeroom . . . I'm trying my best, aren't I? Look at the size of that balloon! Everyone's going to notice her now. What more could she want?!"

"It was very generous," Kenna assures her, but Zanna clears her throat.

"Siobhan," she says, adjusting her glasses. "Don't take this the wrong way. But maybe Millie doesn't actually like you? In her story, you're probably the main villain. Although actually, in my story, you're not exactly a hero, either—"

Siobhan gasps, whirling round to Zanna like she'll have her scalp as a tea cozy, so I hastily step between them. "Um, all Zanna means, Siobhan, is that maybe Millie doesn't like *attention*. Maybe she'd rather you just . . . you know . . . left her alone?"

Siobhan frowns after Millie, who's stumbling to math with her enormous balloon bobbing behind her like a UFO. Frankly, I'm worried she might take off and float away! She might prefer that because she looks deeply embarrassed. She even tries concealing the balloon under her blazer. But she's wasting her time: that balloon is probably visible from Mars.

"I suppose you could be right," Siobhan says eventually.

Zanna smirks at me, and I give her two very supportive thumbs-up. Then Loudmouth Jasmine McGregor shows up, hooting away about Siobhan scoring an own goal in netball last semester, and the two of them start Frisbee-hurling textbooks at each other.

Zanna and I manage to escape to French before getting blitzed to Timbuktu.

Email To: All Students & Staff

Good afternoon,

It has come to my attention that a balloon is present on school grounds. Due to extraordinary reports that an escaped horse is "rampaging through the school, sparing no one," I have made the deans aware and will update them as the situation develops. If anyone is struggling to cope with the excitement and/or hysteria, counseling is available via the Student Health and Wellness Team. Please remain calm.

Regards,
Dr. Woodhouse, MBE, PhD
Headmistress, Queen's School Kent

32

Over and Under, O What a Blunder!

Nobody can stop talking about Millie's balloon. Especially not once it almost blows away with Millie still tied to it at lunch! Luckily, Rich Elizabeth's octopus arms finally came in handy, and Millie "only briefly left the grass," according to witnesses. But then everyone stood up and sang "Happy Birthday" to her in the school cafeteria!

Come assembly time, the Balloon Situation is really getting ridiculous. Millie lets go of the string by mistake, and the school janitor, Dusty Dave, has to retrieve it with a ladder, because it floats in front of the projector and the whole room goes glittery gold.

"I don't know what everyone's getting so bench-pressed about," Siobhan rants when we're walking to the school gates at the end of our helium-heavy day. "No one was listening to Mr. Drew's speech anyway! 'Red Buses of Opportunity'?! What does that even mean?! It was *so* disrespectful toward Cat as well, given her bus-related trauma."

My eyes widen. "Oh, um . . . I didn't really notice!"

"See?!" says Siobhan to Alison. "She's still completely in denial about what happened! Who knows how that could manifest itself later on?! She could become a cosplayer."

"Oh, Siobhan, leave her alone!" Alison laughs, linking arms with me. "Don't worry, babe," she whispers. "Just remember that . . ."

She trails off and I lean closer. "Alison? Remember what?"

"Look!" she gasps. "It's Casper!" Then Alison rushes to the gates, where a red car is parked. It's blocking the entire road. Bus drivers are blaring their horns manically, but the guy leaning on the hood appears oblivious beneath his big sunglasses. Alison hurtles toward him, arms outstretched, and grabs him into a hug, squealing like a dolphin.

"What the Freaky Friday?!" exclaims Siobhan. "Does Alison know him?!"

"Look at that car!" gasps Kenna. "He has a convertible, Siobhan!"

Siobhan splutters with irritation. "Christ on an ACTUAL bike, Kenna, how many times?! A sunroof doesn't count as a convertible!"

Kenna takes out her phone to double-check this, and Alison comes bounding over, *Casper* practically glued to her, giggly and ridiculous as a cloud of soap bubbles.

Beside me, Zanna mutters, "Oh, boy."

"Guys, this is Casper!" Alison drenches us in smiles. "Do you remember, Cat? I told you all about him in London!" Then she gasps, looking between us. "Gosh, *Cat* and *Cass*. I'll have to make sure not to get you confused!"

I go, "HAHAHA," thinking that's hardly likely, unless I look more like Thor, God of Thunder, than I thought. Meanwhile, Casper is greeting Siobhan, Kenna, and Zanna, all manly and Thor-like with his dusty-blond hair and pretentiously brimmed hat.

He turns to me. "Hey there, blondie," Casper says. "Call me Cass."

He flashes me a dazzling grin, then hangs one arm loosely over Alison's shoulder. Gosh, I hate him. He's so *hot*. And yes, obviously I can tell that. I'm gay, not oblivious.

Siobhan is looking very put-out pouty. She eyes up Call Me Cass's car, licking her lips like a lioness with lash extensions. "Is that *your* car?" she demands. "Can you, like, drive?"

Call Me Cass nods. "Got my license for my seventeenth last month . . . Only two tickets so far. *Both* for speeding," he adds, and everybody (aside from me and Zanna) goes all giddy. He speaks like Thor as well, all rumbly. "Thought I'd give this special lady a spin." He jiggles Alison's shoulder, making her giggle and smile so much that I'm genuinely concerned she may explode into bubble-gum-colored goo. "We can listen to my album on the drive."

"Your *album*?!" Kenna practically chokes, then she signs something secretively at Siobhan.

"She says that's amazing, maybe you're rich," Siobhan says out loud as Kenna rapidly tries to shush her. "I suppose she's not *entirely* wrong . . ."

"His album is on iTunes!" Alison gushes. "Right, babe?"

"*Shallow Grave*," Call Me Cass says. "About musical talents taken from this world before their time. Look me up." Then, with a wink that makes me want to hurl myself into a furnace, he leads a practically comatose Alison to his car. "Catch you girls later, yeah?"

They drive off at high speed, finally unblocking the road, and Siobhan gawps after them. Then she turns to me, her face splattered with fury. "You knew about him?! Why didn't you text me?!"

I blink at her. "You were grounded! You didn't have your phone!"

"As if that's important!" Siobhan rages, and I think she might be about to pop a blood vessel, but luckily Lip Gloss Lizzie and her glossy girlfriends show up and Siobhan pounces. "Lizzie! Elizabeth! Eliza! You won't BELIEVE who Alison is necking!"

As Siobhan and Lip Gloss Lizzie give themselves brain aneurysms, I stand very still and silent, gazing down the road after Alison. Zanna appears by my side. Like some sort of Slavic genie. "Well, he was very weird," she says.

I slowly nod. "Zanna . . . can I tell you something?"

"Do you have to?" asks Zanna.

"I think I'm over Alison Bridgewater. I've just realized that I don't like her like that anymore. She's a bit shallow and self-absorbed sometimes actually."

"Too close to home, huh?" Zanna nods.

"And I've been really stupid," I talk over her, because honestly—can't she let me have my moment for once? "I messed up everything with Morgan, and for what?"

I wait for Zanna to tell me that of course I've been stupid, because stupid is what I am by default. But after a moment of considered silence, Zanna links her arm with mine.

"Want to get hot chocolates before going home?" she asks, and like the truly blond and pathetic Aquarius I am, I realize there's a lump in my throat.

"Can we actually?" I ask, and Zanna rolls her eyes.

"Duh," she says. "We need to celebrate somehow."

So we leave Siobhan and Lip Gloss Lizzie squawking like geese and head toward Lambley Common Green together. It's the strangest thing in the world, but now that I've said it, I realize I am totally, utterly, and completely over Alison Bridgewater. Her snow globe is no more. And I finally understand what Morgan meant, saying I've been living in fantasy land.

But now I have a new problem. I am definitely, utterly, and pitifully under Morgan Delaney. And tragically, I don't mean that in a good way.

Horoscope for Myself

According to my *Bible to the Stars*, Capricorn Season is when Aquarians like myself should be cleansing their lives and letting go of baggage . . .

What baggage?! I've literally incinerated all my possessions! I would fully be living Luna's Marie Kondo–inspired Shinto fantasy if I let go of much more. Even so . . . I throw out all my used tissues and a broken hairband—just in case. Oh, and these manky old shoes Mum sometimes wears round the house. I have no idea why Dad bothered to bring them here! Perhaps he inhaled some fumes. Anyway, I'm sure she won't miss them.

But even that doesn't bring Morgan Delaney coasting to my front door! Life is very unfair. It seems that no matter the season, I will have to suffer the enormously enormous pain of being passionately in love with someone who doesn't love me.

"Anyone seen my slippers?" Mum starts shouting.

Urgh! How am I supposed to craft the perfect horoscope with all this racket?!

33

An Anesthetic Love Poem

But what's the use of being achingly in love with someone who doesn't even want to talk to you?! Two tragic days later, I'm none the wiser on how to win back Morgan Delaney's Gemini heart, and my horoscope only tells me to "distance myself from toxicity" . . .

I think that means I should avoid all my problems until they get better on their own, so I jump into a hedge to escape Morgan on the walk home from school. This wouldn't be so bad if there weren't a pigeon nesting there! Pecked almost to death, I march up the driveway with Luna on my tailfeathers. I remove a twig from my hair, and Luna clears her throat.

"You can't keep avoiding Morgan forever, you know. You're going to have to sort this out. You should try *SPASM*. It's a positive-thinking technique: *Self-Improvement*, *Problem-Solving*, *Aspiring to Better Things*, *Slowing Down*, and *Managing Your Time Effectively*. My online friend Willow invented it, and—"

"Luna," I interrupt her.

"Yes?"

"Shut up."

I kick off my shoes in the doorway. My sister may be as bonkers as three chimpanzees in clown noses. Then I drift to the kitchen in search of nourishment and nearly turn inside out from shock! Morgan's MUM is sitting at our table.

"Hello, love!" chimes Mum, beaming at me with a mug of steaming tea. "How was school? This is Caroline from across the road. We bumped into each other this afternoon and couldn't stop chattering!" She laughs reminiscently, then taps Caroline's arm like they're moldy old friends, besties in vesties already. Sappho strike me down. "And you'll never guess what. Caroline can sew!"

Caroline has a Morgan-style edge to her. She's in a tank top and I notice an anchor tattooed on her shoulder. "Your mum's very kindly invited me to her sewing group on Saturday!" she says, smiling at Mum. "It'll be good to get out my needles again!"

Very good. That way, I can use them to stab myself repeatedly! I goggle between Mum and Caroline in speechless horror, then Dad strides in, dressed up like some sort of tragic plumber in jeans and a white T-shirt. He's carrying a toolbox. It's an absolutely spine-chilling sight. Over my shoulder, I hear Luna gasp.

"What in Zendaya's name are you doing, Dad?" she asks.

"I've been putting up some shelves for Caroline here!" Dad says, rolling his shoulders proudly. "She needed a bit of muscle for the heavy lifting, so I got my DIY jeans out."

"Someone bleach my eyes," murmurs Luna, and I'm with her all the way.

Now I'm in trouble. Why, oh why, do my parents have to

be so friendly?! Truly, the most hapless Virgos in town. I just hope, more than anything, that Caroline doesn't decide to bring Morgan with her on Saturday, like some sort of tragic welcome wagon in *The Sims 3*. I might have to relocate to the doubly land-locked Uzbekistan if she does.

Saturday, 12:07 p.m., I spy Caroline leaving her house. Alone, thank Aphrodite. It really would be terribly awkward if Morgan came here, especially since I still have no idea how to earn her forgiveness. I even tried baking a cake, but I slightly messed it up. It turns out you have to *break* the eggs before mixing them in. All very complex.

Mum, Fran, and Caroline are wittering away downstairs at their coffee—sorry, "sewing"—group, and I'm just considering whether I could knit Morgan an astrology-themed quilt when my door opens and Mum pops her head in. "Cat, darling? You have a visitor!"

WHAT?! Wondering if my binoculars missed something and Morgan is here after all, I slam shut the lid of my laptop. Well, Dad's spare laptop. Mine melted in the fire. I hastily plump my hair. I don't even have mascara on—I look like a naked mole rat!

"Um, who is it?!" I ask. "It's just, I'm slightly occupied . . ."

Then Jamie Owusu walks into my bedroom, wearing a different but equally tragic waistcoat and horrifyingly purple chinos. I goggle at him like a fat-eyed goldfish.

I quite literally haven't seen Jamie once since we broke up. In school, he's actually joined the Feminist Society to avoid me—the only club in Queen's that would take me. But now he's here, in my shoebox room. And he's got a guitar.

Jamie nods hello, with this nervous, hopeful shine to his cheeks, and I silently try to scream at Mum with my eyes only: PLEASE DO *NOT* LEAVE ME ALONE WITH HIM!

Mum says, "Let me know if you two want snacks." Then she leaves, chuckling away to herself. Absolutely gooseberry-juicing useless.

"Cat," Jamie says. "Mind if I come in?"

"Um, you're already in," I point out, nervously eyeing the window and calculating my chances of survival should I attempt to somersault out of it to freedom.

"Oh, yeah," says Jamie, shifting the guitar off his shoulder. I pray to every deity in existence that he hasn't got more verses of "Cathleen." "Cat, I know what we had is in the past. But please hear me out. I'm here to apologize."

That takes me by surprise. I'm well within my rights to tell Jamie to guitar-solo his way out of here. He didn't have to put up with the Wildcat comments after all! But this is Jamie, who I've known for years, whose mum is my mum's best friend. So . . . I find myself sighing.

"Go on, then."

He sits on my bed, nervously twiddling his thumbs. "Right. Um, that night at Siobhan's . . . Kieran wanted to know what base I'd got to, and I, um . . . Well, I didn't know what the bases were actually, so I just said, 'Fifth.' Then the lads started cheering and . . . the story got out of hand. I'm really sorry. I never should have disrespected you in that way. I've become a feminist since our time together, and I see now that what I did was wrong."

"Oh," I say, a little stunned. "Well, that's all right. All's well that ends . . ."

Then I notice Jamie is holding a cookie, which he bites into with disturbing enthusiasm. Where did it even come from?! Has Jamie evolved to transform particles into cookies now?

"Mind if I eat this?" he asks. "Need to warm up my vocal cords."

I could point out he's already eaten the entire thing, but I'm more concerned by the last thing he said. "S-sorry," I stutter. "Did you say your vocal cords?"

He swallows. "Yeah. I wrote you a song. To say sorry."

I break into a nervous sweat. "Jamie, you really don't need—"

"Please," says Jamie, his eyes all watery, and once more, my saintly generosity takes over. Resignedly, I nod, and Jamie unzips his guitar case. He even has a guitar pick, which would look kind of cool and pro, only Jamie's has SpongeBob on it. He plucks the strings. I actually think he's still tuning the thing, so I'm taken by surprise when he starts singing.

As if murdering Dolly Parton wasn't enough, he's now stolen the tune of "Don't You Want Me" by the Human League. I'm so glad Morgan isn't hearing this.

"I liked you ever since you said I looked okay,
That much is true.
But spreading round a rumor that we made fifth base
Was quite a lame thing to do.
I'm sorry that I stole some of your socks to smell
Without telling you.
But if you want to be friends, then that would be cool,
But not as cool as you . . .r lovely blue eyes . . ."

When he finishes, dramatically closing his eyes, I slowly clap. It was possibly even worse than "Cathleen."

"That was . . ." I rack my brains. "Very sweet of you."

"Thanks." He pats his heart. "I just read what's in my soul, you know?"

I nod vigorously, and to my relief, Jamie slides his guitar back into its case, then stands. He extends a hand, which I stare at for three full seconds.

"Thank you for this experience, Cat," he says, his voice rattling, like he's trying to sound husky and worldly-wise. "I hope our paths will cross again someday."

Damply, I shake his hand. "I'll see you at school on Monday, Jamie."

"Yeah, that's . . . what I meant." Jamie nods. "I should go. I've got a skateboarding lesson. But thanks for listening, Cat. And thanks for not telling my mum what I did. She'd have killed me."

"That's okay," I say, and he turns to leave. "Um, Jamie?"

He looks round hopefully. "Yeah?"

"It's not completely your fault that we didn't work out. I can't like you because I'm actually a lesbian. Please don't tell anyone! But, um . . . don't feel too bad, okay?"

I wince, waiting for his reaction. He stares at me and then his face lights up! Jamie soccer-punches the air.

"YES!" he hisses. "I knew it! I knew I wasn't ugly."

I stare right back. THAT'S his response?! I snort a laugh. "No, you're all right."

He grins, then pats his guitar. "Guess I should find another girl to be my muse."

I nod as solemnly as possible. "She'll be a very lucky girl."

He grins. "Thanks. And remember, 'Telling our stories, first to ourselves and then to one another and the world, is a revolutionary act.' Janet Mock, *Redefining Realness*." Jamie pats his heart earnestly, then salutes me. "Bye then, Cat."

Then he's gone.

It's only after I've heard the front door shut that I notice he's left his SpongeBob guitar pick on the duvet. I pick it up, wondering if I should run after him, but in the end, I smile and place it on my windowsill. A souvenir, I decide, from when I tried boys for a month.

Later, I call Zanna and tell her about Jamie. We laugh ourselves silly as coots.

"What if you've made a terrible mistake?" Zanna says, midsnort. "He writes terrible songs; you write terrible poetry. You guys should be a match made in heaven."

I know she's trying to badger my beavers, and I almost take the bait. Then it hits me: an idea! In fact, worse than an idea . . . a concept!

"Zanna," I say. "You're a genius!"

"Yes," she agrees. There's a pause. "Why?"

"Poetry!" I exclaim, leaping to my feet. "That's a brilliant idea! I should write Morgan a poem! That will win back her heart! Who could resist an anesthetic love poem?"

"I think you mean authentic," says Zanna. "Also, I didn't say that. Don't you remember what happened the last time you wrote a poem? You were hit by a bus! You seem to keep forgetting . . . Truly, it's a terrible idea, Cat."

"No, Zanna," I reply. "It's a brilliant idea."

"Do you know what brilliant means?" Zanna says. "Cat, I really don't think—"

But I hang up the phone on my Sagittarius soul mate and leap onto the bed, quill pen and parchment already in my hands. By which I mean a pen and a tissue. I'm not a millionaire! But a poet doesn't need money: TALENT is all a real poet needs . . .

NONEXISTENT JOURNAL OF MORGAN'S MOVEMENTS

3:45 p.m.: Morgan arrives home from school.

3:51 p.m.: Morgan shuts her curtains. Maybe she's changing??

4:20 p.m.: Curtains still closed. What's she doing in there???

5:11 p.m.: It's just occurred to me that Morgan could be a vampire. Dark room, goth friends, pale, wears lots of black . . . Have I ever seen her outside during the day?!

6:06 p.m.: Of course I have. I'm so stupid. I must get it from Mum.

7:35 p.m.: If Morgan *is* a vampire . . . her hickeys must be AMAZING!!!

34

Gift from the Gutters of My Heart

I am an artist of enormous proportions! Wait—does that mean what I think it means?! I hurry through to Luna's bedroom to check and she says, "Five foot four is actually average height for your age group, Cat." So I don't think that is what I mean.

It's a good opportunity to call Luna a massive nerd for knowing that though.

Anyway, I am definitely a very big artist, artistically speaking. I stay up all night, sacrificing my sleep to my passion. By morning, I look like a lemur who's been in a pub brawl with a koala, my eyes are so dark and blotchy. I also have an ink stain on my cheek that just won't go away! I scrub my face until I almost don't have a face anymore, but end up just looking worse! Really, it's a good thing that love is blind.

I wonder if I can knock off Morgan's glasses before giving her my poem . . . ?

I practiced writing the poem on tissues before paper. Mainly because I only have one piece of poster paper left, on account of the whole fire thing. But the end result is mesmerizing, each corner filled with intricate drawings of waltzing princesses and swashbuckling piratesses. Around the calligraphy, which I painstakingly copied letter by letter from medieval German Bibles, I've added moons and stars, which glint silver with tinfoil I cut, smoothed, and stuck down.

It's a genuine mistress-piece, a gift from the gutters of my heart! Surely, surely, surely once Morgan sees all the work I've put in, she'll consider forgiving me! I've never done anything like this for anyone before! Not even Alison Bridgewater.

I put the mistress-piece in an envelope, then slide one of the practice tissues into my pocket so I can show Zanna without opening it in front of everyone. Then I head to school with my head held high: in fact, I even walk into a tree on the front lawn.

I am on a mission! Today, I'm going to win back Morgan Delaney.

· ★ · ✦ · ★ ·

"Good grief," says Zanna when I arrive at homeroom. "Are you sick?"

"Yes, I am," I announce. "I am lovesick, Zanna, and I'm following your advice by actually doing something about it. Even though it's not even Libra Season!"

"Was that my advice?" asks Zanna, peering at me over her glasses. "Are you sure you didn't mistranslate something I said again? Like that time I told you to brighten up and you dyed your hair that hideous shade of orange."

I scowl. "That was in sixth grade, Zanna!" I brandish the

huge envelope at her. "And do you see what's in this envelope?"

"Well, no," says Zanna. "I'm not an X-ray machine."

"It's a handwritten poem, Zanna," I explain proudly. "For Morgan Delaney! I illustrated it, decorated it . . . I fell asleep on it for a moment, but you can't really tell . . . I hope. I'm going to give it to her at break! Then she has to forgive me."

Zanna doesn't look convinced, but then Siobhan arrives and nearly faints. Apparently, I look so sick, I've "retriggered her acid reflux." I really should have taken a nap. Morgan will never want to go out with me if I look like "an overripe banana" (Lip Gloss Lizzie's response when Siobhan sends her a picture).

Luckily, I have English all morning—and we're still doing MacSnoozeth. I'm able to take a very satisfying nap for almost two entire hours while Miss Jamison rambles on.

Finally, it's break! Everything is bright and sunny. According to Zanna, it's actually pretty overcast though—so the sleep deprivation must really be catching up to me. It's too late to worry about that though. Break is only twenty minutes and I have to find Morgan!

Me and Zanna skedaddle all over the school looking for her, very wild and exciting scenes, but for fifteen whole minutes, Morgan is nowhere to be found, like a Scorpio's moral compass. We explode out onto the athletic fields, hair flying everywhere in the wind like Kate Bush on Kilimanjaro, and then I spot Morgan: right on the other side of the soccer fields.

"You're going to have to run," says Zanna. "You've literally got five minutes."

"That's all I need," I murmur, clutching the envelope. Then

I take a deep, steadying breath and turn to Zanna. "How do I look?"

"You look like blue cheese," says Zanna. "Off-white, and with bluish stains all over your face. Hey, does Morgan know you have that fungal infection?"

I really don't have time for Zanna's nonsense, so I turn and run. Well, it's a jog. Well, a fast-walk. I am creeping toward Morgan Delaney. She's with the Quadruple M's (featuring Millie Butcher) and looking effortlessly über-licious in her knee-high socks, dark hair blustering about, very wild and dashing and Irish. They're sitting on the grass, facing the river, so no one sees me coming. I stop and hold my breath. Gooseberries. I can't speak!

I'm about to turn on my heel and escape, but then Morgan glances over her shoulder and spots me. Like she has some sixth Gemini sense (or literal eyes on the back of her head, given she's a many-sided Gemini . . .). I'm frozen to the spot, mouth dangling open, and I just pray to Aphrodite that whatever comes out of my mouth is not going to be horrendously embarrassing and stupid. "Um, hello!"

Well, that's an okay start, I suppose.

Morgan looks distinctly unimpressed. Her frown is enough to turn my legs into boneless eels. "You all right?" she asks, in a way that implies she really hopes I'm not.

"I wanted to say something!" I blurt out, which is at least true. "I hope that's okay. What I wanted to say is that I'm sorry about missing your calls at Christmas, and for getting trapped in Alison's snow globe."

"Alison's what?" Morgan frowns.

"Um, never mind!" I lift up the envelope. "I actually made this for you to apologize and, um, I hope you like it."

Morgan and Maja exchange glances. "What is it?" Morgan asks.

I gulp. "Oh! Um, should I open it? I suppose I should . . ." I hurriedly push open the flap and reach inside. Here it is: my creation, my mistress-piece, my last and final hope. I slide out the sheet of paper.

And a gust of wind blows it right out of my hand.

Like a Leo not being the center of attention, I am horrified. Morgan barely has time to blink before my mistress-piece has flown completely over her head and into the river, where it washes away at highly rapid speeds. It might never have existed at all actually.

Me and Morgan stare at each other.

"Um . . ." I go, and Morgan rolls her eyes. I'm losing her! Hurriedly, I reach into my blazer pocket. "Right, well, that didn't go how I thought it would. But I have it here, too!" I hurry over. "Look! It's all there and it's just as good, really . . ."

"Is that a tissue?" Morgan asks.

I stare at what I've just placed in her hand. "Well, yes." I blush. "But it's not used. And it's more about what's on the tissue, to be honest."

But before I can explain, screams and hoots fill the air, and the Quadruple M's scramble to their feet. What now?! I turn around and I'm almost knocked off my feet by Loudmouth Jasmine McGregor. Behind her, Siobhan is brandishing the duct tape! Kenna, Alison, Habiba, and Lip Gloss Lizzie are with her. Behind them, Zanna is looking deeply horrified.

"This is the end, Jasmine!" Siobhan shouts, ripping the tape open. "You really thought you could lock Kenna in a closet and get away with it?! She who hoots last hoots longest . . ." Then she spots me and frowns. "Cat?!"

"Siobhan!" I splutter. "What a coincidence!"

Siobhan's eyes land right on Morgan Delaney. Instantly, her nostrils flare.

"What are YOU doing here?!" she demands, eyes darting between Morgan and me. "Who do you think you are, bothering my friends?! Get lost at once!"

"Get lost yourself!" Morgan snaps back, hands on hips, and I may have swallowed my tongue, for I cannot say a word. "Who's to say your friend isn't bothering me?"

Siobhan passes the tape to Kenna, then cracks her knuckles, squaring up to Morgan Delaney like a Texas cowgirl. "Why would Cat ever speak to a dribbling freak like you?!" she barks. "You can take your lesbian crush and GO. Cat doesn't want to talk to you."

"My what?!" retorts Morgan. ,

And then I say, out loud, "Siobhan, stop! I am the one with the lesbian crush!"

Oh, gooseberries galore. Did I mean to say that?!

Habiba gasps. Lip Gloss Lizzie even stops applying her lip gloss, and Kenna signs, "OMG." Jasmine McGregor gawps along, and I find I'm looking right into the flawless face of Alison Bridgewater, who is staring at me with eyes like Pluto.

"Um, I'm gay," I squeak, my cheeks climate-changing. "Sorry I didn't tell you all before. But, um, I hope that's cool? Thank you for, er . . . listening."

Morgan looks stunned. I think I may have done this with the worst possible timing in the whole history of worst possible timings. But it's done, and I can't take it back now.

Then, bizarrely, it's Lip Gloss Lizzie who breaks the avalanching silence.

"We love you, Cat," she says, then she steps forward to hug me, and everybody wakes up again, nodding earnestly. "You are fabulous and, like, I can't wait to announce this on Instagram."

"We love you so much," simpers Alison. "You're a sweetheart."

"This is fitspirational!" Habiba power walks over and tackles me into an ironclad hug only a netball captain could give. "You're so brave!" she says, although I don't think I am. As Habiba knows, I'm even scared of skipping ropes! But I appreciate where she's coming from.

"I'm so happy for you," Kenna says, and Zanna gives two thumbs-up. I could Pisces-weep. Zanna has been on this lesbian roller coaster since day one after all.

Slowly, everybody turns to Siobhan, who's so still and silent, she could be an out-of-use mannequin.

"I'm sorry," she says, carefully tossing back her hair. "About all those lesbian jokes I made. Obviously, if I'd known you were a lesbian, I'd never have made them. But are you seriously telling me you want to go out with HER?"

I look at Morgan, who narrows her eyes. Then I turn right to Siobhan.

"Yes, I am," I inform her, royally rolling my shoulders. "And if that's not okay, Siobhan, then thank you for your friendship, but it's over now. And those jokes weren't funny. Well, the one about dungarees was quite good, but . . . you need to think about what you say! Because I know you think you're Marie Antoinette, but even she, um . . ."

"Got her head chopped off?" suggests Zanna, and I nod.

"Yes. Thank you, Zanna. So, that's that on, er . . . that."

Siobhan stares at me, truly shawl-shocked. But remarkably, she doesn't self-combust before my eyes. The bell goes off and Siobhan snatches Kenna's trembling hand, then marches away, dragging her frightened-looking friend behind her. Has she really got nothing to say? I open my mouth to call her back, but someone clears their throat beside me.

I turn to Morgan Delaney, and I'm reminded of every dazzling detail: the freckles, the lagoon-blue eyes, the streaks of blond in her dark hair. Morgan tilts her head cockatoo-curiously, but as usual, her face gives nothing away. "You're very unexpected, you know. Credit where credit's due. I did not see that one coming."

"Oh! Um, thank you . . . ?" Then I kick my heels. "So are we, um . . . are we cool?"

Morgan studies the tissue. Then she sighs. "I don't know, Cat. Just keep your phone on. I'll text you or something. See you later, okay?"

Then she gives me an amused smirk before nodding at the other Quadruple M's and heading back toward the school. I break into a giddy smile. She didn't say no! She accepted the poem! I'm as elated as a thousand elevating elephants, very honeysuckle-happy indeed.

Group Chat: The Gang

Habiba, 4:58 p.m.:
Cat babe, do u prefer "lesbian" or "gay" or "queer"?

Let me know by 6 pls!!!

Cat, 5:01 p.m.:
Ummm, what's happening at 6??

Habiba, 5:01 p.m.:
My Q&A Livestream on TikTok!!! xx

Cat, 5:02 p.m.:
GUYS I'D RLLY RATHER NOT MAKE A HUGE DEAL OUTTA THIS

Kenna, 5:03 p.m.:
my sister's nonbinary friend from deaf school said congrats cat ☺

Lizzie, 5:03 p.m.:
Wow so u can be deaf *and* lgbt?

Actually dw, I'll wait for Bibi's livestream!!!

Cat, 5:05 p.m.:
Omg

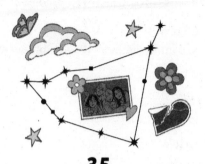

35

Catwoman's Horrendous Sweater

Zanna and I discuss what "I'll text you or something" means for three entire hours on the phone. Which gets on Dad's elderly nerves a lot. Since he put up Caroline's shelves, he hasn't been able to stop. He's now hammering and clattering all over the house! He's already built three tables we don't need, and apparently, my "nonstop yapping" is a distraction.

I tell him that perhaps we should have rented a bigger house or, at this rate, an entire furniture store, then slam my bedroom door.

"What do you think you'll actually do when she texts?" asks Zanna.

"Well, I'm not sure. We'll talk, I suppose."

"Hmm," says Zanna. "Are you sure that's a good idea?"

"Well, what else am I supposed to do?!"

"The problem is that once you start talking, anything could

happen," Zanna explains. "You just ramble your way to disaster. Like that time you ended up as a youth ambassador for Islamic Relief to get out of making a one-pound donation by the train station."

I scowl. "That was completely different. I gave Morgan a poem, remember?"

"That's a good point." Zanna pauses. "You're definitely screwed, then."

I tell Zanna she's a terrible friend and hang up the phone. I have to apologize later though because I can't remember what English homework we have. Some pointless essay, probably. How would I ever survive without my Slavic Sagittarius friend?

I'm still lying on my bed, contemplating what Morgan might text, when Mum comes ramshackling in with a wicker basket over one arm. I point to my crumpled leggings on the chair. "My laundry is right there, thank you, Mother."

Mum scowls. "I'm not your bloody servant, you know! And this isn't a laundry basket. Somebody dropped it off for you five minutes ago. I did call you downstairs."

"I thought you were just calling about dinner!" I protest, and Mum begins ranting and raging, saying I don't know I'm born, I could be milking my own cows, or some such nonsense. Then she drops the basket on my desk and stomps out again.

Has she ever considered yoga?

Even so, I heave my tired bones off my bed and examine the basket, which is genuine wicker! All very impressive. Morgan didn't mention a basket, but maybe this is some strange unknown form of lesbian love language?! Then I see a Post-it Note on the handle. Wait . . . is that Siobhan's writing?! I rip off the tissue paper hiding the contents and gawk. Everything is Post-it-noted—*to avoid confusion*, according to the Post-it Note.

The basket contains a rainbow scrunchie, a copy of *Becoming* by Michelle Obama (*powerful words by powerful women are especially important for lesbians*), some cat earrings (*research has shown lesbians LOVE cats—which is GREAT news for you, CAT!*), knitting needles *to make gay scarves with*, and an actual Polaroid camera. My eyes almost fall right out! It's all wrapped up in a checked shirt—*in case you ever need a tomboy makeover.*

Gooseberries galore. Siobhan is quite blitheringly bizarre. And rich. I mean—a Polaroid camera?! Then I spot the bright pink envelope. Shaky-shocked, I tear it open, and it seems I'm not dreaming: Siobhan Deidre Collingdale, who thinks postcards are for "lonely aunts without families," has written me a letter.

Dear Cat,

I really am sorry for making jokes about lesbians. Boys are useless and ugly, so really, I admire lesbians a lot. You are my best friend. Well, my third best friend at least. I will always support you, even if you choose to wear corduroy. I will even try and be friendlier with Morgan Delaney. She does have a really great nose so it shouldn't be impossible. I can't imagine my life without your chaotic energy crashing all over it 24/7. I hope we are still friends.

Siobhan

P.S. If you ever need me to HANDLE anyone, especially if it's Jasmine McGregor, let me know. I am really good at handling people, naming no names.

Well, it's not quite everything you'd expect from an apology, but for Siobhan—who, we must remember, is a Scorpio—it's a near miracle! She's getting really rather nifty with this apology business. And she wasn't the only one who made lesbian jokes. But she's the only one who's apologized. I send her a text, saying that I'd never wear corduroy, but I appreciate the sentiment. She calls me at once, and it's a weepy and wonderful reunion.

Even if I do have to talk her out of organizing a Coming Out Party in my name.

So, the gang's still ganging, but two whole days pass, and I still have no text from Morgan Delaney. I keep my phone on and wait. As a result, I'm caught off guard when my bra starts vibrating in math on Thursday. I'm actually asleep when it happens!

Eyes fluttering open, I pull out my phone under the table. Finally, a text! I should have known she'd message during school. Very dashing and rebellious lesbian vibes. But before I have time to even read the message, Mr. Tucker rudely clears his throat.

"What are you looking at, Miss Phillips?" Mr. Tucker demands, and I shove the phone (rather painfully) up my skirt and out of sight. Kenna winces.

"Nothing, sir," I say.

"Stand up, Miss Phillips."

Thighs pressed tightly together, I stand. I must look like I'm trying not to pee myself, because there's a trickle of laughter around the class. And then, of course, my phone vibrates again. It slides right out of my skirt and onto the floor like an egg.

"Wait outside, Cathleen." Mr. Tucker turns back to the board, and I grab my phone and hurry out. Kieran and his Lad Friends chortle away like vermin.

At least I can check my phone in the corridor. I open the screen, holding my breath. This had better be worth the detention. If it's not from Morgan, I might scream!

Morgan, 2:50 p.m.:
Hey. Meet me in the park, 7ish?
I read your poem x

YES! I could throw the phone, I'm so elated! But that would be tremendously stupid, so I restrain myself and slip it back into my blazer. All those prayers to Aphrodite are finally paying off! I can't even help myself. I put my hand into a fist and I punch the air.

I also punch Mr. Tucker, who steps out of the classroom just at that moment. My fist hits his nose, and he cries out in pain, then falls to his knees in the doorway.

Oh, gooseberries galore. This is not good.

There's a gasp from the class. Mr. Tucker hisses a word I don't think any teacher is meant to say. I mouth wordlessly at him. If there's a curse worse than "gooseberries," now is the time to say it. "Um . . . cauliflower cheese?"

But I don't think that makes much sense. Mr. Tucker only groans louder.

So what would have been a lunchtime detention for "phone use in class" becomes a Saturday-morning detention for "phone use in class" and "assaulting a member of staff." Mr. Tucker seems to understand that I didn't intentionally punch him in the face. According to him, I was "prancing around in the corridor being very silly indeed." But there's nothing in the system for that.

"YOU DID WHAT?!" Mum shrieks.

"I think she said she punched a teacher," says Dad.

"I heard what she said, thank you, David! Goodness me! Why can't you be more like darling Lilac?" Mum stomps around my shoebox room, raving on about responsibility and my reputation. I'm not overly concerned about either of those things, especially not when I'm meeting Morgan this very evening. Nothing could break my spirits! Then Mum says, "You can stay in your room and think about what you've done for the rest of the evening."

My eyes widen in horror. "Mum, I can't! I have to go to the park!"

"You can bloody well forget about the park!" shouts Mum, then she stomps off downstairs. Dad gives me an apologetic shrug, then follows her, quietly shutting the door behind him. He begins drilling something loudly a few minutes later.

Well, this has thrown a bandanna into the works.

I pace about for the next hour wondering what to do. What would Sappho, the Great Lesbian Poet, do in this tragic predicament? Weep a lot and mope about in some silks probably, so I'm not sure Sappho can be much help at the moment.

I cannot possibly cancel on Morgan. She'd literally never

speak to me again! But Mum doesn't seem to be in the most compromising of moods. I slide down my wall and sit on the floor despairingly.

Then I hear a quiet knock on my door. "Cat?"

I open my door the tiniest crack and peer out. Luna is in the corridor with my black winter coat, a fluffy sweater, and heavy-duty hiking boots. What in the name of Aphrodite's Sacred Goose is she doing?! I open the door further and she steps inside.

"Luna?" I ask. "What's all this?"

"I'm helping you escape!" Luna whispers, eyes dancing. "But it's really cold outside, so I brought you this sweater. Then you can climb out of the window and find Morgan!"

I forgot I told Luna about that. Gooseberries galore! My sister's activist guerrilla tactics are finally coming in handy. Then I notice the sweater she's holding. It's absolutely sickeningly awful, with airbrushed-looking kittens ogling me with dopey blue eyes.

"Luna!" I protest. "This sweater isn't mine! It's some awful thing of Mum's!"

Luna looks at the sweater. "Ah. Well, I was in a rush, okay?! I'm not Catwoman, thank goodness: a prime example of how women are hypersexualized in the comic book industry. No one needs clothes that tight. Then again, she could be Poison Ivy, who in my opinion—"

"Luna, will you hush? I don't have time for your nonsense!" I pull the sweater over my head, then notice my sister is scowling. I sigh, then nudge her with my toe. "Sorry. I am grateful, okay? We'll watch whatever you want on TV tomorrow. As my thank-you."

Luna's face lights up. "Even that documentary on trans representation in Hollywood?"

I close my eyes. Sappho save me. "Yes, Luna," I say. "Even that."

I pull on my boots, then my coat. At least the coat covers up Mum's horrendous kitten sweater. Luna is already opening my bedroom window and peering out into the dark. "Right," she says. "I positioned the recycling outside your window to break your fall. Then I'll tell Mum and Dad that you've gone to sleep early."

I stare at her in awe. She really has thought of everything. Even so . . . "Jumping out of the window?!" I ask. "Are you sure? Luna, I could probably just use the stairs—"

"Are you Catwoman or not?!" Luna retorts, and I frown at her.

"Well, not, obviously." Then I hear Mum shrieking at Dad downstairs. Luna is right. I'm going to have to use my window. Luckily, this isn't the iPhone Box, or else there would be nothing to grip. Even so, I let out a squeal as I lower down my legs until they're dangling completely in midair. I let go of the windowsill and land right in the box of newspapers.

Perhaps Luna isn't entirely useless after all.

THINGS LUNA HAS SAID THAT MADE ME THROW *PRIDE AND PREJUDICE* AT HER BUT MAYBE NEXT TIME I SHOULD LISTEN?!

- "You shouldn't eat so much processed meat, Cat. You're basically digesting plastic. If you went vegan like me, you'd be right as rain! Although not acid rain, which is going to happen a lot if we don't change our—" WHACK!
- "Do you ever worry that those classical depictions of Aphrodite you're so obsessed with actually perpetuate harmful stereotypes that women are innately sexual when actually—" WHACK!
- "Did you know that just one hundred companies are responsible for seventy-one percent of global emissions? That's lots of emissions, Cat. More emissions than you have brain cells, according to Dad—" WHACK!
- "I saw you liked a post on Instagram saying it's great to see more women of color in modeling, but how progressive is it *really* when the fast-fashion brands who use those models are paying their garment makers in Pakistan twenty-nine pence an hour? Really, Cat, your ignorance is—" WHACK!
- "Gross! I just found one of your curly hairs in my—" WHACKKKK!

36
A Highly Romantic and Poetic Ending

If anyone were out to assassinate me, now would be the time. Lambley Common Park is dark and foreboding. Very much graveyard vibes. The sky is clouded over, and I can't see any stars, which isn't ideal, as this is supposed to be my romantic and poetic happy ending!

I text Morgan that I'm here, then wait by the park gates like a loaf-of-bread loner. I wait for ten whole minutes. Gosh, what if she isn't coming?! What if she's Gemin-evil, and the Quadruple M's are her assassination team, waiting in the shadows to pounce?! What if —

"Hey, Cat," someone says, and I jump around with my hands in karate chops.

Of course, it's just Morgan. There isn't an assassin in sight. She's wearing a black padded coat and a black beret, which looks really rather amazing. Her eyeliner is perfect, too. She's in her usual green-rimmed glasses.

"Morgan!" I quickly lower my karate hands. "Um, hello. You look really nice."

"Thanks. You look really nice, too." Then she nods at the park. "I didn't think this through. It looks miserable in there. Want to head to the green instead?"

I nod quickly, and we walk toward Lambley Common Green. There's a few moments of silent salamanders. Then I say, "Um, so not to seem pushy, but was the poem really bad? Because Zanna's been calling me Carol Ann Don't, which is a bit harsh in my opinion—"

"Cat," Morgan interrupts. "Relax. I liked the poem."

I blink at her. "You did?"

Morgan nods, then her smile returns. I notice she's painted her lips gorgeous berry-jam dark red, which turns my stomach into a bucketful of eels. "I loved the poem. It was sweet. No one's ever written me one before . . . Although I wish you hadn't given it to me on a tissue."

"Yes . . ." I waver. "That was, um, unfortunate, losing the proper one. But I did take a picture on my phone! Which I deleted by mistake, but Zanna is confident she can restore it."

Morgan tries not to laugh. But I can see she's smiling. "About Christmas." We pause below a streetlight by Lambley Common Green. "I'm sorry I got mad. But I was trapped on this farm for weeks, then when I called you, you didn't even pick up, you know?"

"Sorry about that," I reply, all wilty-guilty. "I got carried away in London and, um, forgot. Like, how much I actually care. Which is a lot, Morgan. I really like you!"

"I really like you, too," says Morgan, and suddenly, the winter doesn't seem cold . . . Well, it does. But it's still very giddy-licious. "But what about Alison Bridgewater?"

I take a deep breath. "Well, Alison is my friend. And I love her as my friend . . . But I don't like her like *that* anymore. She's wonderful, but I don't think she understands me quite as inter-galactically as I thought she did, and even if she could like me back, Morgan, I'm actually much happier being with, well, you . . . But then Alison was right there and it was like having snow in my eyes! But, well, I think I was brushing up the wrong tree."

As far as passionate speeches go, I don't think that was too horrendous. It's hard to tell if it's done the trick though because Morgan is frowning. Or is she smiling? As usual, she's being very Capricorn Season cool.

"You were what?" Morgan cackles. "Do you mean *barking*? What does brushing up a tree even mean? That sounds super inappropriate." Before I can tell her that of course I know the expression, and I was obviously joking (ahem), Morgan pauses cackling and says, "Listen. I liked you almost as soon as I came to Queen's and saw you at the picnic tables, but Maja and Marcus told me you were just part of the Barbie Brigade, and it was never going to happen. So then, I almost couldn't believe it when . . . you know. It actually started happening."

That's so sweet, I could almost swoon, but . . .

"Wait," I say. *"The Barbie Brigade?"*

Morgan's eyes widen. "Um . . . well, that was their nickname for you, not . . ." She trails off, and I can see she's trying very hard not to laugh again. "Okay, you cannot tell anyone I told you this. But certain people at Queen's might call you Shouty, Shorty, Curly, Airy-Fairy, Glossy, Sporty, and Specks. Don't ask me who's who. I'm literally sworn to silence."

I try to remain composed, although I must admit, those are rather splendid nicknames.

"Well, Queen McFreak, maybe I'm not as shallow and silly as you thought. And maybe your friends are wrong, and you actually do have a fairly decent chance with me."

"Yeah, I'm pretty sure you're sillier," smirks Morgan. "Although coming out to Siobhan like that and sticking up for me . . . that was bold. And romantic." Oh, the tension. I could swoon! I think we're actually about to kiss again, but Morgan narrows her eyes. She reaches out a finger and brushes something small and glittery from my blond curls.

"Look at that," she murmurs. "Is it snowing?"

I look up and realize she's right. Snow is falling all around us, and it's the most hideously stereotypical romantic moment of my life. Which means it's absolutely perfect. I reach out a hand, catching a snowflake. Then Morgan grabs my hand, and we rush to the center of Lambley Common Green. The snow falls quicker and quicker, until it's piling up around the shrubbery, turning the whole world white and fresh and new. I gaze around in awe.

Morgan cackles again. "You're so funny. Smiling at snow like a child."

I blush. "Snow is my favorite weather, I'll have you know,"

I inform her. "Mostly because of *Frozen*. You know. With Elsa?"

Morgan frowns. "*Frozen*? Are you serious?"

"It's a cinematic masterpiece!"

"It's a children's movie," she says.

I cross my arms. "Well, have you seen it?"

"No, because it's meant for seven-year-olds."

"Well, you might have to watch it when we're girlfriends." Wait—WHAT?! I blink at Morgan in panic. "I mean—if you want to be my girlfriend! I'm not saying—"

Morgan places a finger right on my lips. "Cat, can I give you some advice?"

"Hmmph," I say, because I can't open my mouth with her finger there.

"Learn when to shut up." Then she removes her finger, leans in, and kisses me.

I don't think I've ever been kissed quite so beautifully and wonderfully in all my Aquarius Life. Who'd have thought a Gemini could kiss so well? We kiss until our lips go numb. Morgan tells me it's probably just the cold. But I happen to think it's far too poetic and perfect to be "just" anything. It's the moment I finally follow my heart and don't need a horoscope to guide me.

We walk back toward Marylebone Close hand in hand. It's like a daydream, or even like a snow globe . . . but real.

Damp from snow and happiness, we arrive on my doorstep. Luna put a key in my coat pocket, so thankfully I don't have to sleep outside, although that probably wouldn't be so bad, if Morgan were with me. We hover on the doorstep like nervous dragonflies.

"Um, cool," says Morgan. "So, I guess I should . . . head home?"

I don't want this perfect night to end. In fact, I won't let go of her hand, even when she tries to walk away. She gives me a raised eyebrow. It's almost eleven. But who cares about that?! It's not like we're fifty-year-old grandmas! The night is far from over for us.

"You could come in," I suggest quickly. "Sneak up to my room? Like, if you want."

Morgan glances toward her blue front door. "I don't know . . . I probably shouldn't."

Two minutes later, we're sneaking upstairs. I can hear Dad snoring. Although maybe he's still building something and that's the power drill. We make it to my room, and I unzip my coat in relief. Then I turn to face Morgan: an intense and dramatic moment for sure. We're practically undressing! Her eyes flicker down my body. Is she overcome with longing? Then I look down my front and remember the kittens. Ah.

"Good Lord," mutters Morgan.

"It's not mine," I hastily explain.

"That has to be the worst piece of clothing I've ever seen." Morgan raises an eyebrow. "Maybe you should take it off?"

My heart goes *thud, thud, thud*, like a bowling ball falling down the stairs. But Morgan has slid off her coat and her sweater, and now she's just wearing a sleek black top, open at the neck so that her collarbones are showing. The eels in my tummy wriggle.

I tug off Mum's appalling sweater. Unfortunately, this isn't as easy as it sounds: the neck hole is too small and gets caught round my enormous hair. But after a few tugs from Morgan, I manage to pop myself out, and we fall onto my bed. Then we're kissing again, just kissing and kissing and kissing. She snakes her hands right around my waist, moving them OMG-level close to my butt.

I think I might be drunk from kissing! This is über-liciously *hot*.

I kiss her neck. Her collarbones. Hum happily as Morgan kisses my cheeks. My lava lamp is on, and the room is bathed in pink, a bubble of warmth and love. Eventually, when we've kissed ourselves almost into oblivion, Morgan collapses beside me and drapes a sleepy arm across my chest. I can feel her breathing against my neck. It's perfect.

"Morgan?" I whisper, feeling rather sleepy. "You are Aphrodite's Holiest Goose."

Morgan breathes in. I hope I smell nice. Morgan smells delicious. When she replies, her voice is mumbled, very sleepy and sappy indeed. "Babe," she murmurs. "You're beautiful. But I haven't got the foggiest idea what you're talking about."

Beautiful. Morgan thinks I'm beautiful! It's enough to send any pathetic blond clown into a coma. In my head, I send one last prayer to Aphrodite. Then I think about the clean white world, snowy and fresh outside my window. Like a whole new beginning: waiting.

I've heard we come from stardust,

But who can really tell?

All I know is you like me,

And I like you as well.

Venus is a mighty thing,

But I don't really care.

I just want to stay on earth,

Playing with your hair.

The sun won't live forever;

The moon controls the waves.

But I can tell the truth, although

My heart's in retrograde.

I've heard it's written in the stars,

Woven through the sky.

But I can only read my heart,

Who loves a Gemini.

EPILOGUE
Caturday Morning

My eyes flicker open. For a moment, I think I hear a gust of wind or rushing water, but that must have been the leftovers of some dream or other. I wasn't dreaming about Alison though. I'm here with Morgan Delaney and everything is wonderful! Although actually, my arm has pins and needles. Morgan is lying on it! I bite my lip, tug my arm, and—victory!—I think it's finally giving. Then Morgan rolls right onto the floor with a thud.

I sit up in bed. Oops. Morgan is sitting on my floor, looking startled. Which I suppose she probably is. She blinks around the room, then clocks me, ogling her like a lemur.

"Cat?" she murmurs. "What happened?!"

"Um . . ." I hastily clamber out of bed and help her to her feet. "I'm not sure! You must have fallen out of bed! I was asleep, so I didn't see, um . . ."

"What time is it?" Morgan asks.

My phone is on the desk. Apparently, it's half-past seven. Outside, the world is glittering white, a snowy and magical January morning.

"I can't believe we fell asleep," Morgan says, looking out of the window toward her house. "I hope my mum hasn't noticed I never came home. She'll call the police."

That may be true, but Morgan's hair is also very messy and gorgeous, waterfalling down one side of her face. Her eyeliner is smudged, which is so unbelievably dreamy, I'm worried it will send me into a Sleeping Beauty deep sleep of at least three centuries!

I jump onto the bed, smiling. "Worth it?"

Morgan grins. "Definitely worth it."

We kiss again, falling back into the blankets, giggling like happy rainbows, then Morgan breaks away. She's frowning. Have I done something wrong?!

"Cat," she says, slowly. "What day is it?"

I frown back. "I don't know. Saturday?"

"No." Morgan blinks. "Cat, it's Friday."

The tranquility around us freezes, then bursts like a collapsing glacier. Luna would probably weep. Gooseberries galore. It's literally a school day! And then I realize what woke me. That rushing water sound wasn't a dream. IT WAS THE KETTLE DOWNSTAIRS!

I gasp, still poised in prime kissing position above Morgan Delaney and her gorgeous blue eyes, and right at that moment, my door swings open and Mum appears with a steaming mug of tea and her finest "Rise and Shine!" beam.

We stare at her like startled penguins. Mum freezes in the doorway.

I glance at Mum. I glance at Morgan. Right.

Well, we're not naked, so I suppose this could be ever-so-slightly worse. I could say we're having a sleepover! Or that Morgan couldn't travel home in a blizzard?! But our jeans and socks are clearly all over the floor and Morgan lives about six feet away, so I'm really not sure I can babble my way out of this one.

I'm truly going to have to do this again. Does the "coming out" never end?!

I lever myself off Morgan and clear my throat. Mum is gawping at us in her fluffy pink robe and bunny slippers. She looks utterly tragic, but now is not the time to laugh.

"Good morning, Mother!" I begin, hoping that perhaps Mum can be softened by a golden and sunny disposition. I give her my most encouraging smile, but her eyes are getting wider by the moment. "So, there's something I've kind of been meaning to tell you . . . ?!"

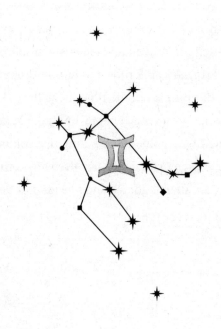

ABOUT THE AUTHOR

FREJA NICOLE WOLF has been writing since she was in elementary school, and at the über-ancient age of twenty-four, she finally wrote her debut novel, *Never Trust a Gemini*, as a joyful, romantic alternative to the issue-led LGBTQ+ stories she grew up with. Her writing is absolutely not autobiographical. (Except for the bits that are.) She lives in London and aspires to be a Capricorn. Unfortunately, she's a Pisces.